To Bob,

THE LONDON
CAGE

next time free copy!

yours aye,

Mark

THE LONDON CAGE

MARK LEGGATT

In his previous adventures, ex-CIA IT technician Connor Montrose felt like a hero after taking on a squad of international drug dealers. After all, he was only supposed to be an IT guy, not an assassin. But when the dust settled, there was no money and no drugs, just three dead bodies. And when he uncovered a major heroin conspiracy between Western powers and the Afghan government, he was set up to take the rap.

So he turned whistle-blower and now the CIA want to make him pay. They have ordered every security agency in Europe to shoot this American psychopath on sight.

Montrose has run to London, the only city where he can feel safe. Under the direction of his boss, Mr Pilgrim, who operates an off-the-grid intelligence network, Montrose is tasked to stay low and monitor a Russian oligarch.

But the CIA will never stop looking for him.

The London Cage
Mark Leggatt

Published by:
Fledgling Press Ltd,
39 Argyle Crescent,
Edinburgh,
EH15 2QE
www.fledglingpress.co.uk

ISBN 9781905916122
Printed and bound by:
Charlesworth Press, Wakefield.

CHAPTER 1

Norway, 1982.

Down in the valley, at the foot of the glacier, the lights of the village appeared through the blizzard then blinked out as thick snowflakes flattened against the windshield. The wipers were losing the battle. *Another mile.* The wind pummelled the windows. He wrestled with the steering wheel, foot hard to the floor, trying to hold the car in a straight line. Keeping his eyes on the overhanging rocks to the right, he traced the edge of the road alongside the glacier that towered above him, leading down to the village. The headlamps dimmed as he ploughed into another drift, slowing the car to a crawl. The snow piled up over the windshield and he pulled the gear stick into neutral before the engine stalled. *One more mile. They'll have a rescue station. And the Norwegian Army.* He glanced in the rear-view mirror, but it was black. *They'll be behind me in minutes.* A gust of wind slammed against the car and pushed the rear sideways.

The gear stick crunched into third and he slipped the clutch. The engine groaned and he could smell the clutch plates burning, but the car remained jammed. The wheels spun as he reversed back, then rammed the transmission into second and shot forward. The hood disappeared under the drift and the engine spluttered to a halt. *For the love of God, just one more mile.* He cranked the engine. The starter groaned then stopped. *Soviet crap!* He switched off the lights and heater and tried once more. The ignition clicked. Nothing happened.

He roared and pounded the steering wheel. *If I try to walk out of here, I'm a dead man.* He peered into the darkness. The wipers stopped as the battery drained. The lights of the village were gone. *There's only one way.* Pulling off his gloves, he took a pen from his pocket, pushed up the sleeve of his jacket and began to write on his arm. *Jesus, just think of something. Don't be too clever.* He read the list of numbers and letters then slid his gloves back on and pulled up his hood. *They'll work it out.* He kicked open the door, forcing it aside enough to squeeze through.

Holding the roof for support, he looked over to where the rocks bordering the glacier ascended into darkness. *Take the high road. They'll never find me.* A hard gust of wind blew him along the side of the car. *Or maybe they'll just find a body.*

In front was a line of thin trees that led up to a small ravine. He struggled forward, pulling on the branches for support, knocking chunks of snow down onto his shoulders. The frozen twigs tore through his gloves as he dragged himself higher. His breathing became heavy and sweat soaked his back under the thick coat. His glove slid off a branch and he twisted right to avoid burying himself face first.

He turned his head and looked back between the trees. *Holy crap, thirty feet? Is that all?* The hood of the car was buried and only the top halves of the windows were visible. *Doesn't matter if it's covered. They'll run straight into it.* He lay still for a moment, gathering his strength. *And if I don't move my ass they'll find me waiting right here.* He rolled over and fought his way through the low branches towards the top.

The wind seemed to lessen in the shelter of the trees and he saw the edge of the glacier above. He managed a short, sour laugh between rasping breaths. *If they don't kill me, the glacier will. Make some distance. Wait it out. This blizzard won't last forever.* He hauled himself forward to where the trees stopped. *Yeah, but long enough to kill me.* Before him was a smooth line of snow that led to the edge of the glacier, protected by a deep cleft in the rock. As he left the tree line the wind caught him, knocking him sideways. He kept his body low and crabbed towards the gap, punching his fists through the crust to give him purchase. At the top, he dragged himself over and rolled onto the glacier. A blast blew the hood clear of his head and he shuffled backwards to the rocks, the bitter wind blinding him. He jammed himself tight into a crevice and stared out over the blackness. The wind was deafening. *All I need is fifty, sixty feet. Get a snow hole going. They'll never find me. Head straight down the glacier and make the village in the morning.* Then the howling stopped and the wind slackened. The moon emerged from behind low, scudding clouds, casting a pale, amber light across the glacier. *Holy shit. This could last seconds. Move!* His blood pulsed in his ears and he could feel his back and legs stiffen as he launched himself forward.

"STOP!"

Twisting his head, he saw a gloved hand jutting out over the edge of the rocks and holding a gun.

A man dragged himself onto the glacier, keeping the gun trained in front of him. He stood up on snowshoes and pulled back the fur-lined hood from his smock. "It is over, Pilgrim."

The wind dropped to a whisper. Pilgrim got to his feet. The black barrel of a Makarov pistol pointed straight at his chest. "So, you worked it out."

The big man shrugged. His guttural Chechen accent was punctuated by wheezing breaths. "I know what you've done."

Pilgrim looked past the man to the lip of the glacier, a mile in the distance and down to the village where lights glowed. "Yeah, I'm sure you do." Above him, thin tendrils of cloud flashed across the sky. The stars shone bright and he searched through the constellations for one pinprick of light.

The Chechen glanced up, following Pilgrim's gaze. "You have stolen from us."

Pilgrim's eyes fixed on the pulsing, rhythmic light.

The Chechen pointed the barrel of the Makarov at the sky. "And you have stolen from me. I want them back. I have given too much to let this slip away." He brought the pistol down towards Pilgrim. "I know how to use this. Now, you will come with us."

He's close enough. And he's no soldier. "You almost make it sound like a good idea. I could die out here." *Wait for the wind, then rush him. Go for the gun. Push him back over the rocks and run for it.*

"Stay where you are. We will wait for my friends."

"Hey, no point hanging about. The weather could

turn nasty. You want me or not?" *I can't wait until the soldiers get here.* Bringing up an arm against his stomach, he could feel where the Browning pistol was tucked into his pants. *You'll never get to it in time.* Pilgrim looked behind. Thick, heavy clouds tumbled across the sky and the moonlight darkened, colouring the glacier a deep caramel. He spun around and made a grab for the Makarov, but his legs plunged through the snow and he caught the man's arm, dragging it down. A crack rang out and a bolt of pain coursed through his leg. He rolled to the side and saw a dark stain seep out from his clothes. *Jesus, he shot me.*

"You'll live, Pilgrim."

Get closer. This isn't over. He leaned forward, but the pain arced through his spine and his head jerked up, throwing his chin into the air.

The big man moved back against the rocks. "I admire you, Pilgrim. But I don't have to shoot you again. In a few minutes you'll be too weak to do anything."

The bastard knows what he's doing. I can live without the blood, but not its heat.

The Chechen leveled the gun at Pilgrim's right leg. "I will carry you. You'll last long enough until we get to the truck."

The wind began to pick up. *No matter. I'll never make it.*

"Pilgrim, come with me. Or you will die here."

Pilgrim looked down. The cold had slowed the bleeding. *They will tear me apart. But that's not the worst.* He began to shake his head, freezing muscles jerking his hood from side to side. Turning to the west, he saw the sky blacken and heavy clouds fill the sky once more. *It'll be dawn in Texas. And warm. I've forgotten what it's like to be warm. The kids will be in bed. My babies. My boys.* For a moment the memory of a scent hung in the back of his throat, their warm, sprawling limbs across the bed, the heat building as the sun came up. He sank to his knees, the snow coming up to his chest. *She'll never know. It will tear her apart.* The single light pulsed in the sky, then disappeared behind the clouds. *But I can't let this happen.*

Russian voices came from below the rocks.

It's over. Make your move. Pilgrim groaned and leaned forward until his chin touched the glacier and keeping his hands buried in the snow, he slid off a glove and pulled the Browning from his waistband. *Do it now, before your hands freeze.* He cradled the gun behind the sleeves of his jacket then lifted it clear and chambered a round.

The Chechen stepped back. "You can't kill us all. Surrender. You have no choice."

Pilgrim smiled and his frozen lips cracked. Snowflakes

gathered on his eyelashes, obscuring his vision as he looked to the West. "I do have a choice." He pushed back his hood with the barrel of the Browning, fixed the muzzle hard against his temple and squeezed the trigger.

CHAPTER 2

Covent Garden, London, present day.

"Would you like to choose your wine, monsieur?"

Montrose glanced at the menu. *What the hell do I order? Get it right. I don't want to blow my cover by choosing white instead of red.* He picked up the wine list and caught the prices. *Holy shit, no wonder the place is nearly empty. A thousand bucks for a bottle of wine?* He ran down a list of unpronounceable names. *I have no idea.* He looked over at the Russians. They sat facing the street, sipping water. A man sat on either side of Arkangel, their seats pushed away from the table, jackets open, legs wide and feet planted on the floor. *They're ready.*

The waiter leaned forward. "Perhaps I can ask the sommelier to give his recommendation? Or perhaps choose a wine for you?"

Montrose grinned. *He knows I haven't got a clue.* "That's a good idea. I'd appreciate it."

"I'm afraid we have no wines from the US, monsieur, they will be all French."

Yeah, you caught the accent. "That's good for me." *I couldn't tell the difference anyway.* He watched another waiter approach the Russians' table, carrying slices of *foie gras* which he laid delicately in front of them.

One of the Russians ripped open his bread roll, forked the entire slice of *foie gras* into the middle of the bread and ate half with one bite.

The waiter stepped back, his mouth open. He stared at the bread roll for a moment, then turned on his heel and marched past Montrose to the kitchen. "Fucking pigs!" he murmured as he smacked open the kitchen door.

Montrose pushed his hair over his ears and tapped the wireless earpiece. A voice crackled in his ear.

"Stop playing with your hair. You look lovely."

He lifted his glass with his left hand, covering his mouth and whispered into his Apple watch. "Thanks, Kirsty. You got me on video?"

"I'm dialed into the restaurant's cameras. There's

nothing happening on the street, but there's a waiter in the kitchen going absolutely fucking mental. He's got a knife. Something I should know?"

"Yeah, don't order the *foie gras*."

"He looks like he's going to go through there and gut someone."

"That would be a bad idea." Montrose shot a glance towards the two bodyguards. They were relaxed, but had angled their chairs so they both faced different areas of the restaurant and out into Covent Garden. *Very professional. Not your usual monkeys for a businessman pretending he's important.* Their jackets were loose-cut and unbuttoned. "Those guys are armed."

"In London? That's a dangerous game. Are you sure?"

One of the bodyguards shifted in his seat and pulled the side of his jacket closer to his body. "Yeah, pretty sure."

"Forget them. Keep an eye on Arkangel."

"I hear you." *Doesn't matter anyway, all I've got is cutlery.*

"Remember, we're just here to watch and listen. That's the order. I want you in one piece so you can take me to dinner tonight."

He stifled a laugh. *I don't even know what you look like. But if you look as good as you sound...* "It's a date."

"And you can tell me all about yourself. Mr. Pilgrim

was very cagey about you. Which makes you all the more fascinating."

The smile faded from his lips. *You don't want to know me. I'm nothing but...*

"Heads up!"

He felt his spine stiffen. "Tell me."

"A car just parked outside. He's watching us."

Montrose slowly turned to the window and saw a small Volkswagen on the opposite side of the street. He watched the door open and a stooping, grey-haired man unfold himself from the seat. Holding a folder in his hand and his chin in the air, he looked first at the restaurant, then down both sides of the street. His thick boots, arctic jacket and woolen pullover seemed out of place for a warm London day.

"He's a copper."

"You sure?" Montrose saw the command-bearing stance of the old man as he stood beside the car. "He seems too old."

"I can smell it."

One of the bodyguards got up from his seat and moved around to the right, leaving the chair next to Arkangel empty.

The old man pushed the door open and stood for a moment, scanning the tables.

Yeah, there's only me and the Russians and some fat

dude stuffing his face in the corner. You're just trying to be cool.

Arkangel got up and graciously beckoned the man to the table. After shaking hands, the old man sat down.

"Hire car. Airport."

"Yeah? He looks like he's from out of town. Wherever it is, it's cold."

"Well, that could be anywhere from Scotland to Canada and everywhere else in between."

The sommelier approached and placed a half bottle of wine on Montrose's table. He cleared his throat and was about to launch into an explanation when Montrose lifted a hand.

"Thanks, I know that chateau." The sommelier nodded and turned away. Montrose whispered into his Apple watch. "Or Russia."

"Fair point. Did Mr. Pilgrim give you any hints?"

"He didn't know the old guy was coming. We've just got to watch Arkangel, that's all."

The old man placed the folder on the table and opened it. Another waiter approached, but was waved away by a bodyguard. Arkangel took the papers from the folder and spread them across the table. The old man handed him a magnifying glass and Arkangel leaned in closer.

"They're looking at photographs. I'm trying to move the camera."

After a few moments, Arkangel nodded then replaced the photographs in the folder and brought out a laptop from his bag. He typed quickly and turned the screen to show the old man.

"Bank screen. Can't see which one."

The old man checked the screen and held out his hand. Arkangel grasped it as they stood up. The old man headed for the door.

What the hell was all that about? "Kirsty? You got that?"

"I'll have to work on the photographs. But I think the old guy is now a very rich man."

"Okay, that folder is the target. Let's find out what Arkangel has just bought." He caught a movement in the corner of his eye. "Wait. Check the fat guy."

From the rear of the restaurant, the fat guy wiped his lips, then walked over to Arkangel's table. He took the empty seat left by the old man.

The voice in his ear made Montrose's blood chill.

"The car!"

Montrose jerked his head towards the window.

The old man was in the car, wrestling with the door, trying to get out. He threw himself to the side and brought up a leg to kick the windshield before a bright blue flash filled the car and the muted thump of an explosion rocked the window of the restaurant. The fire

14

burned fast and hard through the entire car and around the screaming occupant. A blackened hand clawed at the hole left by the sunroof then slid down into the flames. A pall of smoke and debris stained the sidewalk and white tablecloths outside the restaurant.

"Jesus! Connor..."

Montrose felt the adrenalin hit his chest and his breath came short and fast. "Kirsty, keep your eyes on Arkangel."

Arkangel glanced at the burning car and sipped his water then spread the contents of the folder across the table. The fat guy leaned in, his head nodding in agreement as details in the photographs were pointed out to him. They shook hands and Arkangel replaced the photographs in the folder and tucked it into his briefcase. The bodyguards stood and Arkangel fell in between them as they headed for the door.

Montrose pushed back his chair. "Kirsty, tell me which way they go, I'll give them a moment and then follow them."

"Coppers!"

The door of the restaurant burst open and five black-helmeted figures rushed in, brandishing machine pistols. "Hands on heads! Get on your knees!"

The figures spread around the restaurant, covering all the angles. One of them jabbed the stubby barrel of a

Heckler & Koch rifle towards Montrose. "Metropolitan Police," growled the man. "You heard him."

Montrose slipped from his chair and onto the floor, watching the bodyguards and Arkangel reluctantly complying. The cops frisked the bodyguards and confiscated their pistols. The fat guy protested loudly before a policeman kicked him behind the knees and crashed a rifle butt down onto his shoulder.

Two men walked into the restaurant. The first man, dressed in an immaculate grey suit, nodded to the policeman. The fat man was pushed face first onto the floor. The policeman kept his boot down hard between the fat man's shoulders as another policeman ran over and fixed Velcro cuffs to his ankles and wrists then dragged him out of the door to a meat wagon.

The man in the grey suit leaned against the door, rubbing his chin while he scanned the restaurant. Montrose glanced sideways at him. *He's not a cop. He's a spook. What the hell have I walked into?*

Kirsty's voice hissed in his ear. "If they suss you, you're fucked. I know you can't talk. I'm going to try something."

The man in the grey suit stood in front of Arkangel. "Name."

Oh, shit. Montrose caught the accent. *New York. That means I'm dead meat.*

16

Arkangel turned his head slowly to look up. "I think you will find that under English law you must give me a reason for your request and your behavior."

"Yeah? That so? Well, I'm an American, so I don't give a shit. Name."

Arkangel's features twisted into a sneer. "You will find my name on my diplomatic passport. And the names of these two gentlemen are also on their diplomatic passports."

The American nodded slowly. "That right? Show me."

They each pulled out a passport. A small man in a crumpled suit stepped forward and scanned each one on an iPad. He nodded to the American.

The American shook his head and leaned over Arkangel. "Get the fuck out of here. And your boyfriends. I don't want to see you again."

Arkangel and his bodyguards stood, collected their weapons and headed for the door. The American watched them go then faced Montrose.

Kirsty, whatever you have in mind, anytime right now would be a really good idea.

The American walked slowly over to Montrose's table, staring at the roof, deep in thought.

"Excuse me, sir?" said Montrose. "Can I get up now?"

He didn't answer for a moment, then the American looked straight into his eyes. "No."

"I was just eating lunch. I've got nothing to do with this. Whatever it is."

The American took a seat at Montrose's table, picked up the half bottle of wine and checked the label. "Good choice." He scratched his lip. "So, you got a diplomatic passport? ID? Note from your mother?"

"Uh, no, sir. Only my credit cards."

The American nodded at the cop. Two hands appeared from behind Montrose and patted him down. "What's that in your ear?"

"My ear?" Montrose shrugged. "It's a hearing aid."

"Show me."

Montrose pulled the earpiece from his ear, gathering as much wax as he could, then held it out in his palm.

"Just the one ear?" said the American.

Montrose was about to pretend he hadn't heard him then thought better of it. *Might get me shot for being a smartass.* "The other's not too bad. Can I get up? My knees hurt."

The American smiled. "Yeah, have a seat. And leave the hearing aid out."

"Why? I can't…"

"Use the other ear."

Montrose pocketed the earpiece and twisted in the chair so his left side faced the table.

The man smoothed his hand over the snow-white tablecloth. "What's your name?"

Remember the drill. "Fox."

"Full name, Mr. Fox."

If you're gonna tell a lie, make it a big one. "Full name?"

"Go for it."

"Harris Beauregard Claverhouse Fox."

The American grinned. "The first?"

"The only, as far as I know. But call me Harry."

"Right. Yeah. Okay, Harry, let's find out who you really are. Campbell, give me that thing."

The man in the crumpled suit scurried over and placed an iPad in front of Montrose.

"Harry," said the American. "Put your hand on there."

Shit. "Look, I've never been in trouble. Even in college. Although, there was this one time..."

"Shut up. Do it now."

Montrose heard the policeman behind him shuffle his feet, widening his stance. He placed his hand on the iPad. A light scanned his hand and the iPad beeped.

"Okay, let go."

He kept his hand pressed down and saw the word *Dionysus* flash up on the screen before the American grabbed it from the table.

The American considered the iPad for a moment. "Well, I'll be straight with you, Harry. What we have here is something that worries me. But it tells me good things, too. You're on the right side. What it doesn't tell me is who the hell you are. Damn sure it's not Mr. Fox. And that's the thing that worries me."

Maybe, dude. But I'm fucking delighted.

The American looked over Montrose to the policeman. "We'll take care of it from here. Have your guys wait outside." The American watched the policemen leave, then pulled his chair closer, moved the bottle of wine out of the way and rested an elbow on the table. "Let me tell you something."

"But…" *Kirsty, get me out of here.*

"Listen to me. My name is Paul Kane. I control a team in Langley. And you know very well where that is. Now, I don't know what the hell you, or the people on the end of that earpiece are doing here, but this is my operation. What happened here today, who those people were and what your connection is, you will tell me right now. Because, I shit you not, what those people are involved in will make 9/11 look like a pool party at the Playboy mansion."

What the hell is going on?

"So, let's be very clear, you are going absolutely nowhere until you tell me exactly what you and your team are doing and why." He held up a hand. "And don't give me the 'confidential, need to know, higher authority' bullshit. There is no way on God's sweet earth that you have higher authority than me. Now, you tell me and you tell me right now, or I will no longer consider you a friend. And then bad things will happen and they will happen very quickly."

A phone rang. Kane reached inside his jacket and pulled out his cellphone and stared at the screen. He looked up at Montrose while he thumbed the button. "Yeah?"

I know who's calling. That fingerprint scan would have set off alarm bells from here to Virginia. He watched Kane's mouth drop open. *I'm fucked.* He glanced to the door. An armed policeman stood outside, half-turned in his direction, watching a ring of policeman battling the burning car. *Even if I run, he'll see me coming.*

The fire alarm screamed into life and Montrose shot to his feet.

Kane stuck out an arm, shouting over the alarm. "Sit the fuck down!"

Thanks Kirsty, but that's not gonna work. He watched Kane's eyes narrow, but couldn't hear what he said over the alarm, then saw him begin to unbutton his jacket.

Oh fuck, no.

Kane pushed back his chair, shouting into his phone. "You mean here? Right now?" His hand moved inside the jacket.

The fire alarm stopped.

CHAPTER 3

Water burst over their heads from the sprinklers, soaking the tables and floor. Kane instinctively tried to cover his phone while reaching for his gun.

Montrose launched himself forward and smashed his fist into Kane's face.

Kane toppled backwards. His phone slid across the floor towards the policeman at the door who made a grab for the handle.

Montrose spun around and shoulder-charged Campbell over a table, then ran for the kitchen, slipping on the parquet as he kicked open the swing doors. Water was gushing out from revolving jets above the stoves and chefs were shouting and running for the exit. An armed policeman stood in an open doorway to an alley. He locked eyes with Montrose and leveled his machine pistol, but the barrel was forced into the air as several chefs tried to force their way out the door at the same time.

Montrose saw steps to his left and ran up a winding staircase, grabbing a fire extinguisher from the wall. At the top was a door which he shoved open into a small toilet. He slid to a halt before he hit the edge of a sink and a window, three feet in front of him. *Fire extinguisher against a gun. Yeah, that'll work.* He launched the extinguisher through the window then ducked behind the door and kicked it shut. He heard boots on the stairs. *Do it. Make the same mistake I did.* The door flew open and the barrel of a gun came first, followed by a policeman who stuck out a hand before he hit the sink.

Use his weight. Montrose stepped behind and shoved him hard towards the window.

Montrose grasped the policeman's utility belt and hauled him up over the window ledge then leapt to the side as the copper's boots flew past his nose.

He looked down to see boots sticking out of a dumpster. *Okay, not that way.* To his right he could see a low roof. He stood on the sink and kicked away the shards of glass, then levered himself out of the window frame, trying to find his balance on the crumbling brick ledge. *Don't dick around. Jump!* Throwing out his arms, he launched himself sideways, hoping the flat roof would take his weight. He landed and rolled, his hands scraping the rough stone and grit of the tar-covered roof, then ran to the edge and saw the gap. *I can make it. Six feet.*

The gap widened as he got closer. *Ten feet? Oh, man, just go for it.* He glanced down to a filthy alley twenty feet below as he launched into the air. *Leg breaker.* He landed heavily and ducked behind an air-conditioning unit. Shouts came from the alley. Looking back, he saw a policeman's head stuck out of the toilet window, wrestling his rifle clear of the frame. *They're not following. They're not that crazy, they'll take the streets.* He got to his feet and headed for a stone gable, but slipped on the grit and rolled towards the wall. Bricks shattered above his head and hot fragments of metal stung his cheek.

He scrambled behind the corner of the gable end. *Sniper. And a silencer. Not a cop's gun. This isn't an arrest. They've worked it out. They know who I am.* The connecting roofs were a jumble of old, steep, moss-covered slates and flat areas with minimum cover. *Pick a route and stay low.* He got up to run then heard the whump-whump of rotor blades. *Chopper. Get off the roof.*

Keeping low, he weaved between rattling air-conditioning units. To his right there was a long line of windows: an attic conversion. A round table of suited executives stared out at him. The window was open. He reached up and tugged it aside then pulled himself in. He stood for a moment, ignoring the open mouths, then brushed off his damp suit. "Police. Don't mind me, I'm just passing through."

He skirted around the table before anyone could say a word, opened the door and then stopped. "Listen, close that window. There's a bad guy on the roof."

He raced down the stairs. At the bottom was a busy open plan office. Several people looked up from their computers. He grabbed an overcoat from a stand and slipped off his jacket, throwing it into the stairwell. A plain wooden door stood in front of him with an alarmed fire exit sign. *Like I give a shit.*

He pushed the handle and a weak, whining siren coughed into life. *Don't run. Yet.* He stepped out into an alley and turned north towards the main drag. *Where the hell am I?* He pulled the earpiece from his pocket and shoved it into his ear.

"...in because I can't do this through fucking osmosis!"

"Kirsty, it's me. Listen, I'm..."

"I know exactly where you are. I've got four CCTV cameras on you. And don't talk into your Apple watch when you're running, you'll look like a movie extra. And a complete tit. Cross over Long Acre, that's the main road at the end. Take the street at your eleven o'clock. Keep going."

He saw traffic at the end of the road. An unmarked van with flashing blue lights shot past. He stopped in a shop doorway. "Kirsty, any moment now there are going to be police everywhere. I need to get out of London fast." He ran for Long Acre, searching for a gap in the traffic.

"You'll never make it."

He dodged the cars then slid to a halt on the sidewalk. "Jeez, thanks. Should I just kill myself right now? Or wait for them to do it?"

"Keep your knickers on, Yankee boy, you'll never make it because the cops in London have got containment down to a fine art. They'll have your section locked tight in minutes. Vans, dogs, helicopters, the whole nine yards. What you need to do is to get out of the sector. Check the end of the road. See that pillar at the end?"

Montrose looked along the line of shop fronts and yellow brick buildings. "Yeah, I see it. So what?"

"That's the Seven Dials. It's the border of the Covent Garden containment sector. They've been perfecting this ever since the IRA came to town, even if it's now a different enemy. Get there fast. Then you can hide.

Otherwise they'll lock you in and keep squeezing every street until they find you."

"I hear sirens."

"You'll have a lot more to worry about if you don't move your arse."

He stepped off the narrow sidewalk and ran down the street, weaving between the slow-moving traffic. *Just get to that pillar? Is she crazy?* "Kirsty, there are no exits, all the turnings are dead ends. They'll spot me a mile off."

"Probably. Everything will be focused on your sector."

"Got any good news?"

"We'll see. Don't stop. Get to the Seven Dials before the meat wagons."

He glanced behind. Red buses blocked the end of the street.

"Slow down."

He stopped and ducked into a doorway, looking out to the ornately carved pillar in the center of the road. "What is it?"

"It's cool. Only a traffic warden. Thought it was a copper. The bastards all dress the same. Now, walk across the road, take the exit where the traffic warden is standing. See it?"

He could see why the cops would want to control the area. Seven narrow roads converged into a circular junction. Blue lights appeared between the cars at the end of the street. "I see the exit."

"Go for it. Get to the bike rack."

The traffic slowed and he strode straight over the junction then stood in a doorway beside the rack. "I'm there. What now?"

"Get on a bike."

He looked along at the rows of city bikes. "You're joking."

"It's the fastest way across London. Move it."

The sirens were getting closer. He tried to haul a bike from the stand, but it was locked. "Kirsty?"

"You were given a credit card in the name of Mr. Fox. Use that, hold it up to the machine in front."

He fumbled in his pants for his wallet then flattened the credit card against the screen. A slip of paper with a code popped out and he punched in the number to the bike. The lock popped open and he grabbed it from the stand.

"Lose the overcoat."

He tugged it from his shoulders and stuffed it between the bikes.

"Go to the end of the street, turn right then first left. I'm going to keep you off the main drag, so expect a few detours."

He pointed the bike away from the Seven Dials

and jumped on. The wind chilled on his legs and his feet slipped inside his shoes. Trucks and cars lined the street as he flashed past shops and boutiques. The traffic came to a halt at the end of the street. He slowed for the junction and stuck his foot down, sliding along the ground to stop before he ploughed into a bus. He stepped on the pedal again, but his shoe slipped and the pedal spun around and cracked his shin. Pain shot through his leg and he leapt off the bike, pushing it between the bumpers of the stationary cars to the other side of the street.

"Bet that hurt. Take the next left."

"Got it." *She knows what she's doing. If it wasn't for the traffic, the police would have me by now. Or worse, Kane and his goons.* He pounded the pedals, standing up in the seat. "Kirsty, where the hell am I going?"

"Soho."

"Safe house?"

"Soho's never been safe, but as safe as you can get in London right now."

He hauled the bike up onto the sidewalk to avoid a delivery van in the road. "Where in Soho?"

"You'll see. If you knew the address, I'd be worried about you."

"Tell me exactly where, in case I lose comms."

"You won't lose me. I've got five cameras on you. Go

to the end of the street, ditch the bike, then walk down the alley in front."

He dumped the bike in a doorway. At the end of the alley, through a brickwork arch, he could see a busy street. "Wait, we need to check that I'm not being followed."

"Connor, I'm having enough trouble finding you a clear path, so you'll have to take care of what's behind you. You'll be on me in five."

What the f..? He flattened himself against the wall, the sharp, dirty brick pressing through his shirt into the skin of his back. "Kirsty, that's really not a good idea. You don't want to..."

"I've got no idea who you are or what you've done, but I'm here to do a job, so do what I say, you thick-headed Yank, or I'll drop you like a sack of hot shit. This is my territory. Get to the end of the alley."

The stone was cold against his skin as he pressed harder into the wall. *I can't put her at risk. She's just a tech. Yeah, you know what that feels like.* "Kirsty, I can't lead them back to you. Give me a direction and let me go."

"Well, that's sweet, but I can look after myself. And right now, you can't. So shut up and do what you're told. They're going to move containment sectors very soon and you'll be trapped like a rat up a drainpipe."

The sirens had stopped and he pushed himself from the wall. The street behind him seemed calm. He stopped at the archway and looked along the road. It seemed normal, except for the neon signs offering peepshows and porn shops. "Kirsty, I don't want to sound like an idiot, but we've never actually met."

"I know. If we had, you'd remember. I'll be looking out for a panicking Yank in moist trousers."

"Just give me a clue in case I don't spot you."

"Oh, you'll spot me. Besides, I'll be the only chick there. And I don't dress like other people."

He left the alley and stepped out onto the street where the smell of fried food and exhaust fumes surrounded him.

"Twenty yards. And get rid of your watch. They've had enough time to track it down. It's got a MAC address like a phone and once they get it they can tell your heartbeat and nail your location to a few feet. Turn into the bookshop on the left."

He pulled the watch from his wrist and strode forward, glancing into the windows framing the doorway. A display of vintage London books were scattered around, faded with age. Inside, the shop was deserted, only one bored assistant tapping on his phone. The shelves held stacks of haphazardly arranged coffee-table books. On a table beside him a thick layer of dust covered a large hardback edition on sixties fashion. Montrose slipped the watch under a book. He shot a glance around the room. *No doors.* He saw a steep staircase in the corner. The assistant ignored him as he walked past the desk and down the stairs. The lights became brighter and porn posters adorned the walls. He shielded his eyes against the glare and spotted someone at the bottom of the stairs. She wore a long black leather coat and boots, midnight blue lipstick, and her hair was shot through with purple streaks..

Kirsty tapped a jet-black fingernail on the screen of her iPad. "You've got a tail. Follow me." She turned and threaded her way past several stands of latex suits and rubber masks.

He hurried behind her, through a series of small interconnecting rooms lined with DVD boxes and racks of luridly colored objects that he couldn't identify.

She stopped in what appeared to be a dungeon with black paper lining the walls and medieval stocks in the middle of the room. Whips of all sizes hung on metal racks. "Check this," said Kirsty and she held out the iPad, showing a two-camera view split across the screen. "They're at both ends of the street."

He watched a two-man team at each end, talking into their radios. One team took up position and the other made their way towards the bookshop. "Kirsty, they know where they're going." *We're trapped.*

"Well, I hope they know where they're going. I don't want to have to go upstairs and wave to them."

We can't stay here. They'll kill her without thinking about it. Give yourself up and let her run. "Kirsty, they used a sniper. He nearly took my freakin' head off."

She ignored him and concentrated on the screen. "C'mon, boys, stick together."

The men checked their phones and headed for the bookshop. *I need a weapon.* He scanned the room quickly. *I'm in an armory for perverts.* He noticed a long pole with a rubber grip. *That's a fucking cattle prod.* A pair of fur-lined handcuffs seemed the least offensive item. On screen the two men slipped their hands inside their jackets and entered the bookshop. *They'll work it out in seconds.* "Kirsty, we can't hide here. Run for it. I'll take care of them."

"Oh, very macho," she said, concentrating on the iPad. "What are you going to do? Fight them off with a massive dildo?" Kirsty looked up. "They're here. Follow me." She swept a curtain aside and headed along a narrow corridor. "The basements of these shops are over three hundred years old. They go right under the street. The Russian Mafia that own this place have shops either side, so they knocked through. The entrance you came in is a cover for the more discerning pervert." She stopped and pulled a T-shirt, fleece jacket and combat pants from her bag. "Trousers off."

"In here?"

"You shy, Connor Montrose?"

Holding the combat pants in one hand, he tugged at his waistband, pushing down the wet cloth sticking to his legs.

"Just think yourself lucky I didn't buy you underwear. They've got quite a selection in here, if you like leather and your tackle hanging out. Anyway, that was the only decent thing I could find in Soho. Army surplus. It was either that or a gimp suit."

"A what?" He stepped into the combat pants and pulled the damp shirt from his shoulders.

She stopped at the foot of another staircase and watched him struggle into the T-shirt. "You're bigger than you look in the movies. Let's go."

He followed her up the steps and into a brightly-lit room lined with manga comics and magazines. "Kirsty, we should split up." *You have no idea what you're up against.*

She grabbed his hand. "Are you ashamed, Connor Montrose? They're looking for one person, not two lovers." She held on tight and pulled him into the street. "Make sure they can see this. Big Brother is watching. There are half a million CCTV cameras in London, so be cool and just walk normally."

Montrose resisted the urge to look behind. *They'll*

ID me before we get to the end of the street. "Kirsty..."

She pulled him into a long doorway, past a line of glass displays showing faded photographs of showgirls.

A blinking neon sign let him know where she was going. *Peep show.*

"In here," she said and shoved some money under a window at a squinting old man. She pushed open a faded red velvet door, studded with grimy brass.

"Kirsty, this is a..." *How do I say it?*

"Yeah, I know. It's also very dark, has over thirty massage booths, several cinemas and some very attractive fire exits. If the coppers follow us in here, it'll take them all day to search the place and find the escape routes. Places like this need discreet exits. You know what I mean?"

"Yeah, I can guess."

She pulled him by the hand into a stairwell that led down into a dimly-lit corridor lined with identical doors, all closed. At the end was another door, indistinguishable from the others. It opened to reveal a room full of semi-naked women lounging around on cheap wooden chairs, some gazing into brightly-lit mirrors, adjusting their make-up. "Eyes front, Connor."

Montrose locked eyes with one girl. She blinked slowly, her dilated pupils trying to focus on him. He followed Kirsty as she weaved through the chairs to a door at the far end of the room. She flicked a switch by the door and pushed it open into a stairwell. A stone ashtray filled with sand and studded with cigarette butts stood to the side. He looked up. Grimy brick walls towered above him into a clear patch of blue. The faint contrail of a jet traced slowly across the sky.

She kicked the door closed behind her. "That's how you lose the cops. The girls use it when they get a signal." She ran up the worn stone steps, then through an alley so narrow they had to shuffle sideways, brushing past lichen-covered walls. They emerged into a cramped courtyard, with the scent of Indian food coming from an extractor fan. Several covered alleys led off each side into darkness. "If they make it this far," she said, "they'll spend the entire day chasing their own arse down these alleys. Every one has a different exit. Except this one."

He followed her and watched her push open a heavy wooden door set into the wall. He could smell rotting wood, but saw that it was six inches thick.

Kirsty shoved the door closed, turned and set off through a stone archway and into a narrow lane.

The faint noise of traffic and police sirens drifted over them, and through the dim light he saw a metal gate fixed across the exit. "Kirsty, this is a dead end."

"That's exactly what it is, but since this place hasn't

appeared on a map since 1745, we're safe." She stood before the gate and pushed the buzzer.

"They'll find the door."

"Sure they will. But they think we're running from Soho. We're not."

He saw the camera. The grate clicked and opened and he followed her through. *Now I know why she works for Mr. Pilgrim.*

*

Kane dropped onto the seat of the Mercedes, water dripping from his hair and his wet pants sliding on the leather seats.

The driver glanced around but said nothing.

"Thames House," said Kane. "Right now."

Campbell got in the other side, looking down in disgust at his suit.

Kane punched the headrest in front of him. "Fucking MI5! I knew those assholes would mess this up. We should have had our own team doing this. From now on that's how it's going to be. They'll do what they are damn well told. Get a message to Downing Street from Washington. They're our bitch and they better get used to it."

"Sir, Special Branch cops and Met Police have locked down the area," said Campbell. "MI5 have tracked *Dionysus* on CCTV to Soho and have passed the information to our teams. They'll find him, sir." His phone buzzed with a text message. "I have another contact for *Dionysus* and his real name. Connor Montrose."

"Montrose? Never heard of him. And what contact? The Langley dickwipe on the other end of the phone said to kill him on sight. But I need to know what the fuck he was doing there. Whoever this asshole might be."

"Sir, it says Director Spinks must be informed of any new information."

"Spinks, yeah?" Kane tugged the soaking shirt collar from his neck. "Last I heard, he was in a trauma ward. Heart attack."

"That's correct, sir, we think that's why the contact was changed. But the instructions are code red and that Director Spinks must be informed immediately."

"Dial his number. If he wants to know, I'll tell him. You concentrate on bringing Montrose in alive. I don't shoot people because a desk monkey tells me to."

"Uh, the orders are pretty clear, sir," said Campbell. "Terminate with extreme prejudice. At the first opportunity."

Kane turned and jabbed a finger at Campbell. "He's the only lead I've got apart from that rag-head we caught in the restaurant. Bring him in."

"How do we know Montrose is involved, sir?"

"We don't. But he was there for a reason. And Arkangel must be that reason. You know what this means? If Arkangel and his Russian goons have diplomatic passports then we're up against the Kremlin too." He stared out of the windshield at the queue of traffic on Piccadilly. "And that isn't good. Break out the big guns. And I don't mean metaphorically." A ringtone sounded and Campbell handed him a phone.

"Cedars-Sinai Medical Center, Mr. Spinks' room."

"Get me Director Spinks," said Kane.

"Sir, Mr. Spinks can't take calls, he…"

Kane heard Spinks' Brooklyn accent, above the beeping of medical monitoring equipment, telling the nurse to give him the phone.

"This is Spinks. If you're calling this number, it better be goddamn important."

"Director Spinks, this is Director Kane in London. We have made contact with a man, ID verified and the instructions say to call you immediately."

Campbell began to raise a hand, but Kane waved him away.

"Yeah?" said Spinks. "Who?"

"Connor Montrose."

The line was silent for a few seconds then Spinks began to wheeze, forcing out the words. "Kill that fucking traitor! Kill him and bring me his balls, I'm gonna…" the beeping in the background became shrill.

Kane heard a crack, followed by the shouts of medical staff. He waited for a moment then hung up and stared at the phone in his hand.

"What did he say, sir?"

"Not much."

"Is he going to let us know any more about Montrose?"

"You know, I don't think so." He turned in the seat, leaning over until the water dripped from his face and hair onto Campbell. "Listen to me, I don't know who the fuck this Montrose is, or what he's done and right now I don't give a shit. If we can't get to Arkangel, Montrose is our man. Tell him we'll give him protection, but I want him to talk."

"And then, sir?"

"And then what?"

"Montrose, sir?"

Kane gingerly touched the bridge of his nose. "Shit, if it makes you happy, you can shoot him yourself. And make sure it really fucking hurts. That okay with you?"

"Just following directives, sir."

CHAPTER 4

The ancient stonework ascended forty feet into the air, bereft of windows. The carving above the doorway was pitted and worn away, but he could make out the words *Lord have mercy on us*.

Montrose followed her through a wide door, dark with age and studded with bolts. The temperature dropped as he stepped into a long hall, stretching left and right, with a floor of uneven, cracked flagstones. At each end sat a huge blackened fireplace, nearly as wide as the hall. The only furniture was ancient wooden benches lining the walls. "Kirsty, what the hell is this place?"

She didn't turn around and headed for a small door in the opposite wall. "It's a sweat shop. Or it was, anyway. Wait here." The door closed behind her.

Montrose stared up at the ceiling, lined with sagging

oak beams stained by centuries of soot and saw the faded remnants of colorful frescos behind the grime. *This place is medieval. Where the hell am I?* He walked forward and tried the door that Kirsty had used, but it was locked. He looked around. *Cameras? Yeah, I'll bet.* He stepped back, cleared his throat and could hear a faint echo through the room. *Okay, give her five minutes. This is her territory. Shit, by that time the cops will have the whole of Soho shut down. And the goons in the sex shop will be on the street, waiting for me to make a move. The cameras will spot me a mile off. But it isn't just me. I wasn't alone.*

He strode over to one end of the room, his footsteps rebounding off the rough stone walls and stood before the fireplace. The mantelpiece was level with his head. At the side he saw thick rods of iron jutting from the stone, blackened and bent with age. *They could have roasted a whole bull in there.* He ducked his head, stepped into the fireplace and brought up the torch on his iPhone. At one end were rusting metal rungs, just big enough for a child's foot, rising up the greasy, soot-black chimney and disappearing into darkness. *I'd rather face a CIA hit squad than climb up there. Let's hope I don't have to. Is this place really secret? They could come crashing through that door at any moment. Then I'd get a bullet in the brain. And she would be next.*

A jolt of anger made him turn and sprint back down the hall. *What the hell am I doing? I have to get out of here. They're gonna tear her apart.* He stood before the front door which led to the alley and Soho, then gently pushed the handle. It was unlocked. He pulled the door open a few inches but could see nothing past the metal grate. *Go. Right now. She'd be safer here.* His grip tightened on the handle. *But they saw her on the street. And they know there was someone on the other end of my earpiece. And they will want her. Dammit, she's not my problem. Pilgrim got me into this shit. He can work it out. I can draw them away.* He checked the metal gate and noticed the steel bolts lining the frame. *This is a goddamn trap. There has to be another way.* He gripped his phone. *Tell Pilgrim to look after her. Just go.*

The door in the far wall opened behind him and Kirsty stood with her arms crossed. Her voice was low, but it echoed around the room. "Going somewhere?"

"Just checking."

"No need, we have cameras for the alley. Relax, this is the safest place in London right now." She pointed to the iPhone in his hand. "Turn that off." She beckoned him over. "Come with me."

Plan A is fucked. He looked behind her into a dimly-lit stone corridor. *She has the information on her iPad.*

If the CIA want to chase around London looking for bad guys, it's up to them. Worse than 9/11, Kane said. Yeah, maybe, but I'm not gonna let her die for it. When they get the iPad, I can buy them off. That's all I need. She'll be safe and I'll hustle a way out. Okay, Plan B. He hit the power button on his phone.

"Close the door behind you." She led the way along the corridor, then stopped, holding up the iPad. "I have the photos from the restaurant cameras. Connor, you've got to see this." She tapped a code on the screen as she walked.

Just get the information and go. He hurried after her, past small, ornate tables with vases of fresh flowers. Rough masonry blocks arched low over his head and there were openings on either side with steep steps leading down to vaulted subterranean rooms. They were all softly lit, some furnished with antique tables and chairs, others containing Chesterfield sofas. He glanced into one of the rooms as he passed. Several men sat around an empty fireplace, drinks in hand. "Kirsty, where are we?"

She didn't turn around. "Like I said, it's a sweat shop. Or was, anyway." She pointed to one of the rooms. "In old times, these rooms were full of hundreds of men. They rubbed fresh furs down with tallow, then they would trample them in tubs to soften the leather. Like trampling grapes, only with fat and fur. But to make the tallow soft, the place had to be hot."

That explains the fireplace.

"It must have been forty degrees in here when the place was going. And hundreds of naked men working away, inches from each other in front of a roaring fire. That's why they called it a sweat shop."

"And now?"

"Now, it's a bit different. There are still a lot of men, though." She glanced back and smiled, then turned down a set of steps into a long room. "Watch your feet."

The steps were bowed and worn with age. At the bottom, he stepped into an oak paneled room with a long bar at the end. Behind the gleaming wooden surface stood a big man with a full beard, wearing a long silk dress. His bare arms hung from the straps like slabs of meat from a butcher's hook. The man fixed his eyes on Montrose as he followed Kirsty towards a line of high-backed wooden booths that reminded him of a medieval diner. "Uh, Kirsty this place…"

"Think of it as a very private gentleman's club. Now, check this out." She patted the bench beside her. "Sit beside me."

He glanced around as he slid into the booth. No one looked over, but he could feel the barman's eyes boring into him. "Kirsty, we should be going. Right now."

"Don't be such a prude. Connor, there's nowhere better in London than right here. The whole of Soho will be locked down and they can't find us in a place that doesn't exist." She placed the iPad on the table. "I've tracked the old man in the restaurant from his rental car. His flight records show that he flew in from northern Norway, connecting through Oslo. He's a copper. Or was. Retired a few years ago. His station was up near the border with Finland." The first photograph showed a close-up of a crumpled and broken body, half-buried in ice. She flicked her finger across the screen and the photos continued, showing the corpse from a distance, jutting out of the wall of ice above a blue-green lake. "God knows how long he was in there," she said. "He must be about fifty feet from the surface. I heard about a story like this. A few years back, in a different glacier, they found two Italian climbers who had disappeared thirty years before."

"Makes sense. He must have been buried in the snow, further up the glacier. Who knows where. And every year, a fresh layer of snow falls and the glacier slowly advances down the valley to melt into the lake." He flicked through the photos on the screen and stoppped at the naked, twisted body of the man lying on an autopsy table. *The glacier would have smashed his bones to a pulp*. He tried to expand the photo, but the resolution became fuzzy. "There's something not right here, Kirsty. Look at the hair on the right side of his head."

"I know. The darker, matted area. It could be blood. Maybe he was a climber? Smashed his head falling from the rocks?"

Montrose shook his head. "No. I can't see any ropes or equipment." He flicked through the photos. "Can you make these clearer?"

"Not yet, I'm waiting for an app to download." She checked the iPad. "This wi-fi is killing me. But look at his arm. Are those words?"

He leaned in closer. He could make out what seemed to be words scrawled across the skin, but the letters were too fuzzy. He expanded the photo, trying to decipher the symbols. "I can make out *Ekland* and maybe numbers. The other word looks like *pichaq*. An acronym, maybe? I've no idea what that means."

"Arkangel might." She flicked to another photo, showing Arkangel with his finger on the word.

"It's not making sense. We need to know more about how the old guy was involved and why Arkangel killed him. Maybe for the money, or Arkangel might have been covering his tracks. Wait."

"What?"

Montrose pointed to the edge of the photo, at a dark,

rectangular shape sticking out from under a scrap of clothing. "That's the butt of a pistol."

"Really?"

"Maybe a Browning. I need more detail."

Kirsty checked the app download. "This is going to take too long. I need a better signal. The walls in this building are four feet thick."

He sat back against the hard wood of the booth. "Kirsty? You installed the wi-fi, right? Is it always this slow?"

Kirsty shrugged. "It's a big file. I'm not too surprised." She nodded slowly. "I see what you mean. I'll run a monitor. We can't take any chances, but this place is as secure as you'll get." She bumped her hip against him. "Let's go."

"Where are we going?" He slid out from the booth.

"To get a better signal. Don't worry, nobody will track this wi-fi. It changes identity every few minutes."

He followed her up the stone steps and along the corridor into a wide hallway lined with polished antique furniture. Bright sunshine came from an open doorway.

She typed into the iPad as she walked. "*Ekland*. It's a common Nordic name. And it's international. Does it mean something or someone? And *pichaq*? French, no? There's nothing on Google. It doesn't exist."

He shielded his eyes from the sun as they approached

the doorway and could make out a high wall around five meters away. *That's the way out. I get that iPad and I'm gone. She'll be safe here.*

*

"Open it," barked Kane.

The British Army sergeant pushed back the cell door.

In the middle of the room the fat guy sat in a chair, flanked by two men. He jumped up and strode forward. "This is an outrage! I have a diplomatic passport and you must…" He was silenced as Kane punched him full in the face. He toppled back over the chair and lay spread-eagled on the floor.

Kane turned to the MI5 officer beside him. "So, what did he say?"

"Sir, he has a…" The first officer held out a passport.

Kane took it and threw it across the room. "Fuck that. It's fake, right?"

"Actually…"

"If I say it's fake, then it's fucking fake. What did he say?"

"Well, he refused to talk until he was allowed to speak to his embassy."

The fat guy rolled on his side and pushed himself to his knees. Blood streamed from his nose and spilled onto the floor. He stood up, holding his face with both hands and was about to speak when Kane ran over and booted him in the balls. Blood sprayed between his fingers as he toppled backwards and landed on his ass.

Kane turned to the doorway where two men in suits filled the frame. "Get this prick over to Grosvenor Square. Then he'll talk." He looked down. "Yeah, Chubby, afternoon tea is over."

The fat guy retched and curled into a ball.

"You're coming to our place for some fun," said Kane. "We've got the visitor's suite all set up. And I've got to tell you, we've got some really nice toys for you to play with there." He stood over him, then lifted a leg and placed the heel of his shoe onto his ear. "Can you hear me?" He brought his full bodyweight down and twisted his shoe around.

The fat man shrieked.

"I said, can you hear me? Ah, who gives a shit. One ear will do. You know, I've got an ex-marine drill instructor in Grosvenor Square with a baseball bat, just waiting for you to arrive. He's never in a good mood. He lost two of his brothers in a terrorist bombing. I've never seen a guy break bones so fast. It really is a gift."

The fat guy turned his head towards Kane and growled, "Fuck you." He placed both hands under his jaw and twisted until a sharp crack came from his mouth. He screamed and his head jerked back as his body began to spasm. His arms thrashed around and a dirty white froth bubbled from his mouth.

Kane grabbed him by the hair to pull him up, but his eyes rolled back into his skull and his arms dropped lifeless by his side. "You bastard!" He kicked the man in the face, then pointed at the MI5 officers. "One fucking lead, and...you assholes. You can't even do *one* job without fucking up."

"Look, sir, he had a diplomatic..."

"Shove that passport up your ass and get me the head of MI5 right now!"

"Sir, we'll let her know..."

Kane marched forward until their faces nearly touched. "Listen carefully, because I don't think you understand. You work for us. You're just a shitty little island off the coast of Belgium. You think you're a nuclear power? You can't fire a fucking missile unless we say so. We hold the codes, not you. So you do what you are told and you do it right fucking now."

A cough came from the doorway. Campbell was just visible between the two men in suits. "Sir? It's Montrose. I think we have a lead."

*

Nervous glances followed Kane as he strode between the desks.

Campbell scurried after him. "We've got the numbers of all the phones that were switched on in the restaurant and we've discounted the Russians and the staff. One was an Apple watch. We found that in Soho. That leaves only one other number and the last place it connected to a network was right beside the watch. It must be Montrose."

"Where is it now?"

"No signal, sir, it must be switched off."

"Send him a message. And make sure it's loaded, right?"

"I understand. This desk, sir," said Campbell and stood behind a seated technician.

"Show me." Kane pulled the chair back and leaned into the screen.

The technician tried to stand up. "Hey, what the hell?"

"Shut your mouth." Kane pushed him back into his chair.

Campbell ran his finger down the screen. "Where is it?"

The technician shrugged. "It's gone. Must have been a false signal."

"Bring up the signal monitor."

The technician shrugged. "I didn't start the monitor."

"Don't lie to me," said Campbell.

Kane grabbed the back of the technician's chair and pushed it away from the desk.

"Hey, you can't..."

"I told you to shut up."

Two CIA goons in suits moved over and stood either side of the desk, facing the room as Campbell grabbed the keyboard.

A woman ran over from a nearby desk. "Stop this right now! That is a security breach and I'll..."

One of the goons pulled her to the side.

"Listen, sweetheart," said Kane. "If you can't do this shit, then we will. Just don't forget who's in charge."

Campbell pointed to the screen. "This IP address keeps changing. And it's an unregistered wi-fi." He turned to the technician. "Why did you take it out of the monitor?"

"It's a false signal... There's no... It's probably faulty equipment."

Campbell looked up at Kane. "This is the only signal in that area that's behaving weirdly. And it has no address details, no registered owner and it's right in the heart of Soho. The place is full of small apartments and businesses. It's well-hidden."

"I want to know exactly where it is. To the nearest inch."

"We can ping it and measure the response times against the speed of the transmission, then triangulate from the other signals. That gives us location and distance."

"How long?"

"Five minutes. We'll find it."

Kane pointed to the two men in suits. "Get the team ready. I want two hundred cops to close that place down. You go in first. I want Montrose alive. Fuck anybody that gets in the way."

CHAPTER 5

Montrose stood in the doorway to the garden. The tinny sounds of a cello symphony came from speakers above the door and several groups of elderly, well-dressed men sat around tables, nursing their drinks. Five yards in front, the brick wall surrounding the garden rose to around twelve feet high. *Not much of a run up. And I'd have the iPad in my hand. She's not going to let that happen.* A heady scent of flowers permeated the air. He turned and behind him was the barman, filling the whole doorway with his bulk. Montrose nodded. "Nice dress."

The barman said nothing.

Montrose walked over to where Kirsty was seated at a cast iron table in the shade of the wall. The table wobbled around as she laid the iPad in front of her. *If I try and stand on that I'll end up on my ass.*

"Sit down," said Kirsty. "I've got more on the old man in the restaurant. I was right, he was a senior copper. He's mentioned in old news articles." She pointed to a map on the iPad. "And he was based here. It's a town not too far from the Finnish border. If the word written on the stiff's arm is *Ekland* then Finland could be the connection. Or Sweden." She blew out a breath. "This is bollocks. It could be any Nordic country."

"Yeah, but check this." Montrose pointed to the map. "It's also not far from Russia." He glanced up at the top edge of the wall, checking for embedded glass. "I didn't know Norway had a border with Russia. Okay, let's step back a bit. The restaurant. Why did the old man fly all the way to London with some autopsy photos? And why did Arkangel pay a shitload of money for them?"

Kirsty brought up the webpage for a Norwegian newspaper. "Check this out." She pointed to the screen. "The old man was retired, but the glacier where the body was found is near where he was originally based."

She's piecing it together. I can take this to Kane. Maybe it's enough. No, the CIA will hunt her down. They'll want everything. The iPad is the bargaining chip.

"It's only in local news, but not in the nationals," she

said. "Why not? That would make a great story. Body stuck in the ice for God knows how many years. You'd want to get that out, right?"

"Yeah, would make sense. The guy would have been reported missing, even if he was a tourist. Maybe the old cop told them to keep quiet. Because he knew how much it was worth."

"He came all the way to London to hand over these photos personally. He could have emailed them."

"Maybe." He pointed to the webpage of the newspaper. "You speak Norwegian?"

"No, but I'll run a Google translator." Kirsty tapped on the iPad. "It's crap, but it says a body was found in the wall of a glacier and police took it away for investigation. That's it." The iPad beeped. "At last. I've got the download." She opened up a new app and the pictures flashed up, the detail sharper.

"Bring up the photos of the body." Montrose leaned in.

Kirsty shuffled closer towards him, their legs touching as she brought up the first photo of the twisted and crushed corpse.

"His hand," said Montrose. "Look at the fancy ring. There's another photo with a blow-up, check that."

"Sure," she said, "but you're missing the obvious."

"Yeah, what's that?"

She expanded the photo to show the man's face.

"He's got a bullet hole in his skull."

"Shit."

A voice came from behind them. "Ah, there you are."

Montrose turned and saw Pilgrim in the doorway, dwarfed by the barman.

Pilgrim walked over, nodding to several groups of gentlemen who raised their glasses towards him. He took small, neat steps then leaned over the table and kissed Kirsty on the cheek. "Excellent work on the escape and evasion, my dear," he said, in a long, Texan drawl. "That was a very unpleasant surprise in the restaurant, I'm sure."

Yeah, you could say that.

Pilgrim's face was flushed as he nodded to Montrose, his shirt tight around his neck and the precisely knotted tie held in place by collar studs. He brushed the seat of the chair then sat down, his hands folded in his lap.

Kirsty smiled. "It's my turf, Mr. P. We took an unusual route, but we got here. No idea how we are going to get out, but…"

"Leave that to me," said Pilgrim. He held out a perfectly manicured hand. "Good to see you alive, Montrose."

Montrose shook his hand. "Next time, I'd like a gun."

"A weapon would have done you no good." Pilgrim

took off his spectacles, blew on the glass and carefully replaced them. He blinked behind the thick lenses.

"Did you know about Kane?" said Montrose.

Pilgrim shook his head. "I had no idea. And that concerns me greatly."

Montrose nodded. *Whatever shit was going down, it must be serious if Pilgrim didn't know about it.*

Pilgrim adjusted his tie, then brushed imaginary dust from his dark woolen suit. "So, what do we have?"

Montrose was about to speak when Kirsty placed a hand on his arm and cleared her throat. She pushed the iPad across the table. "I couldn't hear what was said to Arkangel. But you've seen the video from the restaurant, yeah?"

"Indeed. They let him go," said Pilgrim. "I saw the diplomatic passport."

"But the fat guy…"

"Let me work on that," replied Pilgrim.

Kirsty pointed to a map on the screen. "The old guy in the car was from this small village here, in northern Norway. Ex-cop."

Montrose saw Pilgrim tense up. His collar seemed to be choking him. *What the hell is going on?* "You knew about this?"

"No," said Pilgrim. "I did not."

Then why is your hand shaking?

Kirsty brought up a CCTV freeze frame showing the cop's face. "This guy delivered and sold the photos to Arkangel before he was killed."

Pilgrim leaned over the table.

Kirsty continued. "The photos are different shots of the body of one guy. Found deep in a glacier. All we know about him is he's got a bullet hole in his head and some writing and a bunch of numbers on his arm."

Pilgrim squeezed his eyes shut and his face paled.

"We have no idea who he is." Kirsty looked up. "Mr. Pilgrim?"

Pilgrim ignored her. He sat back and took off his glasses once more. He gently rubbed his eyes and let out a long, slow breath. He gazed up at the sunshine for a moment, mouth open, then slowly replaced his glasses. "I know who he is." He leaned forward, his chin on his chest and then raised his head, staring blankly at the high brick wall. "He is my brother."

Montrose stared down at the face of the mangled body and up at Pilgrim. *Shit. It damn well is.*

Pilgrim stuck out his chin and gazed calmly at Kirsty. "Go on. The news is not pleasant, but it is not entirely unexpected. I had reconciled myself to his death many years ago. But I never thought…" He closed his eyes.

"That's about all we've got," said Montrose. "When did you last see him?"

"About thirty years ago." Pilgrim leaned closer and gently touched the photo with his finger.

"There's also a gun," said Kirsty. She pointed to the photo.

"Probably a Browning," said Montrose.

Pilgrim cleared his throat and sat up straight. "It may be. And given the nature of the wound, it seems my brother took his own life. I suspect as a last resort to foil our enemies."

"So where," said Montrose, "does Arkangel fit into this?"

Pilgrim tore his gaze from the iPad. "In his youth, Sylvester Arkangel was a Chechen Soviet specialist working in military satellites. He was a genius. He rose quickly in the party ranks. And since the break up of the Soviet Union he is now CEO of a ten billion dollar Russian communications company."

So what is he doing in London buying old photos? Spit it out.

"My brother was a spy, sent to infiltrate Soviet satellite installations during the Cold War. That's all I know. But I think that whatever information he found was valuable enough for him to kill himself to keep it from his enemies and valuable enough for Arkangel to bribe a police officer for over thirty years to deliver this information."

"That's crazy," said Kirsty, "how did Arkangel know that your brother would be found?"

"I don't know. But glaciers are melting faster than ever before. Thirty years ago, the slower rate of warming would have ensured that his body was buried for a hundred years. Things are different now."

But Arkangel still waited. For what?

"I suspect that my brother killed himself in the knowledge that he would never be found in our lifetime. His body must have travelled down the valley with the glacier, being buried further under the snow each winter."

"What was he hiding?" said Montrose.

"I have my suspicions," replied Pilgrim.

I'll bet you do. "One thing I don't understand," said Montrose. "Your brother was a spy and maybe running from the Soviets, right? All the way from Russia. But the gun found in the glacier was a Browning. I'm sure of it. If he was a spy, he wasn't going to last very long in Soviet Russia carrying an American weapon, so where did he get the gun?"

"I don't know," said Pilgrim. "It is a mystery." He nodded towards the iPad. "Let us continue."

Kirsty highlighted a photo and expanded the detail. "We think this is important. There's writing on his arm. It says *Ekland* and maybe *pichaq* followed by a bunch of numbers. Too long for a phone number. Who's Ekland?"

"Ignore the numbers for a moment," said Pilgrim. "Show me the first part."

Kirsty traced the writing and read out loud. "DOBDD TT+14 THE PICHAQ TWO EKLAND."

Pilgrim's mouth dropped open. "*Pee-shack*," he murmured. "That's how the word is said phonetically. It is how we were taught. But it's not how it is correctly spelled." His face twitched. "This message is for me."

"For you?" said Kirsty. "How would he...?"

"I can only assume that when my brother killed himself he hoped it would be the Western security services who found his body. Then they would come to me." He held out his left hand to show a signet ring, adorned with a crest.

"That's the same ring as in the photo," said Kirsty.

"The word is correctly spelled *piseag*. It's Scottish Gaelic." He pointed to the ring. "This is the crest of the clan MacPherson, my mother's family. She gave us these rings on graduation. The motto is *Na bean d'on chat gun lamhainu*. In English it means 'Touch not the cat without a glove'."

"And the numbers?"

Pilgrim nodded. "I think I know what they mean."

"Yeah," said Kirsty. "The groupings. It makes sense. They're coordinates, right?"

"Very perceptive of you," said Pilgrim.

Kirsty grabbed the iPad. "That'll be for the location of the Soviet communications base. I'll find out…"

Pilgrim placed his hand on her arm. "No. Not here. Give Zac those numbers, then set up an audio meeting. Use an encrypted connection."

"I can work them out," said Kirsty. "I'm sure they..."

"This is Zac's expertise," said Pilgrim. "Encryption is yours. Teamwork, my dear."

She smiled and turned back to her iPad, then stopped as it beeped three times. "Oh, shit."

Pilgrim's face tightened. "What is it?"

"Someone's taken over the wi-fi."

Montrose felt his back muscles tighten. *They've found me.*

Pilgrim glanced around. "Here? No, that's impossible, they would never…"

What is this place? A retirement home for gay spooks?

The barman strode towards them. "Kirsty, I just heard there are hundreds of cops in Soho. They're kicking in every door."

She typed quickly into the iPad. "Holy shit, someone is sending data packets to this router from every other wi-fi in Soho."

"Why?"

She looked up. "Triangulation. It's got to be."

Pilgrim looked up to the neighboring rooftops. "Why would they do that?"

"To pinpoint our exact location."

Pilgrim stood up. "How long, Kirsty?"

She didn't respond for a moment and tapped on the screen. "Okay, the wi-fi is down. No more signals. But I don't think that's enough. They'll work it out from what they've got. I'm sorry, they should never have been able to..."

"Tell me, Kirsty, how long?"

She pushed her fingers through her hair. "Ten seconds. Tops."

*

"There's no answer," said the policeman. He stepped back from the metal gate. "We can't break that down." He leant on the buzzer again. Behind him, more policemen pushed back half-naked showgirls as they crowded around the cramped courtyard and blocked the entrance to the alley.

"Get those goddamn whores out of the way." The big man pushed his way through and grabbed hold of the gate, jabbing at the buzzer. He turned to the cops. "This is a US security matter. You stay behind us at all times. But first you tell them to open this gate. Right now." Several men in suits and sunglasses moved to the front.

A voice came from the intercom. "Yes?"

"Do it," said the big man.

The policeman leaned in. "This is the police. We need immediate access to your property."

There was a pause before a refined, elderly voice came over the speaker. "Hello there! The police, eh? How very interesting. And you require access, you say? Well, I think you need a warrant for that, officer. Do you have one? Perhaps you would be so kind as to hold it up to the camera. And let me know the name of the High Court Judge who signed it. I'll check with him personally."

The big man hauled the policeman back, thrust his face into the camera and held up a gray plastic packet. "This is C4 explosive. It's all the warrant I need, so open the fucking gate."

CHAPTER 6

A florid-faced gentleman sporting a red carnation in his lapel and a drink in his hand approached the table. "Had to happen someday, Pilgrim. Bloody technology."

"Lord Jackson, I…"

"Never mind," said Jackson, "all they are going to find is some old duffers drinking too much gin. Unless of course you're still here, so I would recommend you and your chums bugger off sharpish. No offence, of course."

The barman swept the strap of his handbag aside and placed his massive hands on his hips. "Every club is being raided. They're emptying Soho. It's madness out there. There's no way out." A phone rang and he pulled a small cellphone from his bag and lifted it to his ear. "Too late. They're here."

The bent figure of an old man hobbled over, waving his stick. "It must be the bloody Yanks. MI5 would never let anyone near this place. Nor would the Russians. I must say, they'll be bloody furious when they find out."

Jackson stuck out his chin and turned to the barman. "Tell those flatfoot coppers to fuck off. They can't get in without a warrant." He nodded towards Kirsty. "Excuse my language, young lady." He held out his hand to the barman. "Give me that phone. I'm going to call the Prime Minister and tell him he's a spineless little twat."

The barman shook his head. "Lord Jackson, there's a gang of coppers out there with an American in front. He's threatening to blow the gate with explosives."

"Bloody hell," said Jackson. "Fucking colonials. Sorry, Pilgrim, but you need a long spoon to sup with the devil. There's only one thing to do. Start stacking the tables. I'll phone Madame Raymonde."

Montrose tried to lift the iPad from table, but Kirsty slipped it into her bag.

"I've sent the information to Zac," she said. "Unregistered SIM. Let's go."

"Wait. I've got a crazy idea." Montrose leaned in towards Pilgrim.

Kirsty stepped in between them. "Yeah?"

"Why… Why don't we just tell them? Hand over the info, leave them the iPad and then run like hell. They'll stop at nothing to get this. Do we really want to be caught in the crossfire? Or these guys?" He jerked a thumb towards the old men standing around, their rheumy eyes keen for action. "This could be vital to national security. And probably goes all the way to the top at Langley and the White House. We're supposed to be on the same side."

"No offence, Mr. P," said Kirsty, "but fuck the White House."

"None taken," replied Pilgrim.

Kirsty slapped the wall. "They had a chance to be nice, Connor. They used a sniper. If this is a matter of national security they'll kill you anyway. You really are an innocent. Grow some balls and get over the wall."

Montrose turned to Pilgrim. "Look…"

Pilgrim pushed his glasses back hard onto his head. "I concur with the sentiment of Kirsty's assessment, if not the actual phrasing. I know the identity of the Americans you met in the restaurant. Suffice to say that this is the best course of action. Let's go."

Jackson clapped Montrose on the shoulder. "Shift your arse, old boy, they'll be over the barricades in seconds."

An old man shuffled towards them and stuck out

his chin. "Let them come. We'll use the old method of dealing with angry colonials. Fix bayonets and advance by rank."

Several wheezing laughs came from the old men. "They don't like it up 'em!" shouted one, thrusting his cane into the air and almost toppling backwards onto the grass.

Montrose looked up at the wall. *Jesus, get me out of here.*

The barman lifted the cast iron table as if it was cardboard and placed it lengthways against the wall. Several old men came shuffling over to help.

"Everyone over the age of eighty, just stay out of the bloody way," said Jackson and helped the barman place a second table alongside, then lifted another on top. "The last time this happened," said Jackson, "it was Oscar bloody Wilde escaping from the Bow Street Runners with his trousers around his ankles and his spotty arse gleaming in the moonlight." He held out a hand to Kirsty. "Ladies first," he said as he helped her up onto the first table and pushed her firmly on the bottom as she clambered onto the wall.

"You cheeky bugger," said Kirsty. "If I didn't know you so well, I'd rip your arm off."

Jackson grinned. "Apologies, my dear, I dreamt for one moment you were Oscar."

She looked back at Montrose. "See you on the other side!" She slipped from sight.

"Mind you," said Jackson, "last time I did this, it was in Berlin before the wall came down. Trousers up, of course, but with the East Germans on my tail. Happy days." He and the barman lifted Pilgrim bodily onto the second table and pushed him up onto the wall.

Montrose was looking at the shaky pyramid of tables when several hands grabbed him and lifted him into the air. They held the tables as he found his feet.

"Go for it, laddie!" shouted Jackson.

Montrose gripped the edge of the wall and hauled himself up. It was a good twelve foot drop to the bottom.

"Drop and roll," said Kirsty.

He looked out over a patchwork of small back gardens and hedges. There were around twenty doors, but only one was open. At the far end, around a hundred yards away, an old lady stood in a doorway, clutching a long shawl around her and staring directly at them.

"There's no time to lose," said Pilgrim.

"Get over, you bloody chicken!" said Jackson.

Montrose pushed himself over the edge. He tried to roll before his feet hit the grass, but gravity took over and he dropped onto his ass. Pilgrim and Kirsty had already run across the garden and disappeared through a gap in a hedge. He scrambled to his feet and followed them through, just in time to see them clambering over a low stone wall. He sprinted across an immaculate lawn, vaulted the wall and caught up with them as they slipped between two high hedges. He pushed his way through the hedges and stepped into a graveled yard, moving towards the old lady and the open door. He ran, weaving between stone plant pots; he managed to avoid the first few then cracked his shin against the next. He slowed down and shuffled the rest of the way to the door. The old woman smiled as he approached, rubbing his leg.

"That is what they are there for, monsieur." Her face was severe but her eyes twinkled.

Pilgrim held out a hand. "Madame Raymonde, it is indeed a pleasure."

She ignored his hand and leaned forward to kiss him on both cheeks. "Ça *va?*"

Pilgrim shrugged. "Ç*a va*. I see you had a phone call."

"*Exactement.* No more time for pleasantries. Come inside and I will check the street is clear. Then you can go."

Montrose followed them inside. *Who the hell is she?*

Madame Raymonde closed the door behind them and pulled the thick woolen shawl closer around her shoulders. "I am never warm in London." She squeezed past them to the front of the house. "Follow me."

Facing them was a long corridor lined with framed photographs. He studied them as he walked past: a succession of faded black and white shots of British and French soldiers and groups of civilians in front of the Arc De Triomphe. The last was a larger photo of a young woman with Churchill and De Gaulle, standing in front of Buckingham Palace.

She didn't turn around as she talked. "SOE, young man. Not what you are thinking."

I was thinking you've had a hell of a life, lady. But Special Operations Executive? Yeah, the rivals of MI6 during the war. Churchill had them at each other's throats. Lives were lost in the fight between them. And bad blood still runs cold. In the corner of his eye he saw a line of bronze stars on the far wall, underlined with ornate Cyrillic script. *Soviet? Hey, hold on lady...*

"Over here," said Madame Raymonde.

He took a few quick steps and caught up with Pilgrim and Kirsty as they stood behind Madame Raymonde who was now hunched over several small monitors lined up inside the front door.

She glanced up and saw the look on Montrose's face. "Security, monsieur. There are still people out there who would do me harm. *C'est la vie. C'est la guerre.*"

I know the feeling, lady.

"I can't outlive them all." She turned back to the

screen. "The traffic at the end of the street should move soon. If it does not, I shall be concerned." She pulled her long shawl tightly around her.

Montrose glanced back to the rear door. *Those CIA psychos could be over the wall in seconds if they work it out. But the flowerpots and gravel won't help, they won't be creeping up.* "Yeah, we've got to move." He moved towards the monitor.

"Ah, a young man in a hurry. It was always the way." She touched Kirsty's arm. "Look after this one, my dear, he has kind eyes." Madame Raymonde gave him a lopsided smile.

"I'll do my best. If he behaves himself." Kirsty patted him on the butt.

Jesus, this isn't a romantic movie. The CIA will tear you apart.

"Behave himself?" said Madame Raymonde. "Then there would be no joy in life." She turned back to the monitors. "The road is clear. Go quickly. Cross the road and take the alley between the houses. That will take you to Oxford Street. Stick to the crowds. It's more difficult for the cameras." She opened the door and stepped out before Montrose could stop her.

"Let me…" said Montrose and pushed his way to the door. He spotted two figures on the monitor, turning into the street. They pulled out pistols and began to run. "We've got company."

Madame Raymonde looked down the narrow sidewalk and saw them coming. "*Merde!*"

Montrose lunged forward and grabbed her shawl to pull her back. She wriggled free and he fell back into the doorway with the shawl in his hand, revealing a Sten gun hanging at her side.

She gripped the magazine and brought up the stubby barrel then let off a burst towards the men. The bolt in the Sten slammed home and stayed there. She rattled it in her hand. "Stupid British weapon! Why do you always jam?" She tried to tug the cocking handle back to clear the breach, but it was stuck fast.

Montrose saw the figures on the monitor get to their feet, keeping low and bringing up their weapons. Three rounds slammed into the door frame as Pilgrim stumbled forward into the doorway to grab Madam Raymonde. He dropped to his knees and Kirsty leapt over Pilgrim and grabbed the Sten, hauled back the cocking handle, then emptied the magazine down the street in two controlled bursts.

The men lay sprawled on the sidewalk. Madame Raymonde took the Sten from Kirsty. "Go! I am safe here. Once the door is closed, an army could not get in. I shall call for help from my people. They will deal with the Americans."

Montrose checked both sides of the road then turned back and saw Kirsty kneeling beside Pilgrim.

Her face was white as she looked up. "It's bad." She pulled back Pilgrim's jacket revealing his torso drenched in blood.

Pilgrim tried to control his breathing but his gasps came short and fast. "Leave me here."

"No," said Kirsty. "We can't..."

"Just go," said Madame Raymonde. "Now!"

"We'll carry you," said Kirsty.

"*Non*!" Madame Raymonde tore back Pilgrim's shirt to reveal the ragged entry wound. "You may kill him. Leave him with me, *ma puce*. I will take care of him."

Kirsty took a BlackBerry from her bag and pushed it into Pilgrim's hand. "Use this. We'll contact you." It fell from his grasp. She picked it up and pushed it into his pocket.

"Call Zac," whispered Pilgrim.

Madam Raymonde grabbed Kirsty by the shoulder and pulled her up. "*Allez!* There is no time for this." She pulled a phone from her dress and punched in a number. "Elizabeth? I need your help."

CHAPTER 7

Montrose raced after Kirsty down the brick-lined alley. At the end a red double-decker bus passed slowly and a steady stream of pedestrians moved across the exit onto the street. *Oxford Street. Keep to the crowd.*

Kirsty showed no signs of slowing as she neared the corner.

"Kirsty, take it easy."

She stopped and he slid to a halt beside her. "Connor, I'm not going to hang about street corners looking shifty. Get into the crowd, walk at a normal pace. Go with the flow."

"Kirsty, there could be cameras, we have to…"

"Could be?" She turned and laughed. "Central London is swamped with CCTV. They'll be watching us right now. Wait, I've got a better idea." She pulled him onto the street and hailed a taxi.

"Damn it, Kirsty, they'll track the taxi."

"That's exactly what I want them to do. Get in."

"Look, this is not..."

"This is my manor, Connor. Trust me." She opened the taxi door before it came to a halt and jumped in. "Cabby? Liberty's staff entrance." She dropped onto the back seat and connected her earphones into the iPhone. "We're on secure encryption. They can't listen in. I've sent Zac the details." She handed him one of the earpieces.

The taxi pulled out into the traffic, turned into the bus lane and began to pick up speed. Montrose shoved in the earpiece and heard the call going through, then a sleepy Californian accent.

"Yeah?"

"Zac, it's Kirsty. Mr. Pilgrim said to call you."

"Yeah, yeah," said Zac. "That number you sent me. You know what it is?"

"They were coordinates, right? A map reference? Somewhere in Russia, no?"

"No, dude, not a map. At least not one I've ever seen. But I worked it out. It's coordinates for outer space. Or near space, I should say."

"Space?" Kirsty looked quizzically at Montrose.

"It's a satellite," said Zac. "And the weirdest freakin' satellite I've ever seen and satellites are my thing."

"Zac, it's Connor Montrose. What kind of satellite are we talking about?"

"I have no idea. It won't talk to me. Or identify itself. I've tried everything."

"Can't you hack into it?" said Kirsty.

"I've tried. It won't respond, but I know it's listening. It needs an access code and I've no idea what that is. This is seriously old technology, way before Windows and GUIs. Hey, wait a minute, I've got an idea."

"What?" said Kirsty.

"The pictures you sent me. The code written beside the coordinates. That's got to be it."

Kirsty brought up the photos on her iPad and read out the code. "DOBDD TT+14 THE PICHAQ TWO EKLAND. That one?"

"The first part," said Zac. "It's not TT+14. It's *Pi*+14."

"Pi?"

"Yeah, it's the math symbol for Pi. The thing that looks like a little Stonehenge."

Kirsty switched to Wikipedia and brought up the π symbol "Got it."

"This is Math 101," said Zac. "Whoever wrote this was in a hurry. I've broken harder codes than this when I've been stoned. When's Pilgrim's birthday?"

Montrose leaned over to the iPad. *Pilgrim's birthday? What the hell is he talking about?*

"Pilgrim said the message was for him," said Kirsty. "It makes sense."

"I got it," said Zac. "Let me run this through the system. DOBDD is easy, that's the day of your birth. And the DD could mean two digits, like mmddyy."

"Okay, I get that," said Kirsty.

"But that's not going to change, so that's not part of the code. A good code is one that changes daily. The DD is telling us the day it starts."

Montrose shook his head. "We're looking for a code that changes every day?"

"Yeah," said Zac. "You just need to know how to work it out. And I think it's all here. We got the DD, so we know when the code starts. Then the 'Pi+14' could mean the code is the first fourteen digits of Pi on that day, right?"

Kirsty stared down at the iPad. "And the next fourteen digits?"

"Yeah, on the second day after the first DD, then you take the next fourteen digits of Pi in sequence, then on the third day... You know where I'm going with this, yeah?"

"Yeah," said Kirsty, "and right up to today, which would mean a totally new code every day. If you didn't know the sequence, you'd have no chance of hacking it."

Montrose shook his head as he tried to take it in. "Listen, math is not my thing, but that would mean hundreds of thousands of..."

"No sweat," said Zac. "There's no limit to the digits of Pi after the decimal point. The first day's code would be 3.14159265358979, right? If you divide 21 by 7 on your calculator and the readout is long enough, you'll see what I mean. So the next 14 digits after that are 32384626433832. Then you get the next fourteen for the next day and all the way up to today."

Montrose shook his head and looked at Kirsty. "Zac, you just worked this out?"

"No, dude, I'm not that sad. It's on the internet. There's a website that shows Pi to a million digits."

"Is that gonna work?" Montrose heard Zac typing quickly.

"Okay, I know when he was born. So I use the number of calendar days since Pilgrim's birthday, right up to today. I'm guessing the Gregorian calendar, 'cos no one gives a shit about the Julian Calendar except saddos and Russians. Just give me... I got it!"

"So?"

"Holy crap," said Zac. "I'm in."

Montrose felt his chest tighten. *This shit is getting away from me. If Kane finds out what we're doing...*

"What do you see?" said Kirsty.

"Nothing," replied Zac. "But it's asking for a password. Hey, I've seen this before. This is green screen shit. This is ancient technology. Must be the Eighties."

"Zac," said Kirsty. "If the first part of the code was that number, then the second part is going to be that password, no?"

"Got to be. *Pichaq*, right?" They heard Zac typing. "No, it doesn't work."

Kirsty tapped the iPad. "Wait. Pilgrim said that's how you pronounce it, not how it's written." She turned to Montrose. "Gaelic for cat, right? I'll try the translator. I've got it here. *Piseag.*" She spelled it out.

"Hold on," said Zac. "No. Ain't no good. That all we got?"

Kirsty flicked through the photos on the iPad. "Pilgrim's brother wrote that word on his arm for a reason. And that has to be a clue to the password. He gave the coordinates, telling us where to look. There has to be something about *piseag.*

"Yeah," said Montrose, "and that message was meant for Pilgrim. Not us."

"Wait." Kirsty closed her eyes and tapped her fingers one by one. "He told us it was Scottish Gaelic. His mother's language. And her name."

Montrose leaned in. *I can't stop them. Go with the*

flow. The more I know, the more I can sell. And get us out of this shit. "It was MacPherson," said Montrose. "His mother's family. And he said something about a motto. Touching the cat."

Zac laughed. "No man, it's 'touch not the cat, without a glove.' Basically it means don't mess with me."

Kirsty pointed to a photo. "I can see the clan crest on the ring his brother is wearing. The password could be in the motto, but according to Google, there are about seven different translations."

"Kirsty, I'm looking at it now. I'm running a program on all the words and the only one I can find that means cat is '*chat*'. And that doesn't work."

"Shit."

Montrose rubbed his face. "What kind of cat is it?"

Kirsty shrugged. "It's just a... Hold on, there's a cat that lives in Scotland and nowhere else. In the Highlands. And MacPherson is a Highland clan."

"Yeah," said Zac. "I've got it on Wiki. The Scottish wildcat."

Kirsty's fingers flew across the iPad. "That's it, I can see it too. Totally different species. They live in the wild and they're mean as hell. That would explain the line about not touching it. Zac? *Wildcat*. Go for it."

"I'm on it."

Kirsty looked up at Montrose "If that's not it, we could be..."

"I'm in! Holy shit, everything is in Russian. What the hell...?"

The taxi came to a halt and Montrose looked out at the loading bay of a department store.

Kirsty ripped her earphones out. "Zac, do what you can, we'll call you back." She cut the call, took some money from her bag and leaned over to the driver. "Mate, that's for the fare and this," she held up a fifty pound note, "is to pick up a guy outside Vauxhall House. He's in a blue duffel coat and called Paddy. If he's not there then it's yours to keep."

The cabbie shrugged and took the money. They stepped out and stood before the goods entrance to the store.

"There are no cameras here, apart from that one," she said, pointing to a dark glass dome above the loading door. "And that belongs to the store."

"Who's Paddy?"

"No idea, I made that shit up." She grinned and pulled him into a side door. "In here. We need a change of clothes while they go chasing that taxi."

He followed her into the store, past stands of cosmetics reeking of perfume and assistants wearing far too much make up. They entered a central atrium and above him rose four storeys of mock Tudor balconies in a square. *What the fuck am I doing here? Kane said there's an imminent terrorist attack and we're going shopping?*

Kirsty took out a bundle of money from her bag and peeled off several high denomination notes. She held them out. "Cash is king. Cards can be traced. You've got five minutes to change your appearance."

Montrose took the money.

She reached up and flicked his hair into a side parting. "Just clothes unless you find a wig. Menswear is downstairs."

"Sure, do you want me to hold your bag for you?"

She smiled. "You're such a gentleman, but I think I'll manage. Anyone would think you're after my money." She pushed the banknotes into her bag and ran up the ornate wooden staircase.

He watched her go. *What if she gives me the slip? Just get back here before she does. One thing is for sure. I don't care if they shoot me on the street, I'm not wearing a fucking wig.* He headed for the stairs.

*

His sneakers squeaked on the polished wooden floor and the new jeans were tight, but the overpriced designer combat jacket fitted well. He pulled the wrapping from a Timex watch and fixed it to his wrist, then turned into the atrium and looked up. He did a double take when he spotted the blond wearing a sleeveless cotton dress. She walked gracefully along the balcony of the first floor, then descended the staircase, a polished leather bag draped over her left arm, which was covered in a sleeve of black and red gothic tattoos.

If it wasn't for the ink and the Dr. Marten boots, she would fit right into high society. C'mon man, don't let your balls rule your brain. That chick took out two goons with a Sten gun.

She smiled coyly as she stepped off the staircase and crossed the floor, pulling on a cashmere cardigan as she moved.

Yeah, she may be tough, but the CIA will squash her like a bug. I can't let that happen. I've got two passwords. The coordinates of the satellite are on the iPad. I get that and then go. The CIA can take care of the threat. But a satellite? What are the bad guys gonna do? Broadcast shit movies?

Kirsty swept the hair from her face. "I see you didn't choose a wig."

"Blond suits you." He pulled out a heavy black toupee from his jacket. "I'm not sure this works."

She lifted a hand to her mouth and laughed.

"It's the only one that fitted."

"Perhaps not, then. You'd just look like a really shit Elvis impersonator." She took his hand. "Let's go."

"Where?"

"Anywhere that there are no cameras. We need to talk to Zac and Mr. Pilgrim."

Yeah, if he's still alive. The phone rang in her pocket. *They've tracked her phone.*

*

The ice in the glass of vodka rattled in his grip. Arkangel stared blankly out of the window towards Kensington. He spun around as the door opened behind him.

A man walked into the room, ignored Arkangel and sat down on a sofa. He made himself comfortable and placed his hands on his knees.

Arkangel held the glass so tightly he thought it would shatter in his hand. "What are you doing here? Who let you in?"

"Your men let me in. I am Victor Kutuzov. Intelligence attaché at the Russian Embassy in London. And your men know exactly who I am. Shame that you don't. I expected you to be better informed. That is disappointing."

"I don't care you who are, you mind your tongue or

I'll have my men throw you out on to the street."

Kutuzov smiled. "Your men? I think not. Why do you think they let me walk in here?"

Arkangel took a gulp from his glass. "They are idiots, I..."

"Because they are *my* men. You recruited from ex-Spetsnaz troops. A wise choice, you would have thought, but then you never really stop being Spetsnaz, do you?" Kutuzov shrugged. "How would you know? You have spent your career behind a desk. Shuffling paper clips and losing satellites. We haven't forgotten that, you know."

Arkangel strode forward. "I don't have to listen to this."

Kutuzov leaned back in the sofa. "One word from me and they will butcher you like a pig. So, sit down."

Arkangel remained standing. "How dare you..."

"SIT DOWN!"

He found the nearest chair.

Kutuzov straightened his tie. "Your activities have not gone unnoticed. I know your history, *tovarisch*. All those years ago, running around Norwegian glaciers. But we all move on, eh? And as we emerged from the Cold War, you decided to go private. You paid the right people and you made a lot of money using our old Soviet satellite system. It was shit, but good enough for phone calls and pornography. I'm impressed. But you never forgot, did you?"

Arkangel tried to shrug, but his shoulder jerked so hard the vodka sloshed over the edge of his glass.

"The Red Star," said Kutuzov. "You never stopped looking."

"It was my mission. But the trail went cold. Literally. *I* was on the glacier. *I* watched Pilgrim put a bullet in his brain. I went back to get my men to recover the body, but the storm became a blizzard and lasted for three days. We had to escape to save our own lives. There was thirty feet of snow that winter. When the spring came and we returned, a snow plough had pushed Pilgrim's car down the valley. We had no idea where we had left him. There was no way to find his body. And no one could access the Red Star without those codes he had stolen. They died with him. But I never forgot it was my duty to find them."

Kutuzov waved a hand in the air. "That was then. This is now. And a few days ago a body appeared out of the ice of a Norwegian glacier, thirty minutes from the Russian border."

"The Americans tried to trick us, telling us they had the codes. But now we know they were lying."

"You're such an amateur. All that Pilgrim had to do was make a phone call before his demise on the glacier. Or one word to a contact."

"We were close behind him." Arkangel shook his head. "There were no phones."

Kutuzov shrugged. "Another amateurish assumption. Pilgrim talked to no-one? You're sure?"

Arkangel said nothing.

"So, you find the body in the ice and you discover that Pilgrim had written down clues to the code before he died. But do you hand over the information to Moscow? No, you keep it all to yourself and then you tell your friends in the Middle East."

Arkangel shifted in the chair. "No, they heard about..."

"Don't lie to me or I will personally cut out your tongue. You told your contacts. The information is priceless to the right client. And you had one lined up in that restaurant in Soho. He saw the information and agreed to pay. Fifty million dollars. Too cheap, *tovarisch.* You could have got so much more."

Arkangel made to get to his feet, but saw the look on Kutuzov's face. "I need a drink."

Kutuzov nodded.

The vodka splashed in the glass and he drank half in one go. "It was a ruse. I would sell the information and then go straight to you. I would never have betrayed Moscow. But there was no reason I couldn't make good money out of it. It's just business. And I've spent a fortune of my own money looking for those codes and Pilgrim."

Kutuzov threw his hands wide and laughed. "Seriously? You think that would work? You're a fool, Arkangel. You thought you were the only one to know and you killed the old policeman to cover your tracks. But your men were feeding us information all along. Why do you think they were allowed to use government mainframes in Moscow to crack the first password? WikiLeaks has been very generous to us. Once we saw the photographs, all we had to do was check the birthdates in the state records of Texas. We're one step ahead of you. And we were waiting outside the restaurant in Soho. We would have been marching in with a gun to your head. You were lucky the CIA got there first."

Arkangel drained his glass. "You begrudge a man the opportunity to make some money? I swear to you, once I had the funds, I would have handed everything over."

Kutuzov shook his head. "You're a bad liar, Arkangel. And now your friends in the Middle East are asking why their top man is in an MI5 cell. That's not going to go down well. They think you set them up. And they are not known for their forgiveness."

"No money changed hands. They..."

"They are your problem. Not mine. If I were you, I

wouldn't waste money on a pension. You're unlikely to see it. However, if you work for me, I can offer you some protection."

"I have spent years working on this. I can't just hand everything over to Moscow!"

Kutuzov stood up. "Sure. You have a choice. Work for me, or be pursued across the globe by fanatics for the rest of your life. You know who they are, don't you? The kind of people that would send a child as a suicide bomber to kill you. I'd give it a month at most before they found you. If you're lucky, you'll get an orange jumpsuit and a video on YouTube. If not, well, I wouldn't like to think about it."

Arkangel stared at his empty glass.

Kutuzov walked over and stood directly in from of him. "That's unless I find you a threat to my operation and shoot you first. So, join the team. Work for Mother Russia once more."

A young man with a laptop appeared in the doorway. "We have the second password."

"Excellent work!" Kutuzov strode over and thumped him on the shoulder so hard the young man nearly dropped the laptop. "What is it?"

"Wildcat. The word 'PICHAQ' which was written on the body. Once we researched Pilgrim's history and his Scottish connections, we ran it through the language databases. It's phonetic, but translates as 'cat'. Then we found a specific Scottish reference to an indigenous species. But there is something else."

"Go on," said Kutuzov.

"Someone else is connected to the Red Star. They also have the first password. And it's the first time in over thirty years according to the log."

"Block them," said Kutuzov. "We can't allow..."

"No," said Arkangel. "The second password only allows normal maintenance access. Red Star needs a third password before it can be activated."

"Another password?" Kutuzov's face tightened.

Arkangel cleared his throat. "That's what I was trying to tell you. The third sequence of words written on Pilgrim's arm seems to be nonsense. We've run it through all the systems in Moscow. And that's what the Middle East were getting for fifty million dollars. Nonsense. We need to crack the third password before whoever else is logged on."

"It must be the Americans or the British," said Kutuzov. "Only they have knowledge of the Red Star."

"No," said Arkangel. "It's obvious that the CIA pretended for over thirty years that they had access, but they did not. Why would they log on now? There has been a leak. And you tell me, Kutuzov, that these are your men?"

"Arkangel, don't fuck with me."

"Don't block the other sign-on. If they have the first password, they'll soon be looking for the second. Track them. Find out what they know."

Kutuzov clicked his fingers. The young man turned and ran down a corridor.

*

Madame Raymonde sat calmly in a wingback chair and sipped her sherry, then placed the glass down onto a polished slate table, the sound tinkling in the cavernous room. She looked over to Elizabeth Purley, gazing out over the Thames. No sound penetrated the thick security glass and the traffic across Lambeth Bridge moved silently. She saw that Purley's broad shoulders had become more stooped as the years had passed. The tailored dark suit now hung awkwardly on her shoulders. Madame Raymonde had never seen her wear anything else, nor any make-up. Only the Gucci purse gave a clue as to her gender. "I never thought I would see this in my lifetime."

Purley turned away from the window. "The Norway operation?"

Madame Raymonde nodded and lifted her sherry glass once more. "So, he died on the glacier?"

"It seems so."

"And Jack Pilgrim?"

Purley looked across the Thames to the railway arches, leading to Waterloo. "He'll live, with treatment. I'm keeping him close."

"What do the CIA know?"

Purley walked slowly across the room and sat behind her desk, glancing at her laptop. "I'm getting updates from my teams, but all we know is that the policeman who was killed in Soho found a body in a glacier, not far from a Norwegian village close to the Russian border."

"We have to be very careful, my dear," said Madame Raymonde, then swallowed the sherry in one mouthful. "There's so much to lose."

Purley said nothing. She opened up her purse and took out a faded and cracked photo. The photo was so worn that only she could identify the face. "There is everything to lose."

"I only heard the Soviet side of the story before I left Moscow." Madame Raymonde settled back into her chair. "And how they lost the codes. I did what I could. If Michael Pilgrim had not been successful in his mission then the US would have attacked the USSR. The threat was simply too great. And he died on the glacier."

"And then the stalemate began. The Soviets warned the US that if the Red Star was ever activated it would be seen as an immediate act of war. But without the codes the Soviets knew the game was up. It was only a matter of time. The US would never have allowed another Red Star in the sky and the Soviets knew it. The death of Pilgrim was the best possible outcome. And then began a game of poker that has been going on for over thirty years. No one willing to show their hand. Until this happened."

Madame Raymonde saw the lines on Purley's face. They had deepened as the responsibility of running MI5 and the passing years had taken their toll. "Did the Soviets ever know for sure that Michael Pilgrim handed over the codes before he died?"

"No, they were never sure. The Americans pretended they had the codes all along and could use the Red Star at any time. By the time the Soviets had worked out the bluff and realized Reagan's SDI Star Wars was also a bluff, the Red Star was obsolete."

"But not anymore."

"No, now the skies are full of satellites. And the Red Star means complete military dominance for any side that gains control."

"They will do everything in their power to get it."

Purley shook her head. "The Russians are no longer

the Soviets. Making money is the new God in Moscow. They may want the Red Star for prestige, but they would never activate it. Such a thing would be bad for business. But with the Americans, anything is possible." A phone beeped on Purley's desk. "He's here. Wait next door." She got up from behind the desk and nodded towards a small door in the wall, then returned to her desk and pushed a button.

*

Kane strode across the room. "I'm not gonna bullshit you, 'cos I really don't have time for that. I need full cooperation from your team. This is our operation and I know you have it from your Prime Minister that your people will do whatever they are damn well told."

Purley sat down, slipped the faded photo into her purse and placed it under the desk. "As the head of MI5, I'm sure my team will give you all the cooperation you require."

Kane stood at the edge of the desk, leaning over. "Yeah? What about that club in Soho? Were you keeping that to yourself?"

Purley shrugged. "We all have our little secrets.

I understand you found nothing in the club. A dead end. It is merely a place for retired gentleman and of absolutely no interest to your operation. As I'm sure you discovered."

"Yeah, that place, I'll deal with it later. Rooms full of freaks and fruitcakes."

"And what of the rest of the operation? I understand MI5 and the Metropolitan Police have supplied you with the required manpower?"

"Oh, yeah, like your asshole geek who forgets to track the only interesting signal in London. And while all that shit was going on, Montrose got out of Soho. But we'll find him."

Purley leaned back in her chair. "What is it you are looking for, Mr. Kane? Apart from Montrose? We may be of more assistance if we knew."

"No way. This is a US affair. We just need your monkeys to do the legwork. The less we tell you, the better. Your whole system leaks like a sieve."

"Does it?" She let her elbows rest on the edge of the chair and brought her hands together as if in prayer. "Like a sieve, you say? Remind me, Mr. Kane, for whom did Edward Snowden work? And Bradley Manning?"

Kane jabbed a finger at her. "I don't have to take that shit. London is a holiday destination for every major terrorist and crook on the planet. There are enemy spooks everywhere."

Purley curled her lips into a thin smile. "Well, you know what they say, keep your friends close and your enemies closer. By the way, it's relatively nice to see you again, Cousin."

Kane stepped back and blew out a breath. "Look, Elizabeth..." He shrugged. "Our countries go back a long way. I can't stress how important this is to the security of the United States. We need the UK to step up to the plate. We're the Cousins, right? You're our oldest ally."

"Are we? What a short memory the Americans have. I think you'll find the French are your oldest ally, historically speaking."

"Whatever. Look..."

"In fact, only five years before we fought the Nazis, your country had an approved and detailed plan to invade Canada, then declare war on Great Britain and destroy our Empire. Of course, you didn't go through with it because the Royal Navy would have shelled New York into rubble, burned down the White House for a second time and then kicked your Yankee arse across the high seas. Operation War Plan Red, wasn't it? Is that the kind of oldest ally we're talking about?"

"Hey, don't get clever with me, lady. If it wasn't for us, Hitler would have kicked your ass."

Purley leaned over the desk. "We stopped Hitler at

the Battle of Britain without your help. And if it wasn't for the Russian front, the Allied armies in Normandy would have been fighting over two hundred Nazi Divisions, not fifty. Do you consider the Russians to be old allies?"

"Bullshit. We saved your country from starving *and* supplied your army. I don't need a history lesson."

"Oh, I think you do. It took us sixty years to pay you for all the tanks and ships. You gave us nothing and we *owe* you nothing, so you listen to me." She got up from her chair and leaned forward, her fingertips pressing down hard on the desk. "For the moment, as promised, we will help you in searching for whatever it is you're looking for. However, if I discover that MI5 is involved in any activity which undermines the security of the United Kingdom, I will ensure that you and your army of sunglasses-wearing arseholes are chased off the White Cliffs of Dover and into the bloody sea. Is that clear?"

"I've had enough of your attitude, I am…"

She ignored him and walked out from behind the desk towards the door. "You will have full cooperation, Mr. Kane. But do not underestimate me. My only concern is the security of this country. If our interests align with yours and they usually do, then we will work together as we have done for many years. But if I find one of your men accessing an MI5 computer and pushing my operative aside at his own desk, I will personally cut his fucking hands off. Do I make myself absolutely clear?"

"Yeah, yeah, just… Trust us. We need you on this."

"Then we shall do our best." She held open the door.

Kane made to reply, then marched out of the room.

A moment later, Madame Raymonde approached her desk. "What a detestable man. I do hope something very unpleasant happens to him. Be very careful, my dear."

Purley dropped down in the chair and covered her face with her hands.

CHAPTER 8

Shoppers weaved around them as Kirsty stood close to Montrose and pulled the phone from her bag. "It's Zac." She plugged in the earphones and handed him an earpiece.

Her hair brushed his cheek as she leaned in. He felt his own phone buzz in his pocket. Static came through the earphone and Kirsty checked the encryption setting on her iPhone. He slipped out his phone and glanced at the text message.

Montrose, we need to talk – Kane.

How did he...? Hey, they have rooms of computers and control of the whole comms network in London. It was only a matter of time. Yeah and easy if your phone is switched on. I might as well be carrying a tracking device. He turned it off.

Zac's voice came over the earpiece. "We need to talk to Pilgrim. This shit just got real."

Kirsty leaned in closer. "What is it? Tell me, the line is secure."

"Kirsty, the freaking satellite is Soviet military issue. It's Cold War. And it's crammed with bombs."

What the fuck?

"Bombs?" Kirsty looked up at Montrose and her cheek brushed his chin.

"Yeah," said Zac, "I can't work it all out, but I can see the technical plans and the outside of the sat is loaded with explosive devices, with their own trajectory motors. But it doesn't make sense. They could never be used to attack targets on the ground. It's three hundred miles up in the air. Anything it launched to earth would burn up on re-entry."

Montrose tried to picture it in his head. "What about fast jets? Or spy planes?"

"Not unless they were old SR-1 Bluebirds. And they took one of those down with a surface to air missile. They didn't need a satellite for that. No, it's totally weird. Bluebirds never flew that high. Oh, fuck. I can see it. I know what this is. Man, if you could have a steampunk satellite, this crazy shit is it."

"What do you see?"

"The Red Star. Oh, man, I can't believe this actually

exists. This is totally legendary. This is like the holy grail of satellite geeks."

Montrose leaned in closer. "Zac, what the hell is the Red Star?"

"It's an MKV. A Multiple Kill Vehicle."

"A what? It's a thousand miles up in the air."

"This is ASAT. Anti Satellite Weapons. This is the space race no-one talks about. Couple of years ago an old US military satellite blew itself to bits. The Pentagon made some excuse about a mystery temperature spike and that it was old kit. But what they really thought was that the Russians had got another Red Star. Things have been pretty nervous since then."

"You reckon it was the Russians?"

"It's possible. Or the Chinese. They took out one of their own satellites with a missile. Totally stupid idea which covered the place in space junk. The Space Station spends half its time dodging all the crap flying around up there. And when the US found out what the Chinese were doing they built a top secret Satellite Warfare center in Dahlgren, Virginia. Let's just say I've got some old friends there."

"The Chinese ain't that crazy, they're too busy making money."

"Maybe, but the Red Star isn't the Ruskies' first attempt. They've been trying to design an attack satellite since Sputnik. They built a primitive version of Red Star in the seventies, called ISTRIBETEL, shooting out bombs all over the place. But it had one fatal flaw."

"What?"

"It was shit. They cancelled the program in 1982. So that's why they designed the Red Star. But since three years ago they've got a new system and a whole new military division called KRET. The Radio-Technology Group. They've stopped trying to blow things up, now they're just going to take them out by jamming all the systems using radio."

"Would that work?"

"Yeah, maybe. The word is they're ready to test it, but they've been saying that for a while. I mean, someone starts that kinda shit and it's war."

"You reckon they'll do it?"

"Man, knowing the Russians, if they say they're ready to test, that means it doesn't work and it's a total bluff. I mean if it did, they'd keep it secret, right? They can't even build a cruise missile without it going walkabout in someone else's country."

"Maybe," said Kirsty, "but that's Crazy Ivan. You never know with those guys."

Montrose gripped the iPhone in his pocket. *Yeah and you never know with our guys.*

"Hey, Kirsty," said Zac, "we really need to talk to Mr.

Pilgrim. I got a feeling the shit is about to hit the fan."

Kirsty checked the iPhone. "I'll try to patch him in."

Montrose could hear beeping on the line as Kirsty tapped the screen. "Zac?" he said.

"Hey, how you doing?"

"What do you know about Madame Raymonde? The old French lady in Soho?"

"Huh. I checked. She's some dude."

Probably the first time she's been called a dude. "Yeah? I need to know if we can trust her. Tell me what you've got."

"Born in Normandy, France, year unknown. Ex-Special Operations Executive during World War II. She was sixteen years old when she gained a reputation for guerrilla warfare and assassination. She was captured and tortured by the Gestapo but escaped. And she was also nearly killed by MI6 in Normandy over a turf war with SOE. They say Churchill saved her. And she was awarded the Soviet Bronze Star. Nobody knows why. The rest, well, I reckon that's still buried."

And if the CIA get their hands on her and Pilgrim, they'll be through both of them and his BlackBerry in minutes.

"There's no answer from Pilgrim," said Kirsty.

It was the first time Montrose had seen her worried. "Can we change the encryption setting? We can't be sure Pilgrim still has the phone."

"I'm on it," said Zac. "Go to encryption setting Five. I'll send out the details. It's fitted with a password that only Pilgrim knows."

"We've been here too long," said Kirsty. "Just let me do this, then we go."

You got that right. He held the phone in his pocket. *If they know the text message got through, they may have already located the phone.* He thumbed the power button. *One last check. It won't tell them anything new. Maybe Pilgrim sent a message.* The phone buzzed and he glanced at the screen.

Tell us what you know. Your country is in grave danger. Keep your phone switched on. We'll come to you. We can forget the past. We need your trust in us. - Kane.

He stopped himself from a bitter laugh. *They would betray me as easily as breathing. They know who I am. That's enough. They'd never let me live. But the kind of manpower they are using tells it all. The US is under serious threat. Pilgrim might be dead and I'm in a department store with a chick and a wig. This is way out of my league. But there has to be a way to give them the information without compromising Kirsty. Yeah and me too.* He powered off the phone. *Why did they let Arkangel go? A diplomatic passport seems too easy. Or it means they have no idea what he was up to. It was just the fat dude that took a dive. And Arkangel walked away. No, that stinks.* "Kirsty, get us out of here."

She pointed towards the ornate glass entrance. "This way."

He looked at the door and a stream of shoppers on the street. *Assume they have your location. Assume they are close. Assume they'll blow your fucking brains out. Move.*

*

The pain made his eyes shoot open and he lay still until it receded. He could hear the muted thumping of insistent music and then the rumble of a nearby railway line. He slowly turned his head to the left and saw the bag of blood and fluids, then traced the pipes leading to his arm and a morphine trigger. On the table next to him his BlackBerry buzzed. He shifted himself to reach for it when he heard a voice and a nurse came into view.

"Good news," she said. "The bullet missed your liver, but it's going to hurt for quite some time. You lost a lot of blood. Keep still or you'll burst your stitches. You can't risk internal bleeding."

Pilgrim saw her long, blood-red fingernails as she

stretched across to adjust the fluids and the latex uniform that stopped way too short on her legs, exposing red suspenders and stockings.

"Relax," she smiled. "I'm a real nurse, but I have to do something to pay the bills."

"Thank you. I, uh, appreciate it," said Pilgrim. "Where am I?"

"You don't look like the type of gentlemen who frequents this kind of place." She tidied his hair and adjusted his spectacles before lifting him gently by the shoulders and propping him up on the pillows. "You have a visitor." Her killer heels clicked as she walked away and another figure approached the bed.

He blinked, imagining a priest.

"Madame Raymonde sends her best wishes," said Purley.

He recognized the black trouser suit. She never dressed in anything else. "Thank you. She is a woman that I endlessly admire. Before I lost consciousness, I heard her talking to 'Elizabeth'. I should have known."

"We have been friends for many years," said Purley. "She made the right choice."

"Am I to assume, Miss Purley, that this conversation is not taking place?"

Purley nodded. "I have a situation where I cannot act as freely as I would wish."

"Ah, the CIA?"

"I couldn't possibly confirm that, I'm sure you understand. I'll come straight to the point, as I know you need to rest. I'm not going to ask you about Operation Red Star, but I understand that you have a man in the field who may require some information. I am making an assumption, Mr. Pilgrim, that you are acting in your country's interest, but not, shall we say, in concert with the CIA."

"I couldn't have put it better myself. I appreciate your candor and let me also be clear that I think Operation Red Star should stay buried deeper than the pits of hell."

She took a deep breath. "Then we have a common purpose."

Pilgrim saw her shoulders relax.

"Let me tell you about your brother. And please, do not ask me where I got this information. We all have our secrets."

"I understand."

"Your brother was the bravest of men. But there are few people who know his name or what he did, not only for his country, but for all the free countries of the world. And now there are powerful forces scrabbling around trying to piece together the information that will reveal his secret." She looked out of the window for a moment as a train whistle blew. "And since the CIA are running around London like gunfighters in a Western saloon, I know that they do not have the information that they require." She closed her eyes for a moment and then edged closer to the bed. "The man you need to talk to is called Warrender."

He heard a slight tremble in her voice.

"Roger Warrender." Her long fingers tightened around her purse. "He was an MI6 agent. He met your brother at the Russian border. What happened that night..." She looked away.

"I know who Warrender is, or was," said Pilgrim. "Where can I find him?"

"I don't know. The only man who may lead you to him is Captain Kenneth Wolff, a retired Naval officer. If anyone knows where Warrender is, it will be Wolff."

Pilgrim didn't reply, allowing her to continue. It seemed, he thought, that this was an operation she could not, or would not, perform herself. Or a bluff to allow the CIA to find his team in the open.

"I'm sure you have questions, Mr. Pilgrim. I will answer them as best I can."

Pilgrim nodded and shifted on the pillows. "Warrender is the missing link that the CIA has been hunting for decades. Why is he still alive?"

"Roger Warrender disappeared. We never heard of him again, although we searched the globe for many years. The received wisdom is that the Russians killed him. But I have always suspected he is still very much alive and living in London, which is the last place they would look for him."

Pilgrim closed his eyes for a moment. Both the CIA and the KGB had spent decades scouring the globe for Warrender. And this confirmed what he had suspected all along. Someone powerful was hiding him, for their own reasons. And he had no doubt that if Purley had wanted to find Warrender she would have done so already. Something was holding her back and had held her back for many years. But he was sure she would never admit it. "Tell me of Captain Wolff."

Purley cleared her throat. "Warrender and Wolff were once the closest of friends. That was many years ago. The fall of Captain Wolff is a tragedy, but... that is a story for another time." She looked out of the window, towards the railway. "Captain Wolff lives on the streets, usually in the railway arches behind London Bridge station."

A bolt of pain shot through Pilgrim and he squeezed the morphine trigger. He felt his muscles relax as the drug took hold, then he pushed the plastic pump to the side, letting it drop down the side of the bed and out of reach. He needed a clear head.

Purley turned back and leaned over the bed. "The

CIA knows you have two people on your team. One of whom is called Montrose. I realize that it is not a name they will be glad to hear again, but personally, I wish him the best of British luck. And you too, Mr. Pilgrim. However, allow me to be very clear."

He heard the steel in her voice.

"The CIA, MI5 and the Metropolitan Police are searching the whole of London for your team. They have every means at their disposal, every security clearance and if required, any method authorized. It is only a matter of time before they are found. If they are, then I will kill them before I allow them to talk to the CIA."

*

Kane stood with his nose against the full-length glass, staring out at the sea of desks in the office. The small room was soundproofed, but his fury was silent. He turned his head when Campbell stood up and looked over. He went to pull open the door then stopped and beckoned Campbell towards him. MI5 had fucked this up from the start. There was no reason to keep them in the loop.

Campbell pushed the door open.

"Give me good news," said Kane.

"Sir, we have the video of the street where two of our men were killed. There was an old woman in a house behind Soho and a younger woman with an automatic weapon. The property is now empty. We're checking all the cameras. Montrose and a young woman left on foot and took a taxi. We've tracked the taxi to this address, right here, but it was empty."

"Fuck! He's winding me up, the prick!"

"The old woman left in a car with another man. There's no trace of them. She has a long security services history and connections with the Soviets. All of which makes me very concerned about how much MI5 are helping us."

Kane felt the blood rush to his head. "Get me Elizabeth Purley. Right now."

"Sir, I'm told she is not in the building."

He thumped the glass so hard people outside jumped at their desks. "Then find her. I want that bitch back here!"

CHAPTER 9

Kirsty fixed a strap to her purse and slung it across her chest. "Move fast. Stick with me for the moment." She stepped off the busy sidewalk and into the narrow road.

"Where are we going?" He looked behind. *Would I spot them? Probably not. Until it was too late. This is what they do.*

"Oxford Circus tube station. Fastest way out of here."

"The underground? Is that a good idea?" *We'll be trapped like rats in a sewer.*

"Staying here isn't. There's no other way. This is the Regent Street containment zone. We have to beat the cops before they close in and shut it down."

"Where's the station?"

"End of that road." She pointed straight ahead.

"We should run." He looked towards a pedestrian zone, devoid of cars, leading to the line of traffic along Oxford Street and began to pick up the pace.

"No." She pulled him back. "Follow me."

"Damn it, Kirsty, that's the quickest route."

"Listen to me. If you run, you'll give yourself away. You see that old lamp post over there?"

Above him he saw an ornate Victorian streetlight at the entrance to the pedestrian zone.

"That isn't a lamp post. And it isn't old."

Below the elaborate twists of metal he saw a black glass dome hanging where the light should have been.

"In here." She turned into a shop and he followed her across the sales floor where he could see an exit to another street. *We're gonna need more than this.*

Her phone rang. She stopped and pulled it from her bag. "It's Mr. Pilgrim. Thank God."

Yeah, let's hope it's him on the line. And not someone who worked out how to use his phone.

She handed him an earpiece then faced him, stepping in close and holding the microphone between their lips. "Mr. Pilgrim?" she said. "You okay?"

Montrose heard a calm assurance in his voice, but not the usual strength.

"Nothing to worry about, my dear," said Pilgrim. "I'm safe. I just won't be running around for a while.

116

Listen carefully, I need to keep this succinct. I have some important information. Don't tell me where you are. Are you safe?"

Montrose was about to speak when Kirsty pressed a finger to his lips.

"We're good. Zac has cracked the access password. You're not going to believe this, but it's a Soviet Cold War satellite loaded with bombs."

"Oh, I believe it," said Pilgrim. "It makes sense."

Then you're one step ahead of us, fella, so spit it out.

"Have you heard of the Star Wars initiative?" said Pilgrim. "Not the movie, the defense project started by President Reagan, perhaps thirty years ago?"

Kirsty looked at Montrose and shrugged.

"Yeah, I know the one," said Montrose. "He was going to have a ring of satellites with lasers to blow any enemy ICBM missiles out of the sky. Specifically to stop any nuclear attack by the Soviet Union."

"Exactly," said Pilgrim. "And it was all a bluff. They never had the technology to make it work, but they convinced the Soviets that they did. And that satellite, called the Red Star, was the Soviet response. Those bombs that it carries can be directed to fly into the path of any satellite orbiting the earth. They could have taken out the Star Wars satellites anytime they liked. The technology was basic, but effective."

"But there are no US Star Wars satellites."

"That's true, but things have moved on from the Reagan years. The Earth is now ringed with every type of satellite that humanity can build. They are integral to the defense of the US and many other countries, not to mention international navigation, the internet and currency transfer and banking. Whoever controls the Red Star has control of near space. The potential for terrorism is incalculable."

"Shit. No wonder the CIA are going ballistic."

"Indeed," said Pilgrim. "Twenty years ago, my brother Michael stole the access codes to the Red Star satellite. When he was found, I assume he killed himself rather than divulge the secrets to the Soviets. You have two of the passwords. I take it that Zac has not yet discovered the third password?"

"Not yet," said Kirsty.

"The third?" said Montrose.

"You will remember the writing on my brother's arm. There are three sections, if I'm not mistaken. First, the code to wake up the satellite. Second, the access password, from *piseag*. Identifying that the first two parts exist leads us to the identity of a third. And the third, I fear, is the most dangerous. That is where we must focus our efforts. And I suspect it is not written in a code that can be easily solved. My brother was a cautious man. He would have deduced that if the Soviets recovered his body, they would eventually work out the code. I think the last part, 'Two Ekland' is rather more esoteric."

"It's someone's name?" said Kirsty.

"In a way, yes," replied Pilgrim. "One of the most popular actresses at the time was a young lady called Britt Ekland. My brother greatly admired her beauty."

"Okay," said Montrose. "Someone called Britt? Near the border where he was found?"

"I believe it may be 'Brit' with one 't'," said Pilgrim. "And I had a visit today that led me to that conclusion. We have a lead. A British agent called Roger Warrender. The only other man known to be involved in Operation Red Star and I suspect the only man who could have talked to my brother before he was captured. His whereabouts are unknown, but the man who may know where to find him is Captain Kenneth Wolff. I'm told he can be found under the railway arches of London Bridge station. And I believe that Roger Warrender is our 'Brit'."

"I know where that is," said Kirsty.

"Go now," said Pilgrim. "Contact me only when absolutely necessary. I will not always be in a position to communicate."

"We're on our way." Kirsty cut the call, pulled the

earpiece from Montrose's ear and headed for the door.

Montrose followed close behind. They emerged into crowds of shoppers under the arches of Regent Street. He could see the underground entrance fifty yards away.

"Cross the road," said Kirsty. "You take one entrance, I'll take the other. They're looking for two people. I'll meet you at the ticket barriers. Don't stand beside me. I'll get the tickets."

"Understood." He dodged a line of red buses crawling through the traffic to reach a concrete curb in the middle of the road, then stood by a streetlight and looked up. There were six CCTV cameras at the top. *They have us in real time. This is a fucking nightmare.* He ran through a gap in the cars and headed for the Tube, weaving around groups of tourists and street vendors. *No wonder Kane is kicking down every door in London.* His mouth became dry as the scale of the threat opened up. *The whole US defense system is based on satellites. Cruise missiles, artillery, smart bombs and every intelligence gathering system. The list was endless. If someone had access to the Red Star they could hold the world to ransom.*

He glanced up as he turned into the entrance to the Tube station and glimpsed Kirsty's head ducking below street level on the opposite side. *And we're looking for some old spook called Warrender? Why is Pilgrim telling me all this?* A chill ran through him. *Because he's going to die. If he doesn't make it, someone has to know. And that's me.* He ran down the steps and along a short corridor, then saw her at the ticket machine. *But he's told her too.* She disappeared behind the stream of people making for the barriers. *Holy shit, if a terrorist cracks all the codes before we do...* He caught her blond wig in the crowd, moving towards him. *I have to get her safe. But I have to tell Kane. No, man, grow a set of balls. This is bigger than her. The whole of the US defense system is at stake.*

She held her hand low, a ticket sticking out from her fingers. "Walk past me and keep your distance," she said. "Victoria line. Northbound."

He palmed the ticket and made for the barrier. The roof above the escalator was lined with CCTV. Keeping his head low, he pulled out his phone. *I'm gonna lose the signal. Just do it. Tell them we can talk. Make sure she's safe and then tell them what they want to know.* His phone buzzed and a text message appeared on the screen.

Montrose, your country is in grave danger. I know your history. I will guarantee protection. For you and the girl. You have my word. The two men she killed were British agents. She can walk away. Trust me. I have authority from the President. We are at DEFCON 3. We need you.

He stumbled as the foot of the escalator came up quickly. *I have to do this. This is no time for Pilgrim's spy games.* He typed into the phone as he pushed his way onto the platform.

When and where?

He hit the 'send' button and watched the progress bar. It shot to the left and flashed up:

Failed to send

Shit. No signal. He looked up and saw her blond hair in the crowd. *Go back to the escalator.* He turned to push past the tide of people when he felt a whoosh of stale air and heard the rumble of a train pulling into the station. He looked down the platform. Kirsty was staring at him.

She shook her head then ducked into a tunnel below a sign connecting to the Bakerloo line.

He shoved the phone into his pocket and pushed his way down the wall as the crowd moved to the edge of the platform.

She was waiting for him when he rounded the corner. "London Bridge and the Bakerloo Line is this way," she said, pointing along the short tunnel to the other platform. "They will have every station on the Victoria Line monitored when they see us on the cameras."

He heard another train approaching and saw the carriages shoot past.

She held out a hand and waited until the carriage doors opened. "Now!"

Montrose ran down the tunnel behind her and jumped on as the alarm sounded and the door slammed shut. "Kirsty, where are we going?"

"The Embankment."

"But that's still on the north side of the river. London Bridge is on the south."

"I know, but if we stay on the train that long, you can be sure they'll have worked it out by the time we get there. And they'll be waiting for us. I don't want to take that chance. We need another route."

He reached up and grabbed the bar as the train lurched forward.

Kirsty held onto his jacket. "So, Mr. Connor Montrose. Those two guys outside the old lady's house. You remember that?"

The two you cut down with a Sten gun. "How could I forget?"

"Both were armed, but one of them had a 9mm in his hand and a Taser in the other. Which means one of them was going to kill someone and the other was going to capture someone. They will have clocked me from the street in Soho." She wagged a finger at him. "Me or you. Would you like to guess who gets to live?"

"Look, Kirsty..."

"I'll make it easy for you. They were trying to kill me. But you?" She moved closer. "What do you know that makes you so important?"

Montrose shook his head. "I don't know. I know as much as you do."

Kirsty laughed. "Evidently not. So who are you, Mr. Hotshot?"

He stared over the heads of the passengers. "Me? I'm just an IT geek."

"A geek? So, you're not a gun totin' super spy? A shadowy figure, saving '*Murica* from the infidel, leaving a trail of broken-hearted women across the globe? I can imagine them on a balcony at dusk, dressed in negligees, looking forlornly out into the sunset, searching for..." She leaned in closer. "Connor Montrose. License to shag."

"Kirsty, please."

"Oh, you're such a wimp. So, an IT geek, yeah?" She leaned back and gave him a quizzical look. "What's your specialty?"

"Networks. Firewalls, monitoring, security. Nothing special."

Kirsty nodded slowly. "Maybe that explains why you didn't kill them when you had the chance."

Montrose turned to face her. "I'm not a killer."

She held up a hand. "Okay, Mr. Geek, don't get the

hump." She smiled and gently jabbed a finger into his belly. "Just as well I'm here, then."

Montrose said nothing.

Kirsty nudged his leg once more. "You don't have to tell me if you don't want to. But I'll kill you if you don't. Several times, if necessary."

He had to smile. "I'm a whistleblower."

"Yeah?" She glanced out of the window as the train slowed. "It must have been some fucking whistle."

Moments later the train pulled into Piccadilly Circus and more passengers jammed themselves into the carriage. He resisted the urge to check his phone. *I have to stop this before a whole world of shit comes down.*

Kirsty lifted her head and whispered into his ear. "I have another idea. Get ready to go."

The train lurched forward and he held on tight. *Do the right thing. If some psycho terrorist gets their hands on that satellite... or the Russians? If the Soviets had lost the codes, they must have assumed it was under US control. Even if they knew Pilgrim's brother was dead. But how? It had to be the other guy. Roger Warrender. A Brit? If the Brits had the access, they would have handed it over to the US, so who the hell is this guy Warrender?*

He felt her shuffle closer and caught the scent of warm patchouli from her skin. He blinked and looked away. *Jesus, how close were we to nuclear war in the Eighties? If Pilgrim's brother hadn't stolen those codes... but when he did, the Cold War was won. Game over for the Soviets. They must have really thought that the US could take out every satellite or missile that they had. Even if they believed Reagan's bullshit about Star Wars and lasers. Yeah and after that, it was glasnost and they were all good ol' capitalist buddies. That didn't last long.*

The train rattled from side to side in the tunnel, slowing as the signs for Charing Cross flashed past. She pulled two tightly-wrapped rain macs from her bag, both a lurid pink and emblazoned with the Liberty logo. "Sorry, they're from the Ladies section. Put it on before we leave the station. We can ditch them later."

"They'll spot these a mile away."

"It's London. If you don't like the weather, just wait five minutes. Look down there."

He turned to the end of the carriage where he saw a group of Japanese tourists huddled together, all wearing blue disposable macs.

"Relax, Mister Fashion Icon, it's only to get us out the station. Next stop. Embankment."

"But this goes straight to Waterloo."

She tapped a finger on his chest. "Remember, this is my turf. Waterloo Station is one of the most secure places in the UK. It's swamped by hi-res CCTV and has its own police station. And cells. You really don't want to go there."

"Then how are we going to...?"

"Go!"

The doors shot open and he followed the crowd out onto the platform, unwrapping the mac and pulling it over his head. He kept behind her and took the steps into the sunshine. Across the road, a high stone wall bordered the Thames and the cool, damp breeze washed over his face. *What the hell is Pilgrim up to? Whatever shit he's got planned, he doesn't know the scale of this. There is a clear and present danger to the US. Time to end this game.*

Kirsty walked fast as she headed west alongside a garden and he hurried to keep pace. "Keep to the side and under the trees," she said.

"They've got cameras here?"

She pointed across the river to a four-hundred-foot-tall Ferris wheel. "Oh yeah. The London Eye and all the high buildings along the Embankment. And up there." She nodded to the left.

Montrose looked up to the Savoy Hotel. *They could spot us any minute. It's not a chance I can take. I have to tell them. Get them onside. Yeah, before they kill us all. That would be good.* He held his phone as he walked.

How many satellites have to go down before homeland security is compromised? Or the international payment systems? Either one and the US is fucked. He brought up his phone. *This shit is over. Do it.* He hit resend on the text message.

Kirsty stopped and backed against the railings to the hotel garden, then ducked under the low hanging branches of a tree. She pulled the plastic rain mac over her head and stuffed it through the railings.

Montrose stood beside her and began to pull off his mac with one hand.

She looked down at his phone.

"I can't get a signal," he said.

"You don't need one. I'll run comms. Switch it off. It's not secure."

"How are they gonna...?"

"Connor, see that?" She pointed to a streetlight in the middle of the road. "The grey box under the CCTV? It's for mobile phones, right?"

"Yeah, but..."

"Yeah, but it's not from a phone company. Those are radio monitors set up by the government. This isn't some conspiracy shit just because it doesn't have a phone company's logo on it, those receivers are real. The police and MI5 can put them anywhere they like. There are no rules. And they can see every email, text, call and internet connection. There are hundreds of them across London. Thousands across the country. If you think you can have a private conversation in the UK, you're bonkers. You might as well stand outside MI5 headquarters with a megaphone."

He hurried behind her. "Where are we going?"

"The Savoy Pier. We can get a taxi to London Bridge."

"A taxi?"

"Trust me, Connor, they'll never catch us."

*

Kane looked up and saw Campbell approaching, almost running between the desks. A phone buzzed in his pocket. He pulled out an old Nokia cell phone and held a hand up to the glass. "Maybe I don't need you, you little shit," he murmured.

Campbell stood outside the glass, pointing to his iPad.

Kane shook his head and held up three fingers. He turned his back and brought up a text message on the phone.

We have an agreement. Tracking of Red Star intruder underway.

He resisted the temptation to punch a fist into the air and typed **Proceed** into the Nokia, then slipped it into his pocket and pulled open the glass door. "You've got another chance at giving me good news. Go for it."

Campbell brought up the iPad. "Montrose agreed to your text. He's asking where and when. We've tracked his phone to the Embankment Tube Station."

Kane felt a burst of adrenalin. He stared at Campbell, his mouth open, then recovered. "Get a fucking army down there."

"We have two men in the vicinity. Do you want him alive, sir?"

"Yeah, I want to talk to that prick before I shoot him in the face. But if you bring me a corpse, I'll still be happy. Do it now." Kane turned away.

Campbell stood in the doorway. "Sir? What about the girl?"

Kane shrugged, but didn't turn around. "Whatever."

CHAPTER 10

"Stay under the trees, Connor." She glanced up to a streetlight where two cameras covered their side of the road.

"Okay, so where's the pier?" He scanned the wall bordering the river.

Kirsty pointed east along the Embankment. "Near that bridge, you can't miss it. The Ladies Bridge."

"Isn't that Waterloo Bridge?"

"That's the official name. My grandmother helped build that bridge. Hard hat and hammers."

"Your grandmother?"

"Yeah." She punched the air. "Girl power! It was built by women during the war, when the men were away fighting." She lifted her phone into the air, holding it up as she walked.

"You looking for a signal?"

"Nope. As Elvis Costello used to say, *I'm watching the detectives.*" She screwed her face up at him. "You'll never take me alive, copper!"

He smiled awkwardly. *She took down two guys with a Sten gun. That wasn't a lucky shot. It looked like two controlled bursts. Yeah, whatever. Kane agreed she's not a target, so get your mind on the job at hand. Pick your spot. She said a taxi? Okay, then wait until it stops at the lights, then grab the iPad and jump out. This game is over. They can find out about Wolff and Warrender later.* He looked up at her phone. "What do you mean, watching the detectives?"

She ignored him and concentrated on the phone. "Connor?"

"Yeah?"

She showed him the iPhone screen.

Is that video? Real time? Here?

"Connor, whatever is about to happen, I want you to keep a clear head and look for opportunities. One of us has to survive." She looked quickly around. "Preferably me. Now, I need a tourist with some big fuck-off luggage." She nodded at a Chinese woman walking towards them, dragging a wheeled suitcase.

"Kirsty, what the hell?"

"There's a car about to pull up on our right. I've been

watching them behind me on my phone. Take care of the driver. And remember, we drive on the left."

"Jesus, no. Run for the river."

She gripped him by the arm. "Connor, a wee lesson from Napoleon Bonaparte. 'Never interrupt your enemy when he is making a mistake.'" She lunged to the side and grabbed the woman's suitcase, then spun around, lifted the suitcase into the air and launched it behind her.

Montrose jerked his head around and saw a man ten feet away pointing a bright yellow plastic gun directly at his chest. *Taser!* The suitcase slammed into the man's knees and he pitched forward. Kirsty ran over and kicked the Taser out of his hand as he pulled the trigger. Montrose heard wrist bones snap and the barbed projectiles flew past his legs, trailing thin cables and fifty thousand volts sparking across the sidewalk as they hit the ground.

A black Jaguar squealed to a halt at the curb beside him. Montrose saw the driver holding a gun in his hand. The driver made to open his door, but a bus passed on his right and hemmed him in. He launched himself across the front seats and kicked open the passenger door.

Montrose turned but the door slammed into his ass. He dropped to the ground and twisted around, bringing up both feet. He booted the door back towards the driver, who fell back into the car, then pointed his gun through the gap in the door.

Montrose threw himself at the car, trapping the driver's arm between the door and the roof. He reached up for the gun, but the door edged open as the driver slammed his weight against it. Montrose kept his head low, his sneakers slipping on the sidewalk as he pushed with all his strength. "Kirsty! Get out of here!"

She already had the Taser in her hand. The first man jumped up from the sidewalk holding his wrist, then went for his gun, but Kirsty stood her ground and fired the Taser into his face. The barbs pierced his eyes and his whole body convulsed as 50,000 volts coursed through his brain.

Montrose slipped to his knees, his weight against the door. A loud crack deafened him and he saw the sidewalk shatter as the round flew past him, missing Kirsty by inches.

She ducked and scrambled around the car, then leapt on the roof and threw herself flat, grabbing the driver's gun and sliding backwards, wrenching it from his grasp. She rolled off the trunk and brought up the pistol in one move, her face a mask of cold rage.

"Kirsty, no!"

The driver wrenched his arm free, threw himself

across the seat and shoved his hand into the glove compartment.

She shoved Montrose out of the way and emptied the magazine into the driver until the breech slammed back and the trigger clicked empty. Cartridge smoke drifted from the open door.

Pedestrians scattered in all directions. Montrose got to his feet.

Kirsty looked down at the gun. "Shit." She released the breech. "I should have saved ammunition. I'll check him for any spare magazines."

"Jesus, no. They could be here in seconds. Move!"

"Okay, follow me." She wiped the gun on her dress to remove any fingerprints, then threw the empty pistol into the car and took off down the sidewalk. She ran between the traffic and crossed the road to the wall bordering the Thames.

Montrose sprinted behind her and saw her dart through a gap in the stone wall towards the water. He caught up and turned onto a wooden jetty where she stood waiting for him.

"Walk," she said. "We're just a couple of lovers about to go on a romantic water taxi ride." She pointed to a rigid inflatable at the end of the jetty and waved to the pilot. "Let's go."

*

Kane leaned over the technician's desk watching the grainy video of the house in Soho and saw a figure bring up an old machine gun and take down two men. "Who the hell is that?"

"We think it's the young woman seen with the target."

"Hey, no shit, Sherlock."

"Sir?" Campbell stood at the entrance to the glass-fronted office.

Kane strode over. "Bring Montrose to me. I want a word with this prick."

Campbell closed the door. "No. They saw them coming. Two men down. One dead. One brain-dead."

"Our men?" Kane looked out to the technician behind the desk. "I just watched the CCTV video from the house in Soho. That's four men down. What the fuck is going on?"

"It seems Montrose is more than an ex-CIA technician, sir, and the girl knows what she's doing." He pulled the iPad to his chest as Kane advanced until their faces almost touched.

"Where are they?"

Campbell cleared his throat. "We're searching right along the Embankment, but there's no sign of them. We still have the signal on Montrose's phone. It seems he's on the water."

"The water? You mean the goddamn river? What the hell is he doing, swimming? Hijacked a boat?"

"We've got men on the way. We'll cover both sides of the river."

"Shut the fuck up. Get the Blackhawks in the sky."

CHAPTER 11

A squall of rain came in from the east. Kirsty stood up on the prow as the wind kicked up the spray from the dark waters of the Thames.

Christ, we're not on a day out. He craned his neck to look back to the Embankment, but could see nothing behind the high wall. He heard sirens in the distance. "Kirsty, we better keep our heads down."

"It's only weather!"

"Yeah, I guess you London girls are born to this."

"Not me." She dropped onto the seat beside him and slumped against the side of the boat. "I'm a valley girl." She turned and grinned. "The Welsh valleys," she said, drawing out the vowels.

The sing-song accent caught him by surprise. "You're a long way from home."

Kirsty shook her head. "This is my home now."

He could see the look in her eyes that told a story. Not a good one. "You know, I've got to ask."

Her features relaxed and a cheeky grin crossed her face. "You mean in case we end up in a body bag before lunchtime? Go on."

"Those guys in Soho, the ones you dropped with the Sten gun. That wasn't a lucky shot, was it?"

"You're part of the team. Mr Pilgrim trained you too, no?"

"Not really."

"Oh, so you are a gun–totin' super spy after all, eh?"

"No, Kirsty, I'm just an IT guy." He looked out over the water. "But you're more than just some hacker chick. The guy in the Jag?" He jerked his thumb back towards the Embankment. "You emptied a clip into his head. That's not exactly in the training manual."

"Yeah, well, sometimes I get carried away."

He pictured the rage on her face when she opened the door of the Jag and pointed the gun. "I ain't got a problem with that."

She sat silent for a moment, staring out across the water. "I was once a victim." Her shoulder twitched and she tried to hide it by shaking her head. "Never again." She blew out a breath, then pushed her legs straight, resting her hands on her lap. "I came to London ten years ago. A runaway. My father... abused me. It started when I was too young to remember. Yeah, far too young."

Montrose sat still, but felt a tremor down his spine. Her childhood voice and her accent was one of the sweetest things he had ever heard, but it was laced with sorrow.

"My mother was a drunk. But she was also a victim. The endless beatings, I..." Kirsty closed her eyes and stretched her neck, resting her head on the side of the boat. "When she died, it got worse. Then there was only me." She let her head fall to the side, resting against his shoulder. "That was then. This is now."

He looked down to where her hands were clasped tight in her lap.

"It was worse when he was drinking. And that was most of the time. But he was a policeman. And when I was old enough to know the law, I was old enough to know I had no chance. I knew how it was going to end, one way or the other. As I got older, I started going out, down to the village, trying to have a normal life with my friends, but knowing that if I came home late he would beat the shit out of me. Or worse, if the drunken bastard could manage it. Then one night, in the winter when the valleys were thick with snow, I came home early, before the weather closed the roads. I waited in the dark, pretending I wasn't home. After a while he came home, drunk out of his mind. I saw him lose his keys as he was walking through the garden. I watched him from the window, crawling about in the snow. Eventually, he gave up and sat on the step, waiting for me to come home. He fell asleep. I watched him all night. It must have been minus fifteen. And I watched him freeze to death." The spray brushed her face, but she didn't move, then she sat up with a jolt and clapped her hands together.

"Kirsty..."

"Best bloody thing I've ever done." She wiggled her bottom on the seat and bumped him with her hip. "And then I packed my bags and ran. Through the snow, down to the village. I hitched a lift on a tractor, right down the valley and took the first train to Cardiff." She held out her hands and gazed around. "And the runaway came to London Town."

"But nobody followed you? Looked for you?"

She shrugged. "It was a natural death. Happens every winter. Anyway, I didn't give a shit. There's plenty places to hide in London, if you know the streets. I made them my home. Nobody was looking for me. I did it right. I rebuilt my life here. Then I got a job and saw a shrink to find out who I am." She pointed her chest. "This killer. And I found out I'm a nice person.

I didn't tell her everything, but it turns out I'm a really nice, gentle, sweet person, who has absolutely no qualms about killing any man that threatens me. I can live with that."

Or any man that betrays you. He felt a chill and knew it wasn't the weather. "How did you meet Mr. Pilgrim?"

"I was a hacker. I still am. Those guys are my people. I went for the sick bastards in power, all the perverts that hide behind their position and status. I pursued them across the internet. I dragged up every sordid secret they had. The abuse, the beatings and the murders. The orphanages where they preyed and the people who ran them. I uncovered a pedophile ring that led right up to Downing Street. Right up to the desk of the fucking Prime Minister. And the Secret Service who killed people to keep it quiet." She slumped back into the seat.

He watched her eyes, fixed on the horizon, never wavering. "What happened?"

"I was an amateur. A very clever amateur. But a lamb to the wolves. I tried to tell the press, but GCHQ caught me. They had been following my every move. I'm lucky to be alive. They destroyed everything I had and they would have destroyed me too, but I had a guardian angel. Zac. I met him at university. I didn't know he worked for Mr. Pilgrim. They both rescued me. And Pilgrim showed me how to use a gun. Amongst other things."

142

"And the pedophile ring?"

She wagged a finger in the air. "One day I will have them. The lords in their ermine robes, the cabinet ministers, the vile, sick bastards and murderers sitting in that pile of shit down the Thames called the Palace of Westminster." She stared straight at him and her voice shook. "And I will fuck them up. With or without the law." She turned away and blew out a breath. "All the evidence is gone. But they're still out there, most of them. Some died naturally." She smiled at him. "And some just died." She sat back and pulled out her phone.

The sun came out from behind the clouds. The boat bounced as it passed the bow wave of a long barge and Montrose held on to the side rail. *They had a gun and a Taser. One to live, one to die.* He glanced sideways, but she was engrossed in her phone. *Kane said she could walk. But he sent his goons to shoot her in the street.* He pulled his phone from his pocket. *This is all fucked up. Kane is going to have an army of people trying to kill us and Pilgrim is lying somewhere in a hospital bed. Or a morgue.* He rubbed his forehead. *Kane showed his hand. Now I'm going to play mine. The good ol' US of A is big enough to look after itself for a few hours. And when we get clear of here... If we get clear of here, I'm going to find Kane and nail his fucking throat to the floor.*

He checked the phone, but there were no messages. *Yeah, he'll know.* The battery level had dropped. *That isn't right.* He flicked through the apps and spotted a blank browser running. *Shit. The text message.* He began to hold the phone up to Kirsty, then pulled it back. *You don't want to show her. You know what it is.* He tucked the phone into his palm. *Don't fool yourself. You need her.* He glanced down, but her gaze was fixed on the far bank. He lifted his arm to the side of the boat and let the phone slip from his grasp. *You can't find me now, shithead.*

"Your turn, Connor the Whistleblower. How did Mr. Pilgrim find you?"

He pulled his arm back into the boat. "Shit-scared in a café in Casablanca is how he found me."

She laughed and sat up in the seat. "Really? My, you get around. So, how did you get from Morocco to a boat on the Thames with a crazy Welsh chick?"

Montrose shook his head. "Long story."

"You know what you are?"

He half-turned his head towards her.

"You're a nice guy. I'm not sure you've got the balls for this, but I like you. And you know that. But something flicked your switch, Connor Montrose. One day you went over to the dark side, long before you became a whistleblower. Or you would still be behind a desk staring at a screen and eating a tuna sandwich. What happened?"

"What do you mean?"

"I have a degree in psychology. I can see right through you. And I like what I see. But something set you on a path and brought you here today." She shrugged. "You know, if you don't want to talk about it, I understand. I'm interested, that's all. I care."

He cleared his throat and pictured a pale, white body lying on a mortuary slab, remembered walking out into the midday heat of a Californian summer, unable to breathe. "My sister."

Kirsty held his hand. "You lost her?"

"She got caught up with the wrong people. People in Mexico and Colombia. When they had finished with her she was too far gone. She died before she got back to the border."

She squeezed his hand.

"I didn't know. I couldn't save her."

She rested her head against his shoulder.

"And when I found the CIA and the US government covering up a shipment of enough Afghan heroin worth enough money to feed all the kids in Europe, I... I went off the reservation."

"I hear you."

"A lot of people died. A lot of people deserved to die. And one day I will find who took my sister."

The pilot throttled back the engine and the boat edged towards the shore.

Kirsty sat up. "One day, Connor. Let's make sure you live to see it."

Montrose cleared his throat. "Where is this place? Where are we going?"

"Southwark. The old railway arches under London Bridge station. There are hundreds of them, but I know the ones that Pilgrim means. The ones in the best locations have been converted to coffee houses or artisan shops selling overpriced crap jewelry. Others are small businesses or auto repair yards. But there are some that are too dark and damp for anyone. And that's where the homeless go. And have done for a hundred years. Southwark was always edgy. This side of the river deserves its reputation."

The pilot pulled into a dock and Montrose found his feet on the damp wood as it rocked on the choppy water. He heard the whump-whump of rotor blades and looked up.

Kirsty caught him looking and turned towards the west. "Too low for tourists. Let's go."

*

There was a soft knock at the door. Purley sat bolt upright at her desk. "Enter."

A young man in a tweed suit pushed open the door and quickly crossed the room to stand before her desk.

"No pack drill, Lockhart, spit it out."

Lockhart glanced over at Madame Raymonde who was sitting in a wing-backed chair to the right of the desk.

"My guest isn't here," said Purley.

Lockhart nodded. "I overheard the Americans, ma'am. They were asking why you were seen walking over Lambeth Bridge. They intimated that they expected you to be available at a moment's notice."

Purley let out a bitter laugh. "They have control of my entire department and they're wondering where I go for lunch? No matter. To quote one of my friends in Lambeth, I'm as welcome in this investigation as a bacon sandwich at a bar mitzvah. Any other news?"

"They are keeping things tight to their chest, ma'am, but I know there was an incident on the Embankment. CIA agents are reported dead."

"Any other casualties?"

"No, ma'am. And there are no reports of any arrests, but helicopters are searching the Thames and they have a tracker leading towards Southwark."

Purley leaned forward. "They're too damn' close."

Lockhart shuffled his feet. "Earlier, ma'am, there was some activity regarding a search for, how shall I say, an elderly lady in Soho." He flicked his eyes over to Madame Raymonde.

"I'm sure there was," replied Purley. "And I do hope that there have been absolutely no sightings of this lady?"

"None whatsoever, ma'am."

"Good man, carry on."

Lockhart nodded and headed for the door.

Purley waited until the door closed behind him then slumped down in her seat. "I can't take the chance. They may have tracked me to Lambeth. If they have, they'll find Pilgrim."

"Move Pilgrim to the East End," said Madame Raymonde. "They'll take care of him."

"Maybe. But his team? Montrose and the girl? They're heading for Southwark." She scratched the nape of her neck. "Kane is too close. It's only a matter of time."

"Then you may have to clean down everything. I know what it means to you, but it is the only option. We have come to the last resort. Prepare to give the order, Elizabeth. Before it's too late."

Purley held her head in her hands.

"And Pilgrim too."

"No." Purley stood up. "One last chance. But if Captain Wolff is compromised, I'll do what needs to be done." She felt her mouth dry. "The East End boys can pick up Pilgrim. They won't like it, but they know the score. And they can take care of him if required." She reached down to the desk and a copy of *The London Times*, opening it at the crossword. "You know what this is?"

"I can guess."

Purley lifted a pen from her desk and her hand hovered over the paper.

"If my assumptions are correct," said Madame Raymonde, "that will only work if he is listening."

Purley dropped the pen.

"Don't leave it too late, Elizabeth. We cannot let them win. At any price."

"I understand." She picked up the phone on her desk and punched a button. "Major Salter, I need the Blue team. One target Holland Park and three targets Southwark. Mobilize for action. Wait for my command."

CHAPTER 12

The switch from fashionable waterfront to the grimy back streets of Southwark was just a case of turning the wrong corner. Montrose followed Kirsty past the over-priced artisanal shops, through a car park and into a narrow back street. On one side of the street a high fence enclosed a junkyard, barely holding back the haphazardly stacked hulks of rusting cars.

"That's second on our list," said Kirsty, pointing to a rotting wooden shed, just inside the entrance to the junkyard. "We need a motor as bent as a nine-pound-note." She crossed the road and turned into an alley at the side of a boarded-up video store, walking to a yard at the back, strewn with rubbish, broken furniture and a stained and torn mattress. She squeezed past a burnt-out dumpster and stepped carefully through a gap in a broken wire fence.

Montrose looked over her shoulder at an overgrown wasteground where ramshackle huts lay at all angles, held together with plastic sheeting. Outside the huts, groups of men gathered around braziers made from oil drums, Slavic and North African faces tracking their every move. Several dogs sniffed around, occasionally turning their heads towards them. At the far end he saw a line of railway arches below a wide span of tracks leading into London Bridge station. He counted the overhead power lines and worked out there must be at least twenty tracks converging into the station, just visible above a line of warehouses. "What is this place?"

Kirsty pointed to the east. "London Bridge Station is over there. As for here, what do you think it is? Welcome to the United Nations."

Montrose scanned the long line of low arches, framed in sooty black bricks.

"Some go back a quarter of a mile," said Kirsty. "You could hide an army in there. Watch your feet. Syringes."

Montrose stepped gingerly around the trash and wished he wasn't wearing sneakers. Some of the arches were boarded up, but had large holes roughly cut into the plywood.

Kirsty headed for an open arch. The sun was behind the railway line and daylight only penetrated a few yards inside. She pulled a small Maglite torch from her bag and took out her phone. "Switch your phone off and hide it," she said. "They're as good as cash in here."

"I ditched it."

"Yeah?" She had only stepped forward a few feet, when a voice, thick with drink, came out of the gloom. "What the fuck do you want?"

Kirsty turned on the torch and pointed it at the floor. "Relax. Just visiting a friend."

"Visiting, eh? You think this is the fucking Ritz?"

Another voice sniggered and joined in. "Yeah and I'm the doorman, so have you got the entrance fee, sweetheart?"

Kirsty flashed up the torch and scanned two bearded young men crouched over a cardboard box, littered with scraps of tin foil and syringes. "Listen, mate. I used to sleep here. I had enough of your shit then and I've had enough of it now. So, you can help me or you can get out of my fucking way. Captain Wolff. Where is he?"

Montrose widened his stance, knowing they would only see his silhouette. *Let's hope that's enough.*

One of the men rolled a syringe between his blackened fingers for a few moments, weighing up the options. "Down on the right. He's in his office."

The other man stood up. His eyes were glazed and he rocked back and forward on the balls of his feet. "So, you used to live here, eh?"

"Yeah," said Kirsty. "And I've got to say, it's gone downhill a bit since then."

Montrose followed close behind as she stepped around them and into the darkness. She traced the torch along the walls, scanning quickly over bags of rubbish and discarded furniture. A few faces turned away from the light with muttered curses. Some lay still, their mouths open and eyes glazed, hardly registering the beam.

Too young. This guy's got to be in his fifties at least. He stopped and looked back into the darkness. *Yeah, far too young for this shit.*

Kirsty shone the torch on a heap of rags and flattened cardboard boxes wedged into a gap where bricks had collapsed. Rotting mortar lay strewn across the floor and green stalactites hung from the broken bricks where the wall had collapsed. The edge of a hat peeked over the stained and threadbare blankets.

As they approached, Montrose could make out part of a face, just visible between a matted grey beard and the brim of a battered trilby.

"Excuse me." said Kirsty.

A filthy hand slipped from under the blankets and gently pushed up the hat.

"Captain Wolff?"

The bloodshot eyes gave a flicker of recognition as they came into focus.

Kirsty squatted beside him and held the Maglite to her side.

The old man's eyes opened slowly to reveal piercing blue pupils in a sea of red. He studied her for a moment and the crow's feet around his eyes cracked into a smile. "I don't know what I've been drinking, but you're the loveliest thing I have seen in many a year." His refined accent was at odds with a voice that sounded like a corpse being dragged across gravel.

"Thank you," said Kirsty. "You're very kind."

Montrose squatted down beside her. The stench was overwhelming, but Kirsty seemed not to notice.

"I'm sorry to bother you, Captain Wolff. We're looking for some information."

He pulled the blankets down past his face and a full beard sprang out. He began to talk, before a bronchial cough stopped him in his tracks. "It's been a long time since I've been of any use to anyone, but fire away, my dear. Although, I must say, a little *quid pro quo* wouldn't go amiss. I have an extensive wine cellar that needs to be replenished." He laughed at his own joke.

"What did you have in mind?" said Kirsty.

"Well, a contribution to the Mess Fund would be most appreciated."

Kirsty took out her purse. "I'm sure we can stretch to a few bottles of claret and something hot from the galley."

154

"How very kind," said Wolff. He grasped the money she offered. "I admit it's been some time since the nectar of Bordeaux passed my lips, but we shall see."

Montrose looked left and right. A faint sound of footsteps came out of the darkness, but he couldn't tell how far away. "My name is Montrose. You're Army, sir?"

"Good Lord, no. Navy. *Pusser's Rum* and several wives left me high and dry, amongst other things. Talking of which…" He pulled a plastic bottle of cider from below the blankets. "To wives and sweethearts," he said and took a long pull on the bottle. "May they never meet."

"Your good health," said Kirsty.

"Sincere apologies, my dear," said Wolff. "But have we met before?"

Her Welsh accent became deep and lilting. "I didn't think you'd remember, but you chased me out of here. Best thing that ever happened to me."

"I don't remember much, but there was something in your voice. And your name? Let me think."

"That was then. For the moment, it's Kirsty."

"Of course it is," he grinned. "What can I do for you, Kirsty?"

"I'm looking for some information."

"Fire away." He tucked the bottle back beneath the blankets.

"We're looking for a man."

The old sailor was already flicking through the banknotes. "Hmm?"

"Roger Warrender."

Wolff's hands froze. His teeth clenched together. "That bastard! May he rot in hell."

"Are you saying he's dead?" said Montrose.

"He was still very much alive the last time I saw him, the sanctimonious little shit." He pushed the money back towards Kirsty. "Take it. I will accept nothing from him."

"No," said Kirsty. "That's not from him. It's from me. We need to find Warrender."

Wolff's features relaxed and he tucked the cash under his blankets. "Is he in trouble?" he said with a smirk.

Kirsty nodded. "He may be."

"Good. That's made my day. Well, that and a fistful of beer vouchers."

"It's a matter of life and death," said Montrose and instantly regretted it.

"How very dramatic. His, I hope," said Wolff.

"So you've seen him?"

"If you tramp the streets of London as I do, you see him now and again. Though he's changed his appearance. Several times in the past few years. But you can't mistake his walk, the fucking weasel. Pardon my French, young lady."

156

"His walk?" said Montrose.

"He has the gait of a French Legionnaire, you know. Long slow strides that eat up miles of desert. Well, it did in the old movies."

Kirsty edged closer. "Does he know that you...? I heard that you were once a friend of his."

"A long time ago. In a different world."

Save us the saga, old man. "Can you tell−?" began Montrose, but Kirsty put a hand on his knee.

"What happened?" she said.

The old man shrugged. "It was different in those days." Wolff scratched his beard. "It concerned a romantic liaison I had with a young chap. Turned out he was Russian. Bugger me, I thought he was Swedish." He grinned at Kirsty. "Honeytrap, you see? Warrender squealed on me. I was drummed out of the service. No job, no pension. Then my dear wife spent what money I had and then took off with what money *she* had. The rest is history. And not very pleasant."

Montrose glanced around, but he couldn't see shit. *Okay, story over. Spit it out.*

"Why do you want him?" Wolff pushed himself up from the blankets.

"Well," began Kirsty, "he has information we need."

Wolff grinned. "I'm sure he does."

"Where can we find him?" said Montrose. "Do you know roughly where he's living?"

"Roughly? Oh, I can do better than that. He's currently shacked up at number 42 Spey Gardens, Kensington. He changes address whenever he spots me. I have a habit of finding him, following him home and then standing outside his window, just to let him know. If he sees me, he moves house. But I always find him again. I'll give him another few weeks and I'll find a comfy spot outside his window. Frankly, I've got nothing better to do. I haunt the bastard. And I hope it eats his soul."

"And you've never spoken to him?"

"Not a chance. He has the most powerful of friends. I'd be dead within hours if I ever tried to talk to him. I'm surprised he hasn't had me killed already. They're probably waiting for the cider to do that. Besides, I have nothing to say to him. He's not exactly on my Christmas card list."

Kirsty pulled more notes from her purse. "Thank you, Captain Wolff. You have been of more help than you could possibly imagine. I hear the year two thousand was a good year for Bordeaux."

The old sailor grinned. His teeth were like a row of mossy tombstones. "It may well have been, but I can't remember much about it. Still, as long as Somerset is growing apples, I'll be all right." He pulled down the brow of his trilby. "Be careful, my dear. He really does have friends that you don't want to trifle with."

"I will. I've met them already. They're not on my Christmas card list either."

"I suspect you are one step ahead of me."

She smiled and touched his arm. "Goodbye, Captain Wolff." She moved the torch back along the tunnel.

Montrose spotted two figures silhouetted against the entrance. *So, you went to find some friends.* He flexed his hands and quickly scanned the floor for a weapon.

Kirsty quickened her pace and moved to walk around them.

Another figure appeared out of the darkness and stepped forward. "You leaving so soon? We haven't had tea." His friends laughed.

Montrose saw that their hands were hidden. *Go for the tallest. Then run.*

Kirsty moved closer to the wall to get around them. "Yeah, knock yourself out. Just move."

The tallest of them held out an arm, blocking her way. "Maybe you'd like to pay a little tax before you leave. You know, to help with the bill for the fancy cakes."

Kirsty stopped and held the torch under her chin. Montrose was about to step forward when she held him back. "Looking for a little cut, are you?"

Montrose heard her accent deepen once more.

"You remember Shitty Ferguson?" she said. "Used to

live here. Woke up one morning with his balls missing. You remember that?"

The men said nothing, then one piped up. "Yeah, I heard about that. So what?"

"Well, I've still got them. I keep them in a jar at home."

The big man stepped back. "Fucking hell, you're that mad Welsh bint."

"Less of the bint, matey. Shitty got what was coming. And if you want to keep your shriveled nuts, you better get out of my fucking way."

The man dropped his arm and Kirsty stepped out into the light.

Montrose took a deep breath of fresh air. A train clattered above their heads.

"Relax, Connor. I lied."

"Yeah?"

"I haven't really got his balls in a jar," she said as she found the path that led back towards the fence. "That would just be weird."

He kept his eyes on the ground, picking his way through the rubbish.

"I fed them to the dogs."

*

Lockhart pushed the door closed and hurried over to her desk. "They're in Southwark, ma'am. We have a man in the area. They were seen in the railway arches near to London Bridge station. The Americans are not far behind."

Purley nodded. "How did they find them? Cameras?"

"No, they had a tracker on Montrose's phone. They lost the signal on the river, but they worked out he was heading to Southwark. They tracked and triangulated all the phone signals that were closest to him and found one of interest. They were following that, but the signal has gone too, although not before it was tracked to the railway arches. I assume that's his female companion, ma'am."

"No doubt. Anything else?"

"They're going through the CCTV and they have police and Special Branch on the way to the area."

"That will be all. Keep me informed."

"It's only a matter of time, ma'am."

She didn't look up. "I said, that will be all. Carry on."

Lockhart nodded and headed for the door.

Madame Raymonde shifted in her chair. "Elizabeth, they're too close. If they find Wolff then they will find Warrender. You understand what you may have to do?"

Purley leaned forward and held her head in her hands. "I understand."

"I cannot help you, but if Warrender is taken alive, the Americans will show no mercy. And I know this may seem insensitive, but think of yourself. Clear down the threat. And Mr. Pilgrim."

Purley jerked upright and grabbed the phone. "Bring my car to the rear entrance." She took her mobile phone from her purse and typed in a text.

It may be necessary for your patient to die of his injuries. Wait for my command.

CHAPTER 13

Pilgrim opened his eyes and saw the nurse standing over the bed.

"I have to say goodbye," she said, her bright red lips squeezed into a thin line.

"That is a shame. It has been an unusual pleasure." Pilgrim smiled as she gently lifted him by the shoulder, placed his pillows flat, then laid him back down.

"Some men are coming to move you, which is a bloody stupid idea." She touched him gently on the hand. "Good luck. Be safe."

The door opened and two burly men approached the bed.

The nurse whispered. "Your phone is under the blankets."

One of the men spoke in an East London drawl.

"Leave it, nursey. We have to move. And you're coming too."

Pilgrim caught the look in her eyes. She said nothing and turned away.

The two men stood either side of the bed. One blew out a breath and nodded to Pilgrim. "I don't know who you are, guv'nor, and it's none of my business, but we have to move you. And it's going to hurt. There was no time to get the proper equipment, it's gonna be lift and shift."

"Where are we going?" said Pilgrim.

The man shrugged. "We'll find out when we get there."

For a moment, Pilgrim regretted discarding the morphine trigger. "This isn't a very good idea, gentlemen, perhaps you could make other arrangements?"

The man pushed the stand carrying the fluids closer to the bed. "You know, you aren't happy, we aren't happy, but *c'est la vie*, as the Frenchies say." They grabbed the edge of the bed.

"Where are my other friends?"

"No idea. And to be honest, I'm not sure you have any friends left."

"And you?"

"Just following orders, guv'nor."

164

"Where is she?" Kane stepped out of the Mercedes and stood in front of the boarded-up video store.

Campbell didn't look up. "Elizabeth Purley, sir?"

"Yeah, the fucking Virgin Queen of MI5."

Campbell continued to tap the screen of his iPad. "We don't know, sir. She left the building."

"Listen, asshole, you're supposed to find her. What about her phone?"

"Sir?" Campbell ignored him and held up the screen. "We have the information from the archives in Langley. All the operatives in MI5 and MI6 who were involved in Operation Red Star are now dead or retired. Everyone can be accounted for, except two."

"Spit it out."

Campbell read from the screen. "Roger Warrender was MI6. Defected to the Soviets in 1982 and then there's no trace of him. It is strongly suspected that the Soviets lost track of him and have no idea where he is. We have no reports from our sources in Moscow or London. He dropped off the face of the planet."

"Yeah?" Kane gnawed on his fingernails. "Another British traitor. No surprise. But Montrose came here for a reason. And now he's moved on. And you've lost him."

Campbell said nothing for a moment, then continued. "Every camera in London is looking for him. Every policeman, every taxi driver, even the traffic wardens. We'll find him." He focused on the information on his screen.

Kane slammed his hand on the roof of the Mercedes. "Do it! We need to find out the reason he was here. Then you'll know where to send your army of little helpers. This Warrender guy makes my Spidey-sense go fucking crazy. No one disappears unless someone makes it happen. If it wasn't the Russians then it must have been the British. They're the only other people that would have wanted him dead. And you say there's nothing?"

"We've trawled the British files, sir. The records only show his defection to the Soviets and then the history stops."

"You see, that's what's wrong. They should have been searching for him and leaving a trail. Goddamn Brits. Probably his Commie pals in MI5 looked after him. I swear that when this is over, I will go through MI5 like shit through a goose." Kane rubbed his face, then looked up. "You said two people. Who's the other?"

"It's not confirmed, but the archives say that the only connection between Red Star, Warrender and the time frame is Purley, sir. Elizabeth Purley."

"That bitch!"

"It's a tenuous link, but the records say she was a junior officer at the time of his disappearance. She knew Warrender. They were at university together."

"Right, leave her to me. If this Warrender guy is alive, he is your immediate priority. Find out what he knows and then deal with him. And the others, for Chrissake. Get it over with." Kane turned his back and headed down the alley where an operative was waiting. "Give me the good news."

"Montrose was here about twenty minutes ago, sir."

Kane glanced back at Campbell. "Why are you still here?"

"We are trying to identify the phone signal that was next to Montrose's when it cut. We find that, we'll find him."

"Good. Fuck off."

Campbell walked slowly back to the car.

Kane watched him for a moment then pointed to the operative. "Walk and talk."

The operative led the way past the dumpster and through the fence. "Montrose was in one of the arches, sir. He was with the girl. They talked to an old hobo. We've identified him as Captain Wolff. Ex-Royal Navy. The records say he was an old friend of Warrender."

"What is this place?" Kane looked around at the

broken down huts and the smoldering braziers.

"Illegals, sir. They cleared out when the cops approached. That's the archway over there."

"He's alone? This hobo?"

"There are still a few people around. Junkies. Too comatose to move. They won't be an issue."

Kane could smell the occupants as he approached the entrance to the arch. The Nokia buzzed in his pocket. He took a few steps inside and checked the screen.

Estimate two hours until password cracked.

He began to take a deep breath, but thought better of it. "Let's do this. Follow me." He checked left and right; there was no one around. "Sure he's alone?"

"Affirmative," said the operative. "The others are too far gone to notice. You asked for these, sir." He handed Kane an unmarked whisky bottle and a smartphone.

"Cask strength?"

"Yes, sir." The operative shone his torch and Kane followed the beam. "Ten yards down."

Kane scanned the notes on the smartphone and took the torch. "Wait outside." He brought up the beam and saw a bearded figure sitting amongst a pile of blankets. A trilby was pushed back on his head as he chewed on a burger. "Good afternoon, Captain Wolff. I'm from American Intelligence."

Wolff grinned as he chewed, then took a swig of

cider. "Good afternoon, whoever you are. I shall do you the courtesy of not referring to the oxymoron in your first statement."

"Yeah, right." Kane checked the notes on the smartphone. "Helluva story, Captain Wolff. Decorated veteran of the Falklands war. Conspicuous gallantry."

"Conspicuous stupidity more like. Anyway, cut to the chase, old boy. I've got a new bottle of cider that needs my urgent attention and I'd hate to disappoint it."

"Understood, Captain. Two people visited you earlier."

"Did they? Well, perhaps they did. It's all a bit of a blur, frankly. Buggered if I know. Today, you say? Well, I believe you. My calendar is such a riot of activity."

"You spoke to two people. And you gave them information. I'd like to know exactly what that information was."

Wolff finished his burger. "You know, I had a feeling I'd be getting a visit." He took a pull on the cider. "I thought it was going to be one of those days, you know? You wake up lying in your own piss and think, yeah, it really is one of those days and it's only going to get worse."

"Look, Captain Wolff. I don't have time to dick around. Our countries are involved in a mission of the utmost importance. We need to work together on this and fast. Tell me what I can do for you and it will be done. But I need that information. Then I can get you out of here. Back on your feet."

Wolff shook his head. "My dear boy, my previous visitors were not so gauche as to patronize me in such a manner. A bath and a suite at the Ritz won't heal this." He tapped his head. "And if our two countries are working together on this, you wouldn't be here standing in my piss and spouting nonsense. It would be some pompous twat from MI5."

"Captain Wolff, I have been given both the responsibility and the authority to work on behalf of the United Kingdom, straight from Downing Street. This is for your country, sir."

"I've had the honor of fighting for my country and, quite frankly, it can go fuck itself."

Kane shook his head. "Roger Warrender. Where is he?"

Wolf shrugged. "No idea. Do I look like I frequent his social circles? Frankly, old boy, I struggle to remember what happened yesterday, so you're barking up the wrong tree."

Kane heard heavy footsteps and turned away from Wolff who was opening a new bottle. "What is it?"

The operative spoke in a low voice. "Sighting in Westminster, sir. Sixty percent facial recognition on a traffic camera. If it is them, they're north of the river and heading west. They're not showing a phone signal."

"What the fuck does sixty percent mean?"

"It means highly likely, sir. The camera was high definition, on the outskirts of the Westminster containment sector. The teams are combing the other cameras. The cops are on the way."

Kane stared into the darkness for a moment. "Fuck the cops. Keep them clear. And those MI5 assholes. I don't want any witnesses. They're going for Warrender. Find them first and send in a team. You know, knock knock, who's there, bang bang. Get me?"

"Understood, sir."

"Wait for me in the car." He pulled the bottle of whisky from his pocket. "You know, I don't think we'll need to trouble you anymore, Captain Wolff."

Wolff belched and replaced the cap on his cider. "Really? Just when my social life was taking off. I was so looking forward to getting to know you."

"Perhaps I can offer you something stronger?" Kane unscrewed the top of the whisky bottle and palmed a tiny tablet into the upturned cap. He poured in the whisky and held it out. "Here, no hard feelings. Have one on me."

Wolff's trembling fingers took the cap and knocked it back in one. "Good God. What the hell was that?"

"Cask strength Scotch, 120 proof. Straight out of a Highland distillery. Strong enough to forget all your woes. Fancy another?"

Wolff held out the cap, his eyes flickering between his hand and the bottle. "*Alba gu bràth*." He threw the whisky down his throat then leaned forward, gasping as he tried to catch a breath. "Strewth, that's strong, even for an old matelot like me."

"Believe me, Captain Wolff, it's absolutely lethal."

A hacking cough burst from the old sailor's throat, but his gaze didn't leave the bottle.

"Think of it as a parting gift," said Kane.

Wolff began to wheeze.

"Incidentally, what do you know about Operation Red Star?"

"Red Star?" spluttered Wolff. He sat for a moment, his eyes squeezed shut, trying to breathe slowly. "As in 'I had an uncle who once played for Red Star Belgrade'?" He tried to sing the line, but bent forward as his chest tightened.

Kane laughed. "You know it? Operation Red Star?"

Wolff pushed a hand against the wall, trying to steady himself. "Never heard of it. Now, how's about some more of that firewater?"

"Sure you can handle it?"

"I relish a challenge." Wolff tried to reach for the

bottle, but slumped back against the bricks. "What, what did you just give me?"

Kane held up the bottle. "Meet my friend. Mickey Finn. And he had to be at his best for a drunken old shit like you."

"But..." Wolff's mouth dropped open and his head began to drop.

"We know where your friends are. And who they're going to see." Kane held the bottle high, dousing the blankets with whisky. "I'm afraid, as my old drill instructor used to say, you are one man surplus to requirements."

Wolff tried to push himself up, but slumped down, whisky splashing across his clothes and beard as he tried to shove the blankets back.

Taking a handkerchief from his pocket, Kane poured the last of the whisky onto the cloth.

The trilby fell from Wolff's head and rolled across the filthy ground. "No, don't... I'll tell..." He tried to roll away, his breathing turning into a high-pitched whistle. He fell back, his eyes wide open, saliva and whisky dripping from his beard. "Please."

Kane took a lighter from his pocket, stepped back and lit the handkerchief. He waited until flames began to creep up the cloth, then threw it at Wolff. The whisky erupted into a pale blue flame, turning to yellow as the blankets ignited.

CHAPTER 14

Montrose jabbed continuously at the window button. The smell of damp and mold was overwhelming. Eventually the window opened a few inches. He looked back into the rear of the van, covered in dust and unidentifiable debris. "How much did you pay for this?"

"A hundred quid."

"You were robbed."

Kirsty laughed. "It'll do for a few miles before it grinds to a halt. Someone brought it into the junkyard this morning which means it's probably still insured and registered for the London congestion charge. The cop cars and traffic cameras scan the license plates of every car that passes them so they'll ignore us." She pointed out the window to where an identical van was parked. "That's what I'm looking for. Let's hope it's unattended."

"Why? You going to steal it?"

"Nah, it would take too long and I'm not driving about in a stolen van when the cops are looking for us." She reached down and brought up a screwdriver. "Take this. Get the license plates. You do the front."

"What for?"

"Just a bit of insurance. If the cops start sniffing around Southwark, it won't be long before they give the junkyard a visit. That's why I picked a white van. London is full of them." She pushed the door open and headed towards the parked van. "We'll use them later. The old plates got us through Westminster. These plates will get us out of here."

The plastic bolts came away easily. Montrose pulled off the license plate and shoved it into his jacket, then walked back to the first van. "How far?"

"Five minutes."

*

The van swung into a wide road lined with white-painted Victorian apartments, four storeys high. Montrose placed his mouth against the gap in the window and took a deep breath. "Anything from Zac or Pilgrim?"

"I'll check." She shoved her hand into her bag and switched on her phone, then craned her neck forward, scanning the buildings. "There's the address." She swung the van into the curb.

"Not here," said Montrose.

"Why?"

"There's one road in and one road out. All we need is a delivery truck in the wrong place and we're boxed in. Go down to the end, around the corner, we need a T-junction."

"Okay, super-spy." Kirsty pulled out and accelerated to the end of the road, turned right and stopped just before a junction.

Montrose got out of the van and looked over a wall to a garden at the rear of the building. *Exit route. Just in case. I doubt he'll be pleased to see us.* Kirsty was already walking towards the corner and he hurried to catch up with her. "Let's hope he's at home."

"We'll soon find out. But I'm going in anyway." She led the way up the steps. There were four names on the intercom, but none was Warrender.

"Pick a name," said Montrose.

"Nope," said Kirsty and pushed the button marked '*Services*'. "Post." The buzzer clicked and she pushed the heavy door open into a marble-lined hall.

"Fancy place," said Montrose. "Beats the crap out of Southwark." Before them was a wide staircase and two doors either side of the ground floor. Several pairs of kids' shoes lay scattered around outside one of them.

"Not that one," said Kirsty, approaching the other, looking closely at the lock. "One Yale lock. This isn't a person in hiding. He'd have better security than this."

Montrose followed her up the staircase to the next floor. Another two doors, one with potted plants standing sentry. "You think he's a gardener?"

"Nope." Kirsty turned to the other door. It had three locks: a Yale, a mortise and a deadlock. "This is it. Got to be." She looked at the spy-hole and held her face close as she knocked on the door. "Let him see my face. I'm slightly less threatening than you are."

After a few moments, a voice boomed out. "Who is it?"

"Kensington Council. Can we speak to the home owner, please?"

He noticed her accent was back.

"I'm busy."

She held up her iPad. "Sir, if you please, we only need two minutes of your time."

A bolt shot back and the door opened. A tall, elderly man with a tired, lined face and a shock of white unruly hair peered at them. "Make it quick. The council, you say?"

"No, Mr. Warrender. Not the council. We really need to talk to you." Kirsty pushed open the door and walked past him before he could reply.

Montrose saw the fury on the man's face and followed quickly behind, holding up his hands. "Sir, we come in peace. We just need to talk to you. We are unarmed."

Kirsty held out her arms and purse. "You can check."

"Feel free, sir." Montrose held open his jacket.

Warrender stood, his grey face reddening. "I don't know what all this is about, but if you don't leave now, I shall call the police."

"No, you won't," said Montrose. "Look, can we talk? That's all we want. We're not from the government. We're not journalists and we're not crazies. We have a situation. We really need your help." Through the open door, Montrose heard voices on the stair. "I'm sure your neighbors don't want to hear this."

Warrender closed the door. He glanced around for a moment, unsure. The apartment smelled musty and neatly stacked piles of newspapers ran along the corridor. "Follow me," he said and led them to a large sitting room. Every surface: floor, tables, chairs, was covered in neatly stacked newspapers.

"Now, listen to me." Warrender stood in the corner of the room and crossed his arms. "I have absolutely no idea why you're here and I do not have the first bloody clue what you're talking about. Whoever you are, if you intend to rob me, you'll find very little of value, so get it over with."

Montrose sat down on a pile of newspapers. "Mr. Warrender, Captain Wolff told us where you live. He has seen you many times in London, although he said you'd changed your appearance. He said your walk gave it away. Long slow stride, like a legionnaire. The same way you walked when we came into the room. But Wolff never told anyone. You're safe."

Warrender raised an eyebrow. "Safe, eh? That's mighty big of you."

"You might want to check with your contact in MI5," said Montrose. "That's where we think the information about Captain Wolff came from and led us here. But I'll be straight with you. We don't really know where the information came from. If I did, I'd tell you. We've got nothing to hide."

"Oh, laddie," Warrender gave a bitter laugh. "We've all got something to hide."

Montrose shrugged. "Yeah. Guess that's true."

"You're not wrong," said Kirsty. "Mr. Warrender, would you mind if we sat down? It's been, uh, an interesting morning. And if there's one thing I would kill for, it's a cup of tea."

Warrender's shoulders dropped and he slowly

lowered himself onto a chair next to an ancient bureau, strewn with paper and worn down pencils. He stared into a fireplace, empty except for a pile of grey ashes in the grate. "The kitchen is through there."

"White with?" said Kirsty.

Warrender nodded. He sat for a moment, head bowed.

Montrose was about to speak when he saw the wallpaper. It hadn't struck him at first, but the entire wall was covered in tiny writing. Pencil stubs lay strewn across the stacks of newspapers. He looked closer. Every wall surface was covered in long lists of numbers grouped together in five digits. He was so transfixed, he forgot to speak.

"Well, get on with it," said Warrender. "Ask your questions. Tell me what happens next, although I think I know."

"I'll be frank with you, sir, I have no idea what happens next." He tore his gaze away from the faded wallpaper.

Warrender looked up at him. "That wasn't the answer I was expecting. So cut to the chase. What do you know about me?"

"Not much, sir. But one thing we do know, is that the body of Michael Pilgrim turned up this week in a glacier in Norway."

Warrender didn't move. Didn't blink. "You are assuming that I am familiar with this person?"

Pilgrim's words. This guy must have talked to his brother before he ended up on a glacier. Go for it. "Sir, both of you were involved in Operation Red Star. That night, you met him at the border between Russia and Norway. He gave you a password and kept another to himself. Then you went your separate ways."

Warrender didn't reply.

Kirsty appeared in the doorway with a tray of tea.

"We need the other password," said Montrose. "And we need it now, because MI5 and the CIA are running riot through London trying to find it. The Russians have already killed the Norwegian cop who brought them the information on Pilgrim. Burned to death in a car."

"In Soho? I heard about that."

"Yeah, I was there. They nearly got me too."

Warrender slumped in the chair and let his chin drop down to rest on his chest. "I am tired. I am so very tired."

Kirsty placed the tray on top of the pile of newspapers then knelt beside him and held his hand.

Warrender recoiled at the touch, took a deep breath and stared blankly across the room. "This is the end of days." He leaned back in the chair and gently took her hand.

It might just be, fella. "Sir, if we don't get the password before they do…"

Warrender turned towards Kirsty. "I met him at the border. We split up in case one of us was captured. I was the only agent in the area. They didn't expect him to go north. He told me there was someone on his tail. I hoped the Soviets would follow me on the main road south. I left tracks. They were supposed to follow." He shook his head. "But they didn't. Someone must have known. Must have betrayed him." He lifted a hand and traced his fingers down a newspaper on his desk. "I never saw him again. For weeks, I had no idea whether they had captured him or not."

Yeah, but who did you tell? "You reported this back?"

"I'm not a fool. By the time I got back to London I worked out he had disappeared. I thought he'd be safe. I gave him my gun."

A thought flashed into Montrose's head. "A Browning?"

"Yes."

Montrose thought for a moment. "He had it when he died." *But what did he tell you?* "Ekland," said Montrose.

Warrender lifted his hand from the newspaper and rubbed his eyes.

"Did he say the word *Ekland*?"

Warrender looked up. "Pilgrim? No."

"I have to ask you. Who did you tell? Who betrayed Pilgrim?"

"You don't understand." Warrender stared up at the writing on the wall. "Pilgrim was betrayed, just as I betrayed Captain Wolff. The stupidity of youth. I was not alone. I thought it was the right thing to do. I was so sure. We all were."

Yeah, it's so sad. Whatever. "Who did you tell? About Pilgrim?"

Warrender didn't seem to hear him. "I was only a message boy. I knew nothing of the gravity of the operation. I spent the whole time wondering why the hell they had sent me to a godforsaken border post in the middle of a sodding blizzard. And then Pilgrim came hurtling down the road in an old Soviet banger." He looked up at Montrose. "I called and told them what had happened… I mean, I let London know. That we had split up. That I was a decoy and Pilgrim was going north. And when I got back I heard that Pilgrim hadn't made it. He just disappeared. They told me the Soviets didn't have him and I was the only one he had talked to. It didn't take them long to accuse me of being a double agent. But it wasn't me." He shook his head. "It wasn't me, you see, Pilgrim was betrayed after we split up." He straightened up in the chair and smiled at Kirsty. "I'd quite like that tea, if you don't mind."

"Of course." Kirsty poured the tea and handed a cup to Warrender.

He sat with the cup in his lap, then fixed his eyes on Montrose. "What do you want with me?"

"The password. That's it. The password Pilgrim gave you that night before you split up. The rest is of no interest us."

"And then?"

"That's it."

"You'll just let me walk away?"

Montrose shrugged. "Yeah. If that's what you want."

Warrender sipped the tea. "There's a suitcase in the hall. I've had it there for thirty years. Ready to go at a moment's notice. And all this," he waved a hand around the room, "will disappear with me." He tapped an oil heater under the bureau with his foot. "If I hit that button, this place will be an inferno."

*

She looked over the head of the soldier, through the gap in the curtains and clasped her hands tightly together to stop them from shaking. Warrender wouldn't hold out for long. She lifted a hand towards the window, then pulled it back. But there was no other way. If she got any closer, Kane would work it out.

The soldier looked up. "Binoculars, ma'am?"

Purley shook her head. She didn't trust herself to speak. The photo in her bag was of a young man. But she knew what he looked like. She couldn't look at his face. Not now. She let out a long, slow breath and closed her eyes. "Are they in the room?"

"Yes, ma'am. One target. Two others. All out of sight at the moment."

She tried to think of another way. But she knew in her heart there was none.

"There's movement, ma'am. Waiting for the target to appear. Do I take the shot?"

"No." She held out a hand before she could stop herself. "Just give them a moment."

"I'll tell you when I have a target, ma'am."

A radio crackled into life. "OP reports cars approaching at speed on Bayswater Road. It's our Cousins."

Her chest tightened so quickly she couldn't speak. It was over.

*

Montrose stared down at the oil heater. "Well, we'd be much obliged if you let us leave first."

"I still have a friend," said Warrender. "I'll disappear as I did before."

"So they let you go? The Soviets?" said Montrose.

"My God, no. When I escaped from the British interrogation, the Americans worked out where I was headed. The only really safe place in London. They couldn't get to me in time, so they told the Soviets that I was a double agent. Complete rubbish, of course, but it didn't stop them. I knew I had been betrayed. And I knew whatever it was that Pilgrim had told me was going to get me killed. To the British, I was a traitor. To the Soviets, I was a British agent pretending to defect. Whether I talked or not, there would only be one ending to my story. An unmarked grave."

"What happened?"

"I went from one nightmare to another. I had no choice. I escaped the British, but the Soviets were waiting for me. They took me to their Embassy in London. And when the sweet-talk failed, I knew what was coming next. Of course, I denied all knowledge but I heard the screams of the others. I escaped, with some help. People who still believed me."

Shit, this is getting more complicated than a Le Carré novel. It's way out of my league. Threats are not going to get anything out of this guy. He needs to feel safe. Let him talk. Then maybe he'll tell us. But if torture

186

wouldn't make him talk, I haven't got a chance. "And only you knew the password?"

Warrender laughed. "Well, only myself and Colonel Furstenberg. I told him in case they killed me. Carved in stone, for posterity, you see." He smiled and took a sip of his tea. "And he died long before you were born."

Who the hell is Furstenberg?

"Was he the one that helped you escape the British and the Soviets?" said Kirsty.

Warrender sipped his tea. "No, my dear. He was dead before even my time."

This is bullshit. He's protecting someone. If he didn't betray Pilgrim, who did? Maybe the same people who helped him escape the Soviets and the British. And I bet my ass they're still around today and still taking care of him. How else could he have survived for so long, hidden in plain sight, right in the middle of London? Montrose cleared his throat. "Who helped you, sir? Who got you away from the British and then the Soviets?"

Warrender stood up. "When I was young I betrayed Captain Wolff. I would never do such a thing again."

"You got back to London and they thought you were a traitor. Who betrayed you?"

Warrender faced the window, gazing down into the street. "Have you ever read E.M. Forster? One of the pre-eminent English novelists of the twentieth century.

He lived through two world wars, the fall of the British Empire and the rise of the superpowers." He turned to face Montrose and Kirsty, silhouetted against the window. "He once said, 'If I had to choose between betraying my country and betraying my friend, I hope I should have the guts to betray my country'."

CHAPTER 15

The blood atomized across the room in a cloud. Warrender toppled to the floor, a clean hole in the back of his head. The remainder of his face thumped onto the carpet.

Kirsty screamed and scrambled backwards from Warrender's corpse.

"Get down!" Montrose dived towards her. He grabbed her by the waist and tried to drag her to the door.

She wriggled from his grasp and set off in a fast crawl. "Follow me!"

"Keep your head down."

"Listen to me." She wiped a film of blood from her face. "I checked the flat while making tea. There's a rear exit. Move it."

Montrose began to edge forward on his elbows. "Wait."

She dropped to the floor and glanced back. "Are you crazy?"

He looked up at the walls. "Everything we need is here. If we can capture it, maybe we can work it out. Use your phone." He pointed to the oil heater. "Then get clear."

Kirsty rolled onto her back and brought up her iPhone.

Keeping close to the piles of blood-spattered newspapers, Montrose crawled through the pink scum on the carpet. On the front of the oil heater he saw a clockwork timer set to five minutes. He shoved in the plug and pushed the power button. The oil heater hummed into life and he heard the clockwork timer ticking. He rolled over, hit the stopwatch function on his watch then crawled to the door and set off down the hall on his knees.

Kirsty had the window open in a small kitchen and was sitting on the ledge. "It's clear. Let's go!"

He climbed up just as Kirsty jumped. Directly below, he could see the garden with an outhouse and clothes drying on a washing line. Kirsty was waiting when he dropped down onto the grass.

She tore off her blood-stained cardigan and pulled a

T-shirt from the line, throwing it to him when he caught up with her. "You're covered in shit. Put that on." She ran towards the wall beside the van.

"No, this way," said Montrose. "If they have someone on the corner, they'll see us." He ran to the end of the garden and pulled open a gate into a cobbled mews lane. He could almost hear the oil heater's timer ticking in his head. "Run!" He looked up at the open window, then followed her along the lane. "Wait," he said as Kirsty neared the end and pulled her close to the wall. He checked his watch and peeked out into the road. "Clear. Just walk." He could see the hood of the van as they emerged onto the road.

Kirsty jumped into the driver's seat and Montrose ran around to the passenger side.

"Go." he said. "Turn left."

She sat for a moment and shoved the van into gear. "No. We've got to know."

"Kirsty," Montrose shook his head. "Just go. Drive normally and then turn left."

"No." She held the wheel tight in her hands. "You saw what was in that apartment. And whatever the hell that means, they'll work it out." She slowly swung the van out into the road and checked her phone. "Nothing." She switched it off and shoved it in her bag.

"Jesus, Kirsty, I think we'll hear it." He checked the stopwatch on his phone. "Go left. Now."

She turned right, past the mews lane, just as the muted thump of an explosion shook the van.

In the mirror, he saw long tongues of flame erupting from the shattered windows.

*

Kane sat back in the Mercedes, staring down the road towards the apartment. The street was blocked by fire trucks and the sidewalk was awash with water where the fire crews had extinguished the flames before entering the building. Residents wrapped in survival foil were being guided to the end of the road by the police. "How did you find them?" said Kane.

"Phone signal, sir. The one that was closest to Montrose when his signal cut. It must be his companion. We came as fast as we could."

"Not fast enough, asshole."

"Sir, I spoke to the team. The explosion happened just as they kicked the door in."

Kane sat silent for a moment. "Don't tell me. Suicide?"

"No, sir, we had a look at the body. He was shot through the back of the head with a large caliber round.

He was face down and the window was broken from the outside. It was a shooter. Then someone set off an incendiary device." Campbell pointed to the terraced buildings across from Warrender's apartment. "It had to be from there. Judging by the position of the body, they couldn't have hit Warrender from the street."

Kane pressed his face against the glass and looked up at the opposite side of the road. "That isn't random. That's a planned hit. Who knew where he was?"

"We don't know, sir, but someone is one step ahead of us."

"You don't fucking say. Where's Purley?"

"That's the issue, sir."

Kane turned to stare at him. "What the hell are you talking about?"

"She had an unregistered phone. But we found the signal from her movements through Lambeth. It's a very secure device, but we've found a way to track it."

"Yeah? Show me."

Campbell brought up his iPad and showed a map of London with a red line tracing through the streets. "Here are the positions of the cell phone masts that her phone polled when she left Thames House. We've triangulated all the signals and calculated proximity and distance from the signal response times. She was here ten minutes ago."

"That fucking bitch!" He pounded the headrest in front of him, then grabbed Campbell by the lapels. "Find Montrose. Kill that prick."

"Yes, sir. And Elizabeth Purley?"

"She's not your concern. Leave her to me."

*

Through the rear windshield Montrose could see a long column of smoke rising into the clear blue sky and gently drifting east.

Kirsty pulled the van into the side of the road.

"Not here," said Montrose. "Keep going."

"No, Connor." She pointed along the tree-lined avenue of grand villas, bordered on both sides by high railings and walls. "Look down there."

He ducked his head to see past the hanging branches of the trees.

"That's Lancaster Gate, a major junction and a meeting point of three containment sectors. If they have coppers waiting there, we have to be very careful. It's only a matter of time before they search CCTV and find the van. After the fireworks at Warrender's place, false license plates are not going to do it for us. They'll haul over every white van north of the river. Maybe they won't spot us, but we can't take that chance."

"So what if they're waiting for us?"

"Then we walk out and find a safe place." She brought out the phone from her bag and thumbed the power button.

"I'd keep that switched off, Kirsty. You never know."

"They'd have to be a genius to find my phone," she smiled.

"Yeah, well, the CIA has got buildings full of them and they're only looking for one thing. Me." *I hope to God it's only me. No. It's too late for that.*

"Good point." She pulled a new SIM card from her purse and slotted it into the phone, then reset the software. "Stay here." Kirsty stepped from the van.

He opened the door. "I'll come too."

"No, they're looking for two people. Chill out, keep an eye on the mirrors. I'll be back in a moment."

Montrose watched her head down the street. *Where's her bag?* He turned and saw it lying on the passenger seat. *Last chance. Do it now. Bring this madness to an end. Kane will give me whatever I want. This time, I'll make sure. And make sure she's safe.* He looked along the street and saw her sitting on a wooden bench outside a pub. *She can disappear. Get out of London.* Grabbing the bag, he pulled it over. *You won't get another chance.*

He gripped the door handle. *She's a tough chick.* He opened the door.

Doesn't matter what deal I do. He let the handle of the bag slip from his grasp. *Maybe not today or tomorrow, but they'll kill her. They'll never stop looking. The same death sentence as me.*

Kirsty sat on the bench, swinging her leg and watching the traffic.

He jerked his head back to stretch his neck and curled his fists into a ball. *Fucking man up, you asshole. The security of your country is at risk. Any fundamentalist or just plain crazy who gets access to that satellite will cause mayhem on an international scale. The whole defense of the US relies on satellites. It's your country. And you're staring at a chick?* He rubbed his face. Warrender's last words sounded in his head. *If I had a choice between betraying my friends and betraying my country...* He kicked open the door, grabbed the bag and held it tight in his hand, keeping to the cover of the trees as he strode down the road. The sound of sirens came closer. *I'm sick of this shit.*

She looked up as he approached.

"Kirsty, we've been here too long. We need to move. Fast." He handed her the bag.

"That's not a bad idea because, as a matter of fact, there's a fat bloke sitting over there in his car and the traffic wardens are ignoring him. I smell bacon."

"Which way?"

They turned back at the sound of screeching tires and saw a Range Rover slide to a halt beside the van. A black-suited figure stuck a machine pistol out of the window and emptied it through the window of the van.

Montrose felt his legs go weak. "Fuck."

She slung the bag over her shoulder. "I couldn't have put it better myself."

"Your town, Kirsty, which way?"

"Fancy a cup of coffee?"

He wanted to run, but could only stare at her.

"Any moment now this place is going to be cop central. So let's not do anything that would attract attention, yeah?" She pointed to a Costa Coffee at the opposite junction. "They found the van far too quickly. We need wi-fi."

*

The hum of traffic faded as she took a sharp right into a lane. High brick walls lined the sides, set with tradesmen's entrances to the grand villas beyond. At her feet were the cobbled stones where she had played in her childhood. She stopped and brought out the faded photograph, then ducked into a doorway as the first deep sobs racked her body and her trembling hands became wet with tears. She crouched down before she fell and slumped against the door, holding the photo hard to her lips.

She opened her eyes and saw, through the mist of her tears, two boots in front of her. A hand grabbed her by the shoulders and pulled her up. The photo slipped from her grasp when she saw the long thin knife and a huge hand reached behind her head. She lunged to the side, but was like a rag doll in his hands and he pulled her head hard towards him, her nose flattening against his chest. The thrust of the knife lifted her feet from the ground. The blade burst up through her chest and her ribs popped as cartilage gave way.

Her arms hung limp as he held her whole body for a moment, then threw her into the doorway.

Her face hit the cobblestones. She felt cold, but there was no pain. She tried to lift her head and saw a pool of blood moving slowly towards the gutter. The photograph lay beside her. She opened her mouth to say his name, but only a red froth bubbled from her pale lips. Her eyelids flickered, then closed.

CHAPTER 16

Oh, fuck. Montrose watched a police van pull up outside the coffee shop. The rear doors flew open and eight cops in bulletproof vests carrying machine pistols jumped down and fanned out around the junction. Montrose slid down in his chair and squinted between the other customers. *This was a shit idea.* He noticed a stairway to his right, leading to a basement. *That goes nowhere.* He traced a path between the tables to the front door. *There's only one exit. And I'm looking at it.*

Kirsty leaned over the table and handed him an earpiece. "I see them. If they knew we were here we'd be face down on the floor, so cheer up." She held the microphone between their lips. "Come closer or it won't work. We're on. I'm waiting for the line to encrypt."

Montrose heard static and then Pilgrim's voice.

"Kirsty?"

She pulled Montrose closer until their cheeks almost touched and whispered into the microphone. "Yeah, we're here. Where does it hurt?"

They heard him stifle a laugh. "Everywhere. What's happening?"

Montrose was about to speak when Kirsty placed a finger on his lips. "We found him. Roger Warrender."

"The traitor," said Pilgrim. "I need to—"

"He's dead," Montrose interrupted. "Someone put a bullet through his brain while we were talking to him."

There was silence on the line for a moment. "And I hope you managed to escape unharmed?"

"Yeah, we're cool," said Kirsty.

Montrose shook his head. "We're trapped in a coffee shop with the police crawling all over the place, that's not cool."

"They think we're running," said Kirsty. "We're safer in here."

"Listen..."

"I'm sure Kirsty has it covered," said Pilgrim. "We need to concentrate on who wanted to silence Warrender."

"No. What's really pissing me off right now," said Montrose, "is that someone is supposed to be helping us, yeah? That someone gives us the information that leads us to Captain Wolff and then leads us to Warrender and then someone shoots the old man just as he's about to spill the beans. What the hell is going on?"

"Montrose, you're not the only one in the dark. Certain information has been given to me in confidence, the source of which I can never reveal. It is an excellent source, but has its dangers. I have to ensure that we are not being played for fools. Now, I have some information from the people who are looking after me. An address in Holland Park was gutted by fire, just as it was being raided by the security services. I assume that's the address you last visited. The Press have the story that it was a terrorist cell."

"It was Warrender," said Montrose. "He had the place rigged."

"Indeed. I suspect what happened is that, given the imminent arrival of the CIA, Warrender was killed because he would have been captured. I would have very much liked to talk to him."

Montrose heard the menace in Pilgrim's voice.

Kirsty pulled the mic closer. "Mr. Pilgrim, he didn't betray your brother. It was Warrender who was betrayed. We spoke to him. We were in his flat. I really believed him. And the flat, it was totally weird."

Pilgrim didn't respond for a moment. "Tell me what you saw."

"There were newspapers everywhere. Stacks of them all around the apartment. And they were all copies of *The London Times*. The walls were covered in tiny handwritten numbers, in groups of five. There were thousands of them. That's it, apart from a fancy old radio and an oil heater set up as a bloody big bomb. No, wait, there was a photo on his desk. It was a woman. The photo was old and faded. She was tall. I don't know who she is."

"I think I do," said Pilgrim. "Tell me about the radio."

Montrose looked up at the sound of police sirens. He felt a tremor in his spine as a group of armed policemen ran past the window.

"I've got the picture on my phone." Kirsty held it between them and expanded the photo. "It's a Roberts radio. It's got an old red and black LED screen."

"Look closely if you can," said Pilgrim. "Does it have the letters SW on the dial?"

Montrose kept his head low over the coffee. *Shortwave? What's he getting at?*

"Yeah," said Kirsty. "I can see the selector. It's set to SW. Shortwave, right? What's he doing with that? BBC World Service?"

"No," said Pilgrim. "That's not the station he was looking for."

Holy crap. I know what this is.

"Tell me," said Pilgrim. "Are all the newspapers folded to a certain page?"

Kirsty checked the photo. "Yeah. The crossword page. Why would he do that?"

"I know," said Montrose. "Numbers Station. Jesus, that's Cold War shit."

"Correct," said Pilgrim. "In the days before the internet and email, this was the way the intelligence services broadcast secure messages around the globe. And, on occasion, still do."

"But surely anyone could listen in to them?" said Kirsty.

"Of course they could," replied Pilgrim. "But unless you have the ability to decode the message it would mean nothing. The permutation of the numbers is almost infinite. You say his walls were covered by numbers?"

"Everywhere," said Montrose.

"The numbers are transmitted from a military base," said Pilgrim. "They use a powerful transmitter that can be heard anywhere on earth. The message will be broadcast as a series of numbers, but to decode that message into words you need the solution. The normal method was called a one-time pad, where one page of paper, with the answers to the code, would be used to decrypt the message. But the next time a message was transmitted there would be a different code so you'd need a different page of the one-time pad, which is covered in a list of seemingly random letters. That way, even if you discovered the one-time pad, you would only ever able to decrypt one message, if you knew which message it was and how to use the one-time pad code."

"That sounds like a lot of pages," said Kirsty.

Montrose nodded. "Yeah, or a lot of newspapers."

"It's a near-perfect system," said Pilgrim. "Better than any modern encryption device. Its only weakness is that the numbers must be coded using the same one-time pad as the agent who is receiving the message. Cold War spy agencies could get hundreds of pages on a microdot, no bigger than the point of a needle, and then send them to the agent. In the case of Warrender that was not required. He used the London Times crossword and so did the person sending him a message."

"I don't get it," said Kirsty. "So only the person actually broadcasting the message knows what they are sending?"

"No," said Pilgrim. "Only the author. The message would be sent by a military technician. He would only be given numbers to send. He would know nothing of the one-time pad that was used to encode the message, or how to decrypt it."

"Yeah, that would work," said Montrose. "But who

the hell was sending Warrender messages? He escaped from the British because they thought he was a Soviet spy, then he escaped from the Soviets because they thought he was a double agent. They both wanted Warrender to talk. Someone's been helping him all these years. I take it that it's not the CIA."

"I think I know," said Kirsty. "The lady in the photo."

"Exactly," said Pilgrim. "But why? Love or blackmail?"

"Love," said Montrose and Kirsty at the same time.

"And he never betrayed her," said Kirsty. "Okay, what about this for an idea? She was the one who betrayed him. She was the one that Warrender told after he met your brother. And she was the one who told the Soviets where to find your brother. And his escape route."

Montrose nodded. "She got what she needed. Then she saw Warrender was in danger and she helped him escape from the British, then got him away from the Soviets when she realized they were going to kill him. All those years he knew what she was and what she had done. He never betrayed her. That's more than just blackmail."

"It was her," said Kirsty. "*She* was the double agent. Warrender said he called London after he met your brother at the border. She was the one who betrayed him."

"And then she killed him," said Pilgrim.

"What?" said Montrose.

"Assume I know more about this issue than I can tell you, but your hypothesis is eminently plausible. She killed him to stop him from being captured. She let Warrender talk to you, but when she saw that the CIA were at the front door and that Warrender would be captured, she killed him. But she could have killed him at any time. What she did was a last resort. Did Warrender start the fire?"

"No," said Kirsty, "we did."

"Warrender had rigged up the old oil heater as insurance," said Montrose. "I primed it before we escaped. That place will burn clean. And the numbers and all the copies of the newspapers, there will be nothing left."

"Then she'll be safe," said Pilgrim. "I'm not surprised. The numbers that were broadcast would have been recorded. Both the numbers and the newspapers would have been tracked back to legacy transmissions. It would have sealed her fate."

"Which is why he was ready to destroy them," said Montrose. "To keep her safe."

"I'm afraid to say that theory may be rather naive," said Pilgrim.

Hate is clouding your judgment, dude. "No," said Montrose, "he was ready to destroy them because…"

"Mutual destruction," said Pilgrim. "They probably both held secrets that would destroy the other. If one died, then they would somehow ensure that the truth came out and implicate the other."

Kirsty glanced at Montrose. "Then why didn't she kill him before and burn the place down herself? Mr. Pilgrim, I'm right, no? The person who is helping is the lady in the photo. Same age, same place. It all fits."

"I hate to be obtuse," said Pilgrim, "But for your own safety, I couldn't possibly comment."

You asshole. Montrose placed a hand on Kirsty's arm. "Whatever. There's only one thing that makes sense. The strongest bond of all. Love. She knew that he had the password and she protected him all these years. Sounds like everybody wanted to know Roger Warrender. Your brother told Warrender the last password before they split up at the Russian border and Warrender gave him his gun. That's why they found a Browning in the ice. He's not a traitor. He didn't betray your brother. Warrender was the 'Brit' in the clue written on his arm. Your brother trusted him. And Warrender told no one. Not even the British. Not even after they tortured him. He knew the secret was so great he would take it to his grave. And so did she."

Kirsty shook her head. "You know, I don't even think he told her."

Montrose stared at her. "But…"

"Think about it," she said. "She saved his life. She kept him safe all these years. She was a double agent, and if Warrender had told her the password she would have told the Soviets. But she didn't."

"These theories are getting us nowhere," said Pilgrim. "I take it he did not reveal the password?"

"No," said Montrose. "I think he would have told us, but we didn't have time."

Kirsty leaned into the mic. "He said only one other man knew it."

The line crackled and a Californian drawl came through. "Hey, guys, it's Zac. I gotta tell you, this freakin' satellite gets weirder every time I look at it. But give me about four hours and my machines will crack the password."

"We may not have that long," said Pilgrim. "Kirsty, who was the other man that Warrender gave the password to?"

"Colonel Furstenberg. But Warrender said that he had died before his time. What the bloody hell does that mean?"

"Furstenberg. I'm on it," said Zac.

"I don't get it," said Kirsty. "How could he tell someone that he didn't talk to?"

"I got him on Wiki," said Zac. "Colonel Furstenberg. He died in 1946. Natural causes."

"Where?"

"Says here, Astley Ainslie Hospital, Edinburgh, Scotland."

"That makes no sense," said Kirsty. "If it's the same guy, how could Warrender have told him?"

"Well, that's the official version," said Zac. "According to what looks like a range of internet fruitcakes and amateur war historians, he died somewhere else, but it was never proven. I've got a photo of him here. Mean-looking dude, about seven foot tall. His name pops up on a ton of conspiracy theories because, if you believe Fruitcake Central, there are no records of him in Edinburgh and there's no grave."

"Colonel Furstenberg?" said Montrose. "The guy was a soldier, right? He's got to have a record somewhere."

"Oh, yeah," said Zac, "but according to the theories his death was hushed up. Big time. By the British."

"If he died in 1946 then he served in the war," said Montrose. "So why would they try to keep it quiet?"

"This is where the fruitcakes all agree," said Zac. "Because Colonel Furstenberg was a Nazi. A high-ranking SS Colonel, suspected of genocide in Russia. This is one seriously bad dude. And all the amateur sleuths and conspiracy geeks think they know where he's buried. And they're all saying the same thing."

"Where?" said Montrose.

"The London Cage."

"The what?"

"I'm reading it now," replied Zac. "There's lots of websites with black pages and spooky fonts dedicated to the topic. The London Cage was a secret MI9 torture camp run by the British during World War II. You've heard of MI5? Well, MI9 were the guys whose job it was to hunt down and capture senior Nazis. And it looks like the Brits were into some industrial-grade torture too. It was all top secret. All during the war no one ever knew, not even the Red Cross. And that's like totally against the Geneva Convention."

"The London Cage? Where is it? Does it actually exist?"

"Well, according to the net, it's about a five minute walk from Notting Hill Tube station."

"We're not far," said Kirsty. "You got an address?"

"Oh, yeah, I got it all here. It was a private mansion taken over by the government during the war, but it was closed down and sold off when the rumors emerged about the torture. MI9 were disbanded and the Brits pretended all the torture shit never happened."

"Time to knock on someone's door," said Kirsty.

"Wait," replied Zac. "There's an issue."

"Yeah," said Kirsty, "like breaking into someone's house and asking them if they know any dead Nazis."

"No," said Zac. "I'm reading the history. It says Number 8 Kensington Palace Gardens, aka the London Cage, was demolished by developers in 1982."

Montrose slumped down in the chair. "Then it's gone. The password, we can't..."

"That's bullshit," said Kirsty.

Pilgrim spoke slowly. "Kirsty has a point. Warrender was held by the Soviets in late 1982, after the developers are supposed to have destroyed it. Therefore, it may still exist."

"I'm looking now," said Zac. "There's a whole book on the subject written by the dude that ran the place, a guy called Colonel Scotland. It was heavily censored before it made publication. Holy shit."

"What is it?" said Kirsty.

"According to the conspiracy fruitcakes, The London Cage was based in 2 houses, one was destroyed but there was another big fancy house they used."

"Where is it?"

"Next door. Number 7, Kensington Palace Gardens."

"I know that address," said Pilgrim.

"Then that's our next destination," said Kirsty.

They heard Pilgrim sigh. "That might prove rather difficult."

Montrose could hear the resignation in his voice. "Why?"

"Because that's the address of the Russian Embassy."

*

Kane pulled open the door of the Range Rover as soon as it stopped.

Campbell ran around the far side and got in beside him. "We are checking the van for fingerprints, sir."

"Why the fuck are you doing that? We know who he is, asshole."

"The girl, sir, we…"

Kane held up his iPhone. "We have a composite photo taken from the hi-res CCTV. So we know what she looks like. Get this to all the cops and operatives. Right now."

"Yes, sir. We also have the containment sector around Lancaster Gate sealed with men at every exit. Train stations, cabs and the underground are all manned. If they try to run, we'll find them."

"You really are as thick as shit. They were already running when we found the van. Check the sectors they could go to, not the one they were in. They will be long gone from here. Spread out. I want every policeman in London looking for them. Every camera."

"MI5 are being cooperative, sir and we're monitoring them just in case." Campbell looked down at his phone. "Sir, what if they're not running?"

"What are you talking about?"

"They know about containment sectors. We can tell from the route they took out of Soho. What if they're holed up in Lancaster Gate?"

"Then they're more stupid than they look." He sat still for a moment. "Get a team of policeman on it. Check the streets." A phone buzzed in his pocket and he jolted upright. "Stop the car. Now." The Range Rover pulled into the curb and he reached for the door handle.

"Sir, we need to get to MI5 right now."

"Shut up. Stay there." Kane stepped from the car and pulled the Nokia phone from his pocket. A line of coordinates popped up on the tiny screen. His fingers moved carefully on the keypad as he forwarded the message to a different number. "I don't care what the fuck you got, Montrose," he murmured, "you can't stop me now."

*

Madame Raymonde watched the river traffic along the

Thames: the pleasure boats heading to the leafy suburbs and the slow moving barges going east towards the docks. The cars on the bridge crept across at walking pace. She checked her watch, but she knew too much time had passed. She turned and glanced at Purley's empty desk.

A knock echoed around the room and Lockhart stepped inside and closed the door behind him.

"I know," said Madame Raymonde. "I know in my heart. Where?"

"An alley. Not far from where she grew up." He rubbed his face. "They used a knife."

Madame Raymonde pressed her face against the glass. "Dear God, is there no end to this barbarity?"

He shuffled forward. "We have a car waiting for you, ma'am. It will take you to an airfield and then to France. Miss Purley made the arrangements."

"No. We are not finished yet. She told me that I could trust you. I need to make a phone call. The Legacy Transmission Officer in RAF Akrotiri, Cyprus."

"Use the blue phone, ma'am," he said. "I'll dial it for you."

She crossed the room as he dialed the number and sat down in the chair. "Wait outside," she said.

"Yes, ma'am."

She waited until he was gone and then picked up

the handset. "Legacy Transmission Officer? You have an email with a list of numbers for broadcast from Elizabeth Purley. The activation codeword is *regicide*. Do you understand? Yes? Then do it."

CHAPTER 17

"Ready?" Kirsty placed a hand on his leg and nodded towards a young couple entering the coffee shop. She pulled off her blond wig and kicked it under the seat, pulling the pins from her auburn hair.

She's a redhead. Yeah and this isn't the time.

Her hair fell around her shoulders as she tucked the phone into her bag and pointed to the coat rack.

Montrose watched the couple hang their jackets up and walk over to the counter.

"Follow me." Kirsty kept an eye on the couple as she picked out a coat and bundled it into her bag. "Use your jacket as cover."

Montrose pulled a coat down and stuffed it into his jacket.

"Stay ten steps behind me," said Kirsty.

"Where are we going?"

"I know somewhere close to here. There are still places around here that charge by the day."

Montrose was about to ask what the hell she was talking about, but she moved quickly to the door and out into the street.

He saw her go left and caught a glimpse of her turning into a wide boulevard, slipping on the stolen coat just before she turned the corner. He hurried after her and dropped his jacket onto some rubbish bags lying outside the coffee shop. He pulled on the coat, half-expecting a customer to come running after him. *Yeah, I'm wearing stolen gear and this place is crawling with cops.*

He watched her check the porticoed doorways as she passed and then quicken her step, moving towards a hotel. Several tourists hung around outside the door and she slipped behind them as a group of young kids came down the steps, hauling luggage and carrying bulging rucksacks. Montrose ran up the steps, looked over their heads and saw an armed cop take up position on the corner. Two others joined him and pointed along the road. They listened to their radios and then the two cops began slowly walking towards them, checking the doorways. Montrose nudged Kirsty and hid behind a potted plant whose brown leaves littered the entrance. "Cops on the street."

"Did they spot us?"

"No. They're checking all the doors."

"Good. Let's make this fast."

A tarnished brass plaque on the wall showed three stars and Montrose held open the grimy glass door covered in sticky handprints. The last of the kids shuffled past them and down the steps. "Charge by the day?" he said.

"Oh, Connor, you're such a prude." She hurried through the door and into a wide entrance hall.

He looked up at the high roof and the stained and peeling paint. Gaps in the cornicing glared like broken teeth where the plaster had fallen away.

Kirsty stood before a chipped and stained check-in desk, where a shaven-headed clerk was engrossed with his phone. She knocked on the counter. "Hey, time is money. Let's go."

The clerk looked up but said nothing.

Kirsty pulled out a wad of notes and pushed them across the counter. "If you want to put that through the register, that's up to you. I'll be done in an hour." She turned to Montrose. "That okay with you?"

Montrose shrugged.

"Well, I'm not giving you a choice." She tapped the money on the desk and then covered it with her hand. "Are we good?"

The clerk looked around, then reached for the money.

Kirsty kept her hand flat on the desk. "And if the Old Bill come looking, you've never seen us. Understood?"

The clerk nodded slowly.

Kirsty lifted her hand and the clerk slid the notes across the desk and slipped them into his pocket without counting them.

"And give me the wi-fi password. He likes a soundtrack."

The clerk pushed over a slip of paper. "Not too loud," he said in a thick Eastern European accent.

"Hey, you won't hear a thing." She held up a hand and intimated a gag around his mouth. "That's how I like it."

The clerk dropped the key on the counter. "Downstairs. Room three."

Kirsty grabbed the key and made for the stairs. Before them, a wide marble staircase rose up to a landing, the stone balustrades stained with age and lined with deep gouges, the steps covered in a threadbare carpet. Kirsty pushed through a door at the side of the staircase and headed down a flight of plain wooden steps.

Montrose waited until they turned into a narrow corridor littered with service carts. He could smell damp laundry and fried food from the kitchen. "Kirsty, what the hell? Is this going to work?"

"It's working right across London as we speak. He'll keep his mouth shut." She unlocked the door and stepped into a cramped basement bedroom. He felt his sneakers sticking to the carpet and heard the crash of pots and pans from the kitchen next door.

Kirsty dropped onto the bed and jabbed at the iPad screen. She connected to the wi-fi, then hit the encryption app. "Zac?"

"Hey, I'm on," replied Zac. "I've got the photos of the apartment. I can't make out the numbers, but it all fits. Check out the newspaper that's on his desk."

Kirsty brought up the photos on her phone. "It's open at the crossword page."

"He was waiting for the next message," said Zac.

Pilgrim's voice came over the line, metallic-sounding and stilted until the encryption resolved the signal. "Kirsty, your description of the apartment," he said. "The numbers on the wall. It all makes sense. This is more than an obsession with crosswords and you may be right that the motive was love. Perhaps I am too jaded. These things obviously meant a great deal to him. The stack of newspapers indicates the length of his obsession. He may have moved location many times, but he took them with him."

Montrose pictured the flat in his mind. *One newspaper a day. Three hundred and sixty five in a stack. That isn't so high. But he had stacks everywhere.* "I'm looking at the photo now. There might be twenty, thirty years of newspapers."

"He'd been collecting them since the Cold War," said Pilgrim. "It all fits. And he was ready to destroy it all. Both Zac and I are convinced that *The Times'* crosswords are one-time pads. And they correlate to the numbers on the wall. The code changed every day because every day there was a new crossword. Every day a new one-time pad."

"And since Warrender was British," said Zac, "that only means one thing. RAF Akrotiri."

"Where the hell is that?" said Montrose.

"Cyprus," replied Pilgrim. "The last of the Cold War transmitting stations. That's the only transmitter the British have left. They use a special frequency for this kind of work, but anyone can listen to it. And they are broadcasting right now on 14487 KHz. We caught the end of the last message, but it's being repeated every ten minutes. That's not a coincidence. I think someone is trying to contact Roger Warrender. But who? If our theory is correct, the person trying to contact him was the person who killed him. Why would she send a message?"

"14487 KHz. I'll find it," said Kirsty and searched for a shortwave app on her iPad.

"It's time for the next broadcast," said Zac. "I'm offline for five, I have to write this down."

Kirsty started the app and dialed in the frequency. A

synthesized tune began to play single, wavering notes. The iPad shook in her hand.

Montrose grabbed her arm. "What is it?"

"That tune. *The Lincolnshire Poacher*. My mother used to sing it."

He watched her face lose twenty years and her eyes glaze over.

She shook her head and a thin reedy voice came over the air in an immaculate cut-glass English accent.

... nine, three, nine, one, seven....

"How is this going to work?" said Montrose. "Don't you need the answers to the crossword?"

"No doubt," said Pilgrim. "*The Times'* crossword has a reputation of being amongst the most difficult. Perhaps Mr. Warrender was something of a crossword fan and I'm sure after all those years he was something of an expert. But nowadays all the answers are online. The wonders of the internet."

"Okay, so it's a message for Warrender," said Montrose, "But whoever it's from, they don't know the third password. Only Warrender knew the password."

The voice of Zac cut in. "It's not for Warrender. It's for Mr. Pilgrim."

Montrose looked up at Kirsty. *What the hell?*

There was silence for a moment and then Pilgrim spoke slowly. "Read it, Zac."

"*Pilgrim, if you receive this, then I am dead. Our enemies, whoever they may be, will find a way to break into the Red Star in a few hours. If you find what you are looking for, you must destroy it or no one will be safe. You must find it before anyone else. Warrender only told me that the secret he held was written in stone. Nothing else. And you must know, it was I who betrayed your brother all those years ago. But when I found out the nature of the secret, I resolved that no one should know it. I hope I can rely on you, Mr. Pilgrim. I realized too late that your brother's sacrifice kept us safe from the horrors of nuclear war. That threat has never gone away. I wish you all the luck in the world.*"

Montrose stared up at the sagging ceiling. *She kept Warrender safe all those years. And then she killed him. It must have broken her heart.*

Pilgrim spoke. "I can only conclude that Miss Purley left this message as insurance."

"Who?" said Kirsty.

"Our informant."

"The woman in the photo?"

"I believe so," replied Pilgrim.

Montrose spoke. "She was the one who told the Soviets where to find your brother once Warrender had reported back to her."

"So it would seem," said Pilgrim. "In which case I

won't mourn her death, apart from the fact that we have lost our most valuable asset in MI5. I spoke to her today. She was the contact that led us to Captain Wolff."

"There's more to the message," said Zac. "No words, just a bunch of web links and codes. Mr. Pilgrim, I'm copying it through to you."

"Okay," said Kirsty. "I've got an idea." She flicked her eyes towards Montrose. "Bear with me on this. Warrender told us when we spoke to him that he was held in the Soviet Embassy, right? And before that, the Soviet Embassy was an MI9 torture center called the London Cage. The Soviet Embassy is now the Russian Embassy. And this Colonel Furstenberg guy was a high-ranking Nazi…"

"Yeah," said Zac, "and rumored to have died in The London Cage."

"What if," said Kirsty, "Warrender was held in the same cell that Furstenberg had been held in? After all, he said that Furstenberg had died years before. It would make sense."

Montrose stared blankly out of the window at the feet of the passersby, trying to picture the cell. "She said that Warrender told her it was carved in stone. Like a prisoner carves his name on a cell wall."

"Yeah, I see where you're going with this," said Zac. "Condemned Nazi dude carves his name into the wall of his cell. The same cell that Warrender was held in. And Furstenberg died in 1946. Like your guy Warrender said, that was way before his time. And that's the only connection between the two. The cell."

"My God," said Kirsty. "That's where it is. The password is in that cell. When Warrender thought he was going to be tortured to death, he carved it into the wall. Beside where Colonel Furstenberg carved his name. That's what he meant. Written in stone."

"I admire your imagination," said Pilgrim. "I would normally criticize such a notion, but I can see no other explanation."

Montrose blew out a breath. "How the hell are we going to get to it? Sure as shit the Russian Embassy don't do guided tours of British torture cells."

"That's where Miss Purley has left us one last gift," said Pilgrim. "The second half of the message that Zac has just sent me contains links to certain areas of MI5 archives."

"I'm in there, man," said Zac. "And I got to say, this is full of real spooky shit. What am I looking for?"

"Project Orbital," said Pilgrim. "One of the most closely guarded secrets of the past fifty years."

"Searching for it now."

"When the British gave that house to the Soviets as an embassy," said Pilgrim, "the Soviets expected it to be extensively bugged. But they searched the whole building and found nothing. I assume they put it down to the British sense of fair play. But the British had other ideas."

"I'm there," said Zac. "Project Orbital. I got the plans."

"The plans of the building?" said Pilgrim.

"Yeah, that and more."

"That's what we need," said Pilgrim. "Now I understand why the British demolished part of the London Cage. It was to hide the fact that they were building a listening network on a grand scale. It must have been a major feat of construction and hidden by the demolition and development work. When they were finished, the Soviet Embassy was closely ringed by huge utility pipes. Hence the name *Project Orbital.*"

"Utility pipes?" said Montrose. "That's going to get us in?"

"Access was a secondary option. When the old building was destroyed, a new one was built on the foundations right beside the Embassy. During construction they built an entire new utility network: power, gas and water. And upgraded the sewer system around the whole site, including the Russian Embassy. But before they connected the sewer pipes to the public system, MI5 went in behind the construction workers and installed a smaller core through the pipes. The objective was to listen. Every sewer pipe was fitted with an inner core containing the most advanced and sensitive monitoring equipment. Over the years, the technology has been upgraded to a degree where they can triangulate voices to a particular room and computers can recognize and filter out any extraneous noise. Like footsteps or running water."

"I've got the blueprints. This is some crazy shit," said Zac.

"Wouldn't they work it out?" asked Kirsty.

"The whole house was searched for bugs," replied Pilgrim. "Who would break into a functioning sewer pipe?"

"I've got the entire network," said Zac. "And I'll send you the plan by screen capture. But it's going to cut comms if you go underground. I'll talk you down as far as I can."

"I'll go too," said Kirsty.

"No," said Pilgrim. "We will need a distraction."

"A distraction?" said Zac. "You're gonna need a thirty piece jazz band and strippers for this one."

"I take your point, Zac. And I have an idea," said Pilgrim.

"Okay," said Montrose. "Where do I go? How do I get in?"

"Kensington Palace," replied Zac. "And go through Hyde Park. There's hardly any cameras if you stick to the grass. Oh and Connor? Just one thing."

"Yeah?" Montrose got up from the bed.

"I hope you're not claustrophobic."

*

Arkangel stood behind the bank of desks where technicians sat hunched over their laptops. A phone buzzed in his pocket. He pulled out the old Nokia and stared at the screen where a list of digits appeared. He cleared his throat and handed it to a technician. "Here are the numbers. Enter them into the system."

The technician examined the phone. "I haven't seen one of these in ten years."

"Old but basic technology. Unlike a smartphone, it cannot be hacked unless you know the number. And now there are millions of numbers. Hundreds of millions of numbers."

The technician entered the digits into his keyboard. "These are coordinates," he said. Several names flashed up on the screen. The technician sat back and looked up towards Arkangel. "You know what these are?"

"Just do it."

The technician said nothing and hit the keys. "The attack plan is processing. But we'll need the activation password."

Arkangel turned to another technician studying a scroll of letters and numbers flashing across his screen. "How long?"

"Two hours. I have accessed more databanks in Moscow and all the processing power they can give me. We'll crack it."

Arkangel nodded, his head jerking up and down. "And the attack plan? Once we have the password?"

"I estimate thirty minutes for some and forty minutes for others. It's never been tested before."

Another technician got to his feet. "Our friend is online. We are getting closer. Soon we will be able to see exactly what he is doing. We will have his location in the next ten minutes. He is being clever, but not clever enough. We've tracked him to Cambridge."

Arkangel stuffed the Nokia in his pocket. "Get the team airborne. And I want an ETA for Cambridge. Our little friend is about to get a surprise."

CHAPTER 18

"Kirsty?" He pointed to the narrow window near the roof. "Cops." Two pairs of boots stood outside.

"Okay, I have an idea." She skipped around the bed and opened the door to the corridor. "Kitchens were to the right when we came in. Good for weapons, but chefs are particular about their knives so we'll give that a miss. The laundry was to the left. Stay here and keep this door open. I'll be back in a moment." She turned into the corridor.

Montrose poked his head around the corner and saw her wheeling a laundry cart towards him.

"Out of the way!" She pushed the cart into the room and kicked the door closed behind her. "Okay, let's see what we've got." She began to rummage through the white plastic bags, holding them up. "Dirty underwear. Not my thing." She threw the bags onto the bed and ripped one open. Several men's business shirts tumbled out. "Check them for size." She grabbed another bag.

Montrose held up a shirt, noticing the grimy collar and cuffs. "Kirsty..."

"Forget them. Look what I've got." She pulled out a dark blue Pakistani *kurta*, held it by the shoulders and placed it against his chest. The long shirt reached down past his knees. "Put it on."

Montrose held it up. It was a damn sight cleaner than the shirts.

"Bingo!" she said, handing him a white lace *kurta*.

"What is it?"

"A Muslim skull cap. That's you sorted. At least the *kurta* will save you wearing that shit Elvis wig. You're not ready for Vegas." She returned to the laundry cart and pulled out a heavy bag.

Montrose could see the leopard skin pattern through the thin plastic.

She ripped it open and a faux fur coat fell out. The reek of cheap perfume filled the air. "Christ," she said, "if I'm going to pretend I'm a whore, I might as well dress like one."

Montrose pulled off the jacket and slipped the *kurta* over his head.

"There's one more thing I've got to do," she said. "Did you notice that electrician at the end of the corridor?"

"Yeah. What, you're going to steal his tools?"

"No." She pulled out her purse. "He was wearing the best disguise of all. Give me two minutes and meet me at the top of the steps to the hotel lobby."

He glanced up at the window, but the boots were gone.

She saw him looking. "Listen to me. The cops have checked this road and they've moved on. There will be others at the junction, but you only have about one hundred yards until you make it to Hyde Park. It's the end of the street, turn left, straight across the road. You can't miss it, it's a big green thing full of annoying Americans."

"Kirsty..."

"Shut up. Go into the park and take the path that leads south west. At the far end you'll see Kensington Palace. Some minor royals and other benefit scroungers still live there so there will be coppers around, but the last thing the CIA will expect us to do is go sightseeing, so stick to the tourists. Ditch the *kurta* and cap before you go in. Otherwise the fascist bastards will think you're a terrorist. When you're inside, call Zac."

"What about you?"

"I'll be right behind you. I'm going to take the path

directly west, towards the Princess Diana memorial then back onto the street. The Russian Embassy is fifty yards from there. I'll be able to watch you crossing the park. If I see someone tailing you, I'll call." She reached into her bag and brought out an iPhone. "It's clean. Zac has the number."

"Okay and then what?"

"Zac will talk you down. I'll see you on the other side. Go."

*

Montrose slotted the earphones into his ear and then covered them with the headphones handed out by the tour guide. He let the other tourists walk past him as they were called forward by the guide. He looked over their heads to a wide, ornate staircase, its steps covered in checkered marble and the palace walls lined with gilded frescos.

The guide held up his hands to stop the group. "Please ensure you have switched off your mobile phones before we continue." He waved his hands theatrically behind him. "This is the King's Staircase."

Montrose covered the mic with his hand and held it to his lips. "Zac, you hear me?"

"Yeah. Where are you?"

"Grand entrance hall. King's Staircase."

"I gotcha. Okay, lose the tourists."

He watched the guide lead the crowd up the staircase and bent down to inspect his shoelace. He looked up as the group turned at the first level, then he ducked behind the side of the staircase. He listened to the voices fade away and pulled out the folded hi-vis vest and penknife that Kirsty had bought from the electrician in the hotel.

"Ready. I'm at the bottom right of the staircase."

"Across from you there's a door. Go through and go down the corridor to the end."

Montrose checked the front entrance and saw two guides herding the next group of tourists into line and checking their tickets. He darted over to the door and pulled it open. *Let's make this fast*. He closed the door and set off down the corridor. Office doors were open either side, but it was quiet. At the very end of the corridor he saw a door with a push button digital lock. *That's the one.*

A woman carrying a stack of files came out of an office, into the corridor.

Shit.

She stopped and looked at him quizzically for a moment. "Can I help you?"

234

Montrose pointed to the door at the end of the corridor and smiled, then held a finger to his lips. He brushed past her and stood in front of the keypad. He whispered into the mic. "Zac, the code."

"1855."

He punched the buttons. The lock turned and he shot a glance back along the corridor. The woman smiled and turned away. He looked down a stairwell where the plain walls and thinly varnished balustrade stood in contrast to the grand rooms elsewhere. "I'm in. Is this a fire escape?"

"No way, man, it's hundreds of years old. You're in the servants' stairs," said Zac. "They have access to the entire building. Go down. All the way."

His senses on edge, Montrose hurried down the steps. At the bottom he faced another door. "There's no lock."

"Go for it."

He pushed the door handle as smoothly as he could and the door opened into darkness. He stuck his hand around the door jamb and fumbled for a light switch. A forty-watt bulb barely illuminated a dingy cellar, where worn stone steps led down to a floor strewn with rubbish and boxes.

"You there?" said Zac.

"I can see it," said Montrose. "And I can smell it." He

stepped forward and shone the iPhone's torch through a grate in the floor. Below was a circular metal door that reminded him of a submarine hatch. "I got it."

"Listen, dude, as soon as you're in the pipe this signal is gonna cut. Just remember what I told you, okay? The plans are on your iPhone. They're not great, but it's the best I can do."

"Understood." Montrose grasped the cold metal bars and hauled back the grate. It swung to the side and dropped onto the earth floor. He knelt and grabbed the wheel on the hatch. It turned smoothly in his hands. He pulled it back and peered in.

"The sewer pipe is about ten feet wide," said Zac. "But the inner core is about four feet in diameter and lined with equipment, according to these plans. It's a pipe in a pipe. You lie on a tray and move along on rails. So, it's going to be, er, kinda cozy."

Montrose looked down at a wooden tray sitting on rails.

"Lie on your back," said Zac. "That way you can operate the switches above. And ditch anything you're wearing that's going to snag on the equipment."

"Yeah." He stepped in, steadying his feet on the tray as it moved on the rails. "Is this motorized?"

"Don't think so, man. You've got to slide yourself along. Lie on your back, head first and push your feet against the bottom of the pipe. This is Cold War technology."

"Yeah, just one step up from the Great Escape. Is there a light switch?"

"I'm checking."

He pulled off the hi-vis vest and threw it to the side, then lowered himself down, lying flat on his back. The sides of the pipe brushed his shoulders. "Jesus, this must have been built by fucking dwarves."

"You lying flat?"

"Yeah."

"The light switch is above your head. Third one from the left. Maybe."

"Maybe?"

"The diagrams are about fifty pages long. Those pipes are stuffed with all sorts of black ops surveillance shit."

Montrose flicked the switch and several tiny lamps began to glow. "That's it?"

"That's all it says here."

He lay back and looked at his feet, but the amber light barely lit his sneakers. He tipped his head back and could see nothing but darkness. "They can't be serious."

"When you get to your destination there's a red light. Stop there. Above it will be another switch, so you'll see the escape hatch."

"Oh, yeah, great. The height of fucking technology. Anything else?"

"If there is, it's on the phone. That's all I got. Good luck, dude."

He steadied himself on the tray, then twisted his shoulders and reached up to pull the hatch closed. It slid out of his grasp and slammed shut. "Zac?"

There was no response. Montrose saw his breath condensing inches from his face on the cold metal where cable racks hung either side of the pipe and brushed his shoulders. *Don't touch anything. The Brits will know.* He banged his elbows as he shifted on the tray, then pushed with his feet. *This pipe is full of listening devices. Yeah, they're gonna fucking know.* He lifted a hand and turned a metal wheel on the rear of the hatch. The bolts squealed and slid into place. He pushed down with his feet and the tray slid into darkness.

*

Kane stood in the middle of the floor, looking up at a wall covered in screens, turning his head back and forth to each camera view. A row of MI5 operatives behind desks stretched across the floor, scanning each screen and manipulating the cameras with joysticks.

An operative spun around in his chair. "We found her." One of the screens flickered then expanded across all the others, showing a young woman dressed in a leopard skin coat striding down the road.

Kane started up at the screen. "Where is she?"

"Bayswater Road."

"Get her." He watched her stop at a garbage pail and dump her coat, then turn into a street where armed guards stood between tall stone pillars. "Where the hell is that?"

"Kensington Palace Gardens, sir."

"Whatever. I want two teams on her. Right now."

Campbell edged up beside him and shook his head. "No. We can't."

"What the fuck do you mean, no?"

Campbell held out his hands. "Kensington Palace Gardens is the one street in London where we can't charge in. And I think she knows that."

"There's nowhere we can't go. Including Downing Street. Do it."

"Sir, that street is home to a whole host of embassies, including the Israelis, the Saudis and the Russians."

"The Russians?"

"That road is the most sensitive place in London. It's blocked at both ends by armed guards. We have to wait."

"That really is fucking amazing. Get her on camera. See where she goes."

An MI5 technician stood up. "I'm afraid not, sir. It's embassy confidentiality. There are no cameras on that street, apart from those hardwired to the guardhouse. The embassies were concerned about MI5 monitoring their activities. Understandable, really. Besides, the whole street belongs to Her Majesty the Queen. We'd need her permission. The PM was happy to comply with the embassies' request."

"He was happy to fucking roll over, you mean. I want two teams at each end."

"Perhaps she's seeking asylum," said Campbell.

Kane's face turned red as he spun around. "Asylum? If Montrose is working with that bitch and she goes to the Russians, I'll burn that fucking place down." He looked away for a moment, then beckoned to one of the black-suited figures. The man hurried over and Kane leaned over to him and spoke in a low voice. "Listen to me. Operation Spanish King. Just in case. Get the team ready. Understood?"

The man nodded and hurried towards the door.

Campbell cleared his throat. "I think we may need higher authority for that particular operation, sir. Grosvenor Square would certainly need to authorize an escalation."

"Whatever. I know who to talk to."

"As do I, sir. I have a direct line to the people required. I'll make the necessary arrangements." Campbell turned away before Kane could respond.

*

Arkangel leaned over the laptop where a Google Street View image flashed on the screen. "What is that?"

"Student accommodation. We've broken into his laptop registry. We have the IP."

"He's a student? Where?"

"Cambridge University. There are over fifty rooms in the building. We'll have the exact location soon. The team have landed and are standing by."

"Don't do anything until I tell you, understand? I want to know what they know. See what they see. Understood?"

"Yes, sir."

*

He tried to look behind but darkness enveloped him.

Just keep your eyes closed. His head hung back over the edge of the tray and sweat rolled down his cheeks and into his eyes. He stopped for a moment and tried to lift his hands to wipe his face, but his arm smacked into something hard on the side of the pipe. Squeezing his shoulders together, he managed to maneuver his hand towards his face and grab the collar of his T-shirt. Using his thumb and forefinger, he pushed as much sweat as possible from his face and then twisted his arm back to his side.

He opened his eyes, searching for a red light, but there was nothing. *Keep going. The sooner I'm out of this shithole, the better.* He felt his breathing quicken. *No, you're panicking. Cut that shit out. You'll get out of here. Red light. Keep going. And keep your eyes open. If it's anything like the one at the entrance, you could miss it.* His neck ached when he tried to lift his head clear of the track and he stopped, letting his head drop back, blinking as sweat rolled into his eyes once more. His vision cleared and he spotted a dull red glow in the darkness. *Thank Christ.* He kicked his feet down hard and the glow became brighter. The trolley gathered speed and a single red bulb came into focus. His breathing was ragged as he pushed the final yards, then slid to a stop underneath the light and saw the exit hatch above. He stretched an arm up to the hatch.

Okay. Get the hell out of here. He looked at the hatch. There was no handle. *How the...? No, it has to be powered.* A red and black cable was pinned to the side of the hatch. *That's got to be the electrical feed. So where's the switch?* Junction boxes and switches were fixed above his head. *Got to be one of them.* He saw paper labels with faded handwriting. *I can't read that shit.*

He slid his hand into the pocket of his pants and pulled out his iPhone. He switched the torch on and held it above his head, craning his neck to read. *What the hell does that say?* He placed a finger on the first switch. *Don't touch anything, Zac said. Yeah, like I got a choice.* Holding his breath, he flicked the first switch. Nothing happened. *Okay, not that one.* Flicking it back, he placed his finger on the second switch and pushed down. *Nothing. Shit, it's got to be one of these.* He pushed the third switch and the light shut off.

Fuck! He tightened the grip on his iPhone but it slipped from his wet hand and bounced off his face. He tried to grab it but missed and he heard the phone tumble to the bottom of the pipe. His breathing became ragged. *Focus. Be cool. Find the switch. Close your eyes and go slow.* His fingers traced the edge of the hatch, then back towards the bank of switches. His trembling fingers found the third switch and pushed up. The red light flickered into life. *I don't care who gets alerted, I'm getting the fuck out of here.* He clawed at the switches and the sound of a metal solenoid slamming back echoed along the pipe. He lifted his arm and shoved at the hatch. It swung back silently, revealing nothing but darkness. He sat up and made a grab for the edge. *No, you need the phone.* He pushed his hand down, but it was useless. *Shit.* He slid the trolley back, then used the space to arch his arms backwards and drag his fingers across the rails until he found the phone. *Get out.*

He grabbed the edge of the hatch and hauled himself up. The faint red light glowed out from the pipe and disappeared into darkness. He stood on the trolley and groped around, feeling nothing but cold metal. Pushing out a hand into the darkness to check the height clearance, he slowly shuffled out onto the edge of the hatch.

He switched on the iPhone's torch again. Around him he could see brick walls in a twelve foot square. He looked down at the pipe. It stretched ten feet across and three quarters of it was buried in the earth. *Jesus, it's massive. They could have made the inner pipe a bit bigger.* Near one end of the pipe, where it disappeared through a brick wall, he saw a larger metal plate studded with bolts the size of his fist. *That'll be the sewer access hatch.* He pictured the map in his head.

The pipe runs south of the Embassy. He turned to face a wall of bricks. In the middle was a section of lighter bricks, lined with a pale-colored mortar. *That's the one. How the hell am I going to get through that?*

He slid down the pipe and stood before the wall, running his fingers along the bricks, then gave one a push. It moved. He pushed harder. The other end of the brick slid out. The thick mortar crumbled in his fingers. He looked up and saw a wide stone joist above the bricks. *That's what's taking the weight. These bricks sure as shit won't.* Pulling the pocketknife from his pants, he slid it between the gap, levering the brick aside. *They're not fixed.* He picked up a piece of mortar and it instantly disintegrated. *What the hell is this stuff?* He tugged two bricks towards him and the surrounding mortar powdered as they dropped onto the soft earth. *Whatever it is, it's just for show.* Before him he saw a wall of gray stone. He pushed it with his finger and it moved to the touch. *That's just plaster. I could punch right through.* He closed his eyes and listened for a moment, but could only hear water flowing in the sewage pipe. He pushed the tip of the knife into the plaster and twisted it around until the tip broke through, then held up the iPhone and peered through the hole.

CHAPTER 19

The guardhouse stretched across half the street and armed guards stood either side, machine pistols cradled in their arms. Kirsty stepped towards the booth, relieved that she was off the main road. She noticed more guards to the side, tooled up with heavier assault rifles and combat vests. *Just what I don't want*, she thought, swinging the bag in her hand, *but exactly what I need to keep those psychos off my back.*

Behind a red and white horizontal pole, steel barriers covered in studded metal teeth rose up out of the road. She watched a blacked-out stretch Mercedes drive up and the barrier slide into the ground to let it through. She approached the booth and stood before the low window. "Hi, I need to visit the Russian Embassy," she said, rolling out the Welsh vowels.

The guard glanced at the sleeve of gothic tattoos covering her arm. "Do you have an appointment?"

"No, I checked the website and it said just to visit if I was applying for a passport for residency."

"You're applying for a passport? With that accent?"

She smiled. "Absolutely! My father was Russian so I qualify, I hope. I'll be honest, it's a career move. Sick of bloody Cardiff, I am. And I can go over there and take care of him. He's not too well at the moment."

"Can I see what's in the bag?"

"Of course." She lifted the bag up onto a ledge facing the window and took out her iPad and phone and a large can of hairspray.

The security guard held up the bag to check that it was empty. "What's in there?" he said, pointing to a long cardboard tube she'd left in the bag.

"Souvenir. He wants a map of the London Underground. He's crazy about maps. I hope MI5 won't be too bothered about that."

The guard popped both ends from the tube and peered into it, then passed everything through a scanner. "How come your father is Russian?"

Kirsty shrugged. "He was a sailor. A lover in every port. But he said the prettiest girls were from Wales," she smiled at the guard. "He didn't desert us. He kept in touch while he was at sea. Or at least we think that's where he was."

The guard repacked her bag. "ID?"

Kirsty took out her purse and pushed over a driving license.

"Russian Embassy is first on the left." The guard picked up a phone. "I'll let them know you're coming." He smiled and handed back her ID. "My father was in the army. Never saw him either. Good luck."

"Thanks, mate." She swung the bag over her shoulder and stepped through the gate. To her left she saw the high windows and opulent 19th century facade of the Russian Embassy and two uniformed guards watching her through the high railings. She turned into the entrance, past a manicured garden and approached the front door. One of the guards listened to his radio, stepping aside as she approached.

Let's make this fast, she thought. She walked through a polished stone archway and stood before a wide hall, feeling the chill of air-conditioning envelop her. Around the hall, several corridors were cordoned off and directly ahead stood an ornate reception desk where a young woman with a severe expression examined her as she approached. She was the only visitor and several guards turned towards her. *I need a distraction*, she thought, *or someone is going to start asking questions. And the last thing I want to do is talk to that snooty bitch.*

She took her phone from the bag, set it to silent, then talked cheerily as she held it to her head. "Hi? Yeah, I'm at the embassy. What? Okay, I'll hold." She smiled at the receptionist and held up a hand. She stood for a moment looking up at the decor and the row of oil paintings hanging on one wall. A bulky air-conditioning unit mounted high on the roof clunked and whirred into life. *Good cover*, she thought, *the noisier the better*.

She spotted a cable on the wall and traced it to a detector on the roof. *No, that's a smoke detector. I need something more modern than that.* She slowly gazed around and found another cable emerging from a corridor, pinned high on the wall beside the ornate plaster cornice, leading to a small white plastic box fixed above the paintings. *Got it. Ionization detector.*

There was a row of chairs set against the wall under the paintings. She pulled the phone away from her ear and looked at the screen, then spoke into it again. "Are you still there? Yeah, well ask them to hurry up. I haven't got all day."

Keeping the phone pressed between her shoulder and cheek, she crossed the hall and sat on a chair directly underneath the detector. She placed her bag beside her, popped the top from the tube, rested it vertically against her shoulder and placed one end in her bag. She rummaged around in the bottom of the bag and pulled the plastic cap from the other end of the tube. "Yeah, I'm still here. How long's this going to take?" Out of the corner of her eye, she saw a guard moving towards her. She kept her hand in the bag and wriggled on the seat to get comfortable, spreading her knees apart and allowing her dress to ride up.

As the guard approached she brought her knees together quickly and flashed him a look.

The guard turned away, crossed the hall and sat down opposite her.

Nothing to see here, my friend. Just a girl trying to do too many things at once. She lifted up one side of her bag and grabbed the can of hairspray, holding it deep in the bag and out of sight. She pushed the nozzle into the bottom of the map tube. "Yeah, I'm still here." Keeping the phone pressed to her cheek, she adjusted the tube where it rested against her shoulder and pointed the end towards the roof. She pressed the button on the can and heard the hiss as the spray ascended through the tube. "I've been hanging on for ages. Just make it quick, will you?" Her eyes began to sting as some spray drifted down from the top of the tube and her fingers began to freeze with the residue. She flicked her eyes upwards to the ionization detector. *Jesus*, she thought, *this better bloody work.*

The security guard stood up.

*

Montrose gave his eyes a few moments to adjust to the darkness and then stepped back, but no light emerged from the tiny hole. *It's got to be a cellar.* He brought up the map on his iPhone. The screen dazzled him in the darkness. *Get a good look then shut it down, or I won't be able to see a goddamn thing.* The plan showed the sewer pipe and three small rooms, linked by a corridor. He shut off the phone and eased out another brick. It came away easily in his hand. *Whoever built this knew what they were doing.* He pulled out a handful of bricks and they tumbled to the damp earth at his feet. As soon as the hole was big enough he stuck his head through and pressed his ear against the plaster. There was nothing.

He stuck the tip of his knife into the hole and twisted it around. The plaster looked about half an inch thick. *Being subtle isn't going to work. And if they find a fucking big hole, they'll go straight for the pipe.* He turned and shone the torch along the length of the pipe, focusing on the larger bolted hatch at the far end. *I bet the Brits heard every word, the devious bastards. Shit, they can probably hear me now. Yeah and do what? They're not gonna knock on the door of the Russian*

Embassy and ask if they can have a quick look in their basement. But if the Russians come after me... He looked at the open hatch and flicked the torch back towards the sewer hatch. *Yeah. That's it.* He bent down and picked up a brick, then clambered up to straddle the pipe beside the sewer hatch.

He ground the edge of the brick against each of the bolts in turn, exposing a sliver of metal. He brushed away the brick dust, slid off the pipe and shone his torch on his handiwork. *Anyone sees that and they'll just think I could have used a better wrench.* He stood before the wall and picked up another brick, weighing it in his hands. *No. Take it easy. You have no idea what's behind that plaster.* He dropped the brick and pushed the knife into the plaster once more, turning it around until he had a hole the size of a dime. He blew away the plaster dust, squeezed his head past the bricks and pressed his eye against the hole.

CHAPTER 20

An alarm screamed behind the wall and the shock jolted through him like electricity. His head jerked up and cracked against the stone and he tumbled back, stumbling over the pile of bricks. He scrambled to his feet and made a lunge for the open hatch, but his hand slipped on the cold metal and his face smacked into the pipe. He bounced off and rolled to the side to steady himself, then grabbed the edge of the hatch. He tensed, preparing to launch himself forward, but stopped.

Holy shit. She's done it. He leaned against the pipe, listening to the pulsing of the alarm which seemed to vibrate through his body. *That's a fire alarm. It worked.*

He brought up the torch on his iPhone. The beam punched through the brick dust hanging in the air. *Do it. Before they wise up.* He grabbed a brick from the pile at his feet and ran towards the wall, smashing it into the plaster. It spidered and cracked and he ripped the pieces away, shining the torch through the hole. In front of him were two metal sheets. *What the...? Shit. Filing cabinets.* He leaned forward and pushed hard, his sneakers slipping on the loose bricks and earth. His dusty hands slid on the metal, but it began to move and he heard the cabinet base scraping across the floor. *Christ, that's heavy.* He tried the other and it moved easily, until it turned and jammed against the first cabinet. *This isn't going to work. I'll be here all day.* He stepped back and shone the torch on the top of the cabinets. *I'm going over.*

He tore at the bricks above him, tossing them behind him, hearing them bounce off the pipe. *That'll deafen a few Brits.* He planted his feet firmly, leaned back and punched his fist through the plaster using the edge of a brick. *More. Wide enough for shoulders.* Grabbing a row of bricks with both hands, he threw himself backwards. The whole section collapsed, exposing the stone lintel above his head and he jumped out of the way as bricks tumbled down around him. *Jeez don't bring the whole lot down.* The alarm seemed to pulsate through his head. He tore at the bricks on one side, ripped back the plaster and flashed the torch. He could see over the filing cabinets into the darkness beyond where the torch reflected off another wall. *Do it.* He climbed up the pile of bricks and shoved an arm through the hole, reaching over to grip the front edge of the first filing cabinet. He hauled himself through, his shoulders scraping the sides of the hole and his ribs jammed against the edge of the cabinets. He moved forward slowly, then stopped and shone the iPhone into the room. *Don't mess around. Head first.* He reached out a hand to break his fall, then tipped his body over the edge and tumbled to the floor. His shoulder cracked into the concrete and he rolled to the side, then scrambled to his knees and brought up the torch.

A stack of cardboard filing boxes lined the far wall and to his right he saw a thick steel door. *This is it. This is a cell.* He swept the torch behind him. Above the cabinets, on the wall he had come through, was smooth white plaster. *I hope the Brits didn't... Never mind. Get going.* He flashed the beam back to the far wall and crept forward. The wall was whitewashed rough stone and he could see several indentations under the paint. *They must have painted the walls since Warrender was here.*

He hauled away at the cardboard boxes on the floor then held the iPhone close to the wall and shone it upwards to highlight the relief of the indentations. The wall was covered in dents and scratches, but nothing stood out as a name. He arced the torch beam higher up the wall. *Zac said Furstenberg was well over seven feet tall. Hell, if I was that tall, I'd write it high just to piss them off.* Near the top was a line of indentations. Sliding the phone closer, he could make out the words. HEINZ ROSTERG. Below was a number that was too indistinct to make it out, then another row of letters. He held the torch closer. GEFOLTERT. *What is that? A rank? No, I know that word. My grandfather used it often enough when he told me about the Nazis. Tortured. That's what it means. So it was true.*

He stepped back and scanned the wall once more, but could see nothing. *Okay, not this one.* He shone the torch towards the door. *There's no handle.* He stood open-mouthed for a moment and let out a nervous laugh. *Of course there's no fucking handle. It's a cell.*

At the bottom of the door was a rectangular hole, covered by a metal sheet on the exterior. *For food.* He knelt and grabbed the top edge and let his body fall backwards. *Sweet Jesus, don't be locked.* The door swung open and he toppled backwards onto the concrete. *Yeah, about time I had a break. Next cell.*

He stuck his head out of the door. Above him an alarm flashed red and screamed in his ears. The corridor was empty. He darted out and leaned on the handle of the adjacent door. The handle didn't move but the door swung open and he fell into darkness.

He swung the cell door closed and shone the torch around. More cardboard boxes lined the floor and wooden chairs were stacked haphazardly against the walls. *Dammit! It'll take me ages to move this shit. Pick a wall.* He stuck his hand through the chair legs and held up the iPhone. *Nothing.* He took a step back, jammed the phone between the chairs again and saw the first indentations behind the paint. *Go high.* Shadows picked out the bold lettering, each about two inches high.

FURSTENBERG, H.T. GEFOTTENT. MEINE EHRE HEIßT TREUE.

Montrose stood staring it for a moment and the words came back to him. *Meine ehre heißt treue. My honor is my loyalty. The motto of the Waffen SS.*

The phone trembled in his hand and the shadowed letters danced on the wall. At the edge of the beam of light he saw more words below, carved in shallow, hurried writing. He edged the torch closer and read until the words seared into his brain.

GEFOTTENT - RW - MILCHMANN

He stood back. *Tortured. Roger Warrender. Milkman.* For a moment, he couldn't hear the alarm as he stared at the wall. *That's why he wrote it under Furstenberg's name. They'd think it was German.*

*

The technician spun around in his chair. "Sir! We've cracked the intruder's laptop."

Arkangel tried not to run as he hurried towards the desk. The technician pointed to the screen. "The team in Cambridge is still trying to locate the exact spot, but we can see what he sees."

"What about his laptop camera?"

"His camera?"

"Think clearly, you idiot. You get a photo of him, then pass it onto the team."

"I have it," said another technician next to him.

On the screen was the photo of an unshaven young man in a Metallica T-shirt, his hair falling over dark, soft eyes.

"Get that to the team." Arkangel turned back to the first screen. "What the hell is that?"

"He's looking at some sort of map, sir. Bringing it up now."

"A map?" Arkangel leaned over to the screen as the image flashed up, showing plans of a building, with thick red lines bordering the walls. "Can you show me more?"

"We don't have control, sir, we can only see what he sees. I'm working on it." The map on the screen zoomed out and Arkangel saw an address written at the bottom corner.

7 Kensington Palace Gardens. Duct Map Plan Lower Ground.

"My God, that's… freeze that image!" He leaned forward and traced the red line with his finger, along the building and down the dotted line piercing the wall. "What the hell is that?"

The technician shook his head. "It looks like pipe work. What should I do, sir?"

"Shut up." Arkangel stepped back and pressed his hands to his face. Whoever they were, they had the first two passwords. There could only be one reason why they would attempt to break through those walls. He turned to the other side of the room and pointed to a technician. "How long to the activation password?"

"Perhaps another hour, sir."

"Too long. Get Kutuzov on the phone. Now!"

"Where is he, sir?"

Arkangel stared at the address on the screen. "The Russian Embassy."

*

The fire alarm stopped. He could hear himself breathing and feel the blood pumping in his neck. *Get out of here.* He ran to the door and stuck his head out. *Clear.* He slid through and was running to the first cell when he saw the blinking light in the top corner of the corridor. CCTV. He froze. *Oh, fuck.* The iPhone almost slipped out of his sweaty palm, but he pushed it to his chest and raced through the cell door, slamming it behind him.

He launched himself at the cabinets, pushing them back against the wall, then picked up two cardboard boxes and threw them on top. *Might buy me a few seconds. If they're idiots.* Clambering up onto the cabinets, he maneuvered his body, feet first, into the hole and grabbed the cardboard boxes as he edged backwards. The rear edge of the cabinets dug into his ribs. His legs dangled behind him, but there was no foothold. Gravity took over and he raked his ribs along the back edge of the cabinet as he dropped through the hole, cracking his head off the stone lintel and landing on the pile of bricks. He sat stunned for a moment, then reached up and pulled the cardboard boxes back towards him, covering the hole.

He turned, stumbled over the bricks and threw himself onto the pipe, gripping the edge of the hatch and hauling himself up. He swung his legs over and dropped down. His feet hit the trolley and he held onto the edge as it slipped forward. He steadied his feet and grabbed hold of the hatch cover, lowering himself down. The hatch cover slammed shut and the solenoid lock clunked home. He stretched up his arms and gave the cover a shove. It didn't move. *Fuck you, Ivan. Work that one out.*

He shuffled his torso until his head was hanging over the back of the trolley, then steadied his legs and pushed hard. The trolley shot forward. He instinctively looked back down the pipe, but it was black and his nose grazed the roof of the pipe. He dropped his head back. *Wait for the next red light. Get some speed up.*

The sound of spinning wheels echoed along the pipe. He tried to visualize the map in his head. *Fifty meters. Curve to the left. Then one hundred meters in a straight run. Don't think about it. Do it.* His ribs ached where the cabinets had raked them and sweat stung his torn skin. *Keep going.* The muscles in his legs began to cramp and he cracked his knee off the roof of the pipe. He gasped in pain and his cramped thigh muscle began to spasm. *Suck it up.* His vision blurred as sweat rolled back into his eyes. *I have to be able to see that light.* The trolley rolled to a halt and he maneuvered his arm forwards to wipe his eyes. The air felt thick in his throat. He flexed his legs and placed his feet down to push when a low booming sound echoed through the pipe.

He pulled his hand from his face. *What the fuck was that?* Vibrations ran up the pipe and a loud crack echoed past his head. *Shit. They're trying to break the hatch.* His body jerked in panic. He cracked his head off the roof and snagged his T-shirt on a cable tray. *No. They're trying to break the pipe.* He shoved his arms forward and pushed his legs down, his sneakers slipping on the floor. *I'm surrounded by sewer water. They smash that pipe and...* Rapid hammering sounded, growing in speed, punching through the air and a metallic wall of noise rang in his ears as the metal shuddered above his head.

*

Kirsty elbowed her way into the middle of the crowd as they were herded towards the front door and out into the garden. She spotted a black Range Rover blocking the road beyond the guardhouse where the guards stood with their machine pistols raised. The passenger advanced, holding up his ID. She could hear an argument erupt. The shaven-headed driver wore Aviator Ray-Bans, had both hands grasping the top of the wheel and was revving the engine.

People pushed past her onto the road and an embassy guard shoved her through the gates. Kirsty looked along to the other end of the street. The second gatehouse was hidden by the trees, but she knew more Range Rovers would be waiting. She kept her head low and joined a group of people standing by the side of the road. For a split second she thought about turning around and demanding political asylum, but knew Warrender had tried that. It hadn't worked out. She would have the same fate.

Above the heads of the crowd she saw the red and white security barrier lift into the air. She began to run, keeping to the cover of the trees that lined the road, scanning every house as she ran. Each one she passed was bordered by high walls or spiked railings. On the other side of the road she saw a block of flats surrounded by a low hedge. The gates were open. She readied herself to run across the road and then stopped beside the cover of an ancient oak tree. The road was clear ground. They knew who they were looking for.

To her left a Rolls-Royce emerged from a gated driveway, two Indian flags fluttering from the fender. She waited until it rolled past, kept her head down and walked quickly across the road, through the gates to the apartment block and along the side of the building. The driveway began to slope down to a car park and she could see the high rear wall of the property. She ducked behind the corner of the building and looked up at the wall. It was over twenty feet high, but directly below it was a line of parked cars. She ran at full speed towards a Mercedes SUV and jumped onto the hood. Metal buckled under her feet as she leapt onto the roof and threw herself up against the wall. Her fingertips caught the crumbling stone edge, tearing her skin, but she hauled herself up and swung her leg over the top.

From the corner of her eye she saw the shape of a black Range Rover between the trees, then looked down at the roof of a summerhouse below the wall. She lowered herself onto the slates and dropped into a garden.

An old man's face appeared at the window of the summerhouse.

Kirsty smoothed down her dress, smiled at the old man and tapped her nose. "You ain't seen me, right?" She took off across the garden.

CHAPTER 21

His throat tightened as he screamed, the sound ricocheting off the sides of the pipe. His legs flailed from side to side and his head smacked off the roof. He dropped back, stunned into silence. *Focus. Do it. One way out.* The image of a wall of black water flashed through his mind, cascading towards him through the darkness.

He pulled his arms tight across his chest and stamped his feet down. The trolley shot forward. The hammering came louder and sharper. Sweat was blinding his eyes and his legs spasmed in cramp. The trolley rattled along, its wheels just inches below his head. The hammering came even faster. *They've got a team on it.* A sound like a gunshot cracked past his head and the hammering stopped. *It's broken.* His breath became ragged and his chest heaved. *You're not dead yet. Control your breathing.* He kept his eyes wide open despite the pain, searching for the red light. Echoes played around his head then faded into the darkness. Then he heard it: water slapped against the side of the pipe and the stink of the sewer rushed past him and caught in his throat. *Oh, sweet Jesus, not like this.* His sneakers slipped and he arched his head back, gasping for breath.

A dull red glow appeared in the distance. *How far? Jesus, I can't see.* He blinked as fast as he could and the red lamp came into focus. He forced his heels down to stop the trolley, his ankles bouncing off the rails. The metal cable tray tore the skin from his arms and he threw his hands up before the trolley had stopped, scrambling for the hatch. *Find the hatch release switch. The water will cut the power.* His fingers found a bank of switches just as the red light flickered, then died.

He heard his own screams. His hands flailed around in the darkness and the rank, fetid stench of sewage filled his mouth and nose as the roaring sound of water became louder. His fingers grasped a small ledge and he slammed his head against the lid of the hatch as a torrent of water hit his torso and spewed up over his face.

The white light blasted into his eyes.

"Connor! Hold on!" Her hands held him around the chin, lifting his face from the water.

He threw up a hand to the edge of the hatch as she reached down and grabbed his shirt. The trolley slipped away beneath him and he dropped to his knees in the stinking water.

Kirsty thrust her head into the hatch and wrapped her arms around his chest, then threw herself backwards, dragging him upwards.

He landed on top of her and rolled away. "Close it!" he croaked.

Kirsty scrambled to her feet and slammed the hatch shut.

Montrose lay face down, his whole body shaking.

She knelt beside him and wiped his face with her dress.

"Milchmann," he croaked.

"What?"

"The password. Milchmann. Or milkman."

"We have to move." She leaned in to kiss his forehead, thought better of it and stood up, pulling the iPad from her bag. "And, uh, well done. Right, we need to talk to Zac."

"Yeah." Montrose got to his feet and looked around; they were in a bare, concrete-clad room, a single light bulb hanging from the roof.

"You're in West Kensington," said Kirsty. "An old World War II command bunker." The sound of a tube train filled the room. She typed in a number and hit the speaker on the iPad. "That's the Circle and District line on the other side of the wall. Zac?"

"Yeah, what's happening?" said Zac. "Where's the man?"

"Right here. End of the line," said Montrose. "The password is milkman. Or milchmann."

"I'm on it."

Montrose leaned against the wall for a moment, then walked slowly towards Kirsty. Zac's face was on-screen, his hair falling over his eyes as he typed into a keyboard.

"Holy moley," said Zac. "You should see this shit. My screen just lit up like a freaking Christmas tree."

"Don't talk to me about shit," said Montrose.

"It works?" said Kirsty.

"Oh yeah, it works," replied Zac. "Question is, what the hell do we do now?"

"Change it," said Montrose. "Change the password. Then get the hell out. We'll meet up when it's safe."

"Yeah, you're right. Any suggestions?"

Montrose bent over to the screen. "How about...?" The words stuck in his throat as he saw a figure loom up behind Zac, the knife slashing forward then back in an arc across his throat. Zac's eyes opened wide as he was pulled back from his chair and a gout of blood sprayed across the screen.

268

"Zac!"

A hooded figure stared at them from the screen, reached over and closed the laptop.

"Oh, Jesus..." Kirsty staggered back and Montrose grabbed her around the waist and held her up. She stood, her chest heaving, then brushed him aside. A single tear dropped before fury crossed her face. She roared at the iPad. "I will find you. I will find you and I will cut your fucking heart out!"

"Kirsty, we've got to go."

She wiped her face and began to type into the iPad. "Zac's laptop is fitted with a tracker. They won't leave without it." She brought up a map on the screen. "They're moving fast. On foot." She held the iPad closer. "No, in a car." She turned to Montrose. "We're going to Cambridge."

"Kirsty, we need to speak to Pilgrim."

"Listen to me. They have the final password and they're on the move. Wherever they're going, we have to get there first. And drive the bastards off the road. Then they're mine. Don't even think about stopping me."

*

"Milkman," said Arkangel, his phone pressed to his ear. "Type it in." He stepped back from the desk and watched the technician enter the password. The black and green screen burst into life, scrolling through the activation program, then stopped at the blinking cursor.

"Attack program ready to activate," said the technician, his finger hovering over the keyboard. "The choice is 'Yes or No.'"

A voice boomed out from behind them. "Arkangel!" The technician sat back.

Arkangel turned.

Kutuzov stood framed in the doorway. "Come with me."

Arkangel looked down at the screen then turned his back on Kutuzov and nodded to the technician, mouthing the words. "Ten seconds. Do it." He cleared his throat and stepped towards the door. Across the hall, in a sunlit salon, he saw Kutuzov standing before a window.

"Close the door," said Kutuzov.

Arkangel hesitated, glancing back to the technician before he slammed the door behind him.

"Moscow want you back in Russia," said Kutuzov. "There is a plane waiting for you."

Arkangel shook his head and began to laugh.

"Relax," said Kutuzov. "If they were going to kill

you they would have done so by now. You are to be rewarded for locating the spy who broke into the embassy."

Arkangel grinned. "That's very kind of them. Do you know why he was there? The spy? Do you?"

Kutuzov crossed his arms. "Don't play games with me. You're not safe yet."

Arkangel rubbed his face and looked past Kutuzov, out on to the street. "It astounds me how an imbecile like you managed to worm his way into Intelligence." He dropped onto a sofa. "Or maybe it's just that scum always rises to the top."

Kutuzov's face reddened and he spoke through gritted teeth. "I warn you, what you've done will only keep you alive for so long. The President is sitting behind his desk in Moscow, waiting for my call. When someone woke up the Red Star, the supposedly secret US Satellite Warfare Center in Virginia went crazy. Of course, we are saying nothing, but be in no doubt, we want control."

"And do what? Take down their satellites? The Americans will blow you out of the sky, then NATO will crush you like a bug. You think threatening them will work? Tell them you're going to kick their ass around space?"

"What we tell the US is none of your business. When

we control the Red Star, we will deny everything. This is politics, you idiot. Our country has NATO troops on our border with Latvia and Estonia. Our former Soviet allies are now vassal states of Washington. And that is unacceptable. NATO troops are heading for the borders of Poland and Slovakia. But with control over the Red Star, Moscow will ensure they are driven back a thousand miles. Then we'll do business. Just make sure you get that final password. And then you can call the President yourself." Kutuzov held out his phone. "Or you can call him now."

Arkangel ignored him and pulled out his own phone. "Guess who I'm calling?" He leaned back on the sofa and slowly dialed a number. Kutuzov's expression turned to fury as Arkangel spoke into the phone. "Here's the deal. The price remains unchanged. Two hundred million dollars. Fifty for each one. But, for four hundred million dollars, I can make it look like the Iranians. With absolutely indisputable evidence." He listened to the response, his eyes closed. "Agreed. Consider it done." He cut the call.

Kutuzov shook his head. "You're an idiot, Arkangel. You think you can do deals for this? My men will find the password. It's only a matter of time. We don't need you."

"Oh, your men. Of course. Well, you can stop

worrying your little peasant head. We have the activation password."

Kutuzov's mouth dropped open. "You have it?"

"We have it and we have control of the Red Star."

"My God. Moscow will…"

"Moscow won't do anything. Apart from crying into their potato soup. You can phone the President if you like and ask him about his dreams of strutting about the world stage, smiling like a Bond villain because he's got power over every satellite in space. But I wouldn't recommend it."

"What are you talking about? Hand it over. My men will…"

"Your men, Kutuzov, have a price. Twenty million dollars in a Swiss bank account and a US passport with a new identity." Arkangel took a pistol from his jacket. "You see, I have friends too. New friends. In Washington."

The look of horror froze on Kutuzov's face as the bullets pierced his heart. He crumpled to the floor.

Arkangel stepped over Kutuzov's corpse and opened the door. "Clean that up," he said to a guard and marched back across the hall to where the technician sat at his desk. "Well?"

"Attack underway. We should have the results very soon."

Arkangel waved a hand around the room. "Pack up everything. Leave nothing behind. Not a trace."

"Where are we going?"

"Not far. An Iranian diplomat has just died and left us the keys to his home."

The technician smiled. "He has wi-fi?"

Arkangel nodded. "Of course, and is being closely monitored by MI5. It's perfect."

*

"They're moving fast," said Kirsty. "Too fast. What the hell is going on?"

Montrose pulled off his stinking shirt and threw it into a corner. "What do you mean too fast?"

She traced her finger across the screen. "The tracker is supposed to pick up local wi-fi and record the location. But it keeps jumping in and out in seconds. It's gone through hundreds of them. The last time it came on, it had covered two miles in a minute. There's no motorway close enough to Cambridge to get that kind of speed up."

"Helicopter," he said. "Got to be."

Kirsty's eyes opened wide and she brought up a flight

tracker app. "There are hundreds of commercial flights over the south of England."

"Can you trace the fight route?"

She focused on Cambridge. "There's nothing in the sky. It's not logged. Wait." She flipped over to a map where a line of red dots recorded each wi-fi the tracker had found. She zoomed out, then traced her finger down the screen. "They're heading for London. Right to the center. I think I know where they're going." She narrowed the map onto the River Thames. "Battersea heliport. It's a direct line." She shoved the iPad into her bag. "Take your trousers off."

"What?"

"I know, it's the second time I've asked today, but this time I mean it." She took a penknife from her bag. "Cut the legs off your jeans. It'll keep the smell down a bit. And don't bother with a shirt. One glimpse of sunshine in London and the place is half naked, so you'll fit right in."

"Kirsty, we have to find a way of getting out of here. Every cop, every camera is looking for us. And the Brits will know that the pipe is broken. They'll be heading to each exit point."

"I'm working on it. But they know what we look like and you're covered in shit. We'll have to risk it." She pulled her dress over her head and handed it to him.

"Turn that into a skirt." She tossed him a pair of nail scissors. "I've got work to do." She paced around the room in her lace vest and panties, typing on the iPad.

Montrose got to work with the scissors.

"We have to get across London fast and undetected," she said. "And through the traffic."

He hacked away at the legs of his jeans, trying not to look at her, but noticing a bright red Welsh dragon tattooed on her ass.

"Got it." She jabbed the screen. "We've got one hundred yards to go, dressed as a couple of London weirdos. Let's go."

"Where?"

"Cycle shop. Notting Hill."

*

Kane's footsteps echoed off the walls of the ballroom. At the far end, below a fifteen foot high portrait of Nixon, the figure of the Farmer sat hunched over a desk. Kane looked at Campbell's feet, his rubber-soled shoes moving noiselessly beside him. "How come the Farmer gets a bigger office than the US Ambassador?"

"I couldn't possibly say, sir." Campbell picked up the pace.

Kane grimaced as pain shot through his broken nose and he gave Campbell a look. "Might have known you'd be a soft-shoe kinda guy."

"Best not keep him waiting, sir."

Kane lengthened his stride. "Jesus, it'll all be over by the time we get there." The room was bereft of furniture, apart from two chairs in front of the Farmer's desk. A series of high, wide windows tinged the sunlight from Grosvenor Square with an eerie green light from the security glass. As Kane approached, he watched the Farmer trying to type into an iPad, his massive fingers slowly tapping each key. "What do I call him?"

"He doesn't have a title, sir."

"I thought he was CIA?"

"Not exactly sir, higher than that. We just call him Sir."

"We?"

"Have you met him before, sir?"

"No. What is this, a fucking cocktail party?"

"Well, we're in the right place."

Kane bit his tongue as they stood facing the desk. He was about to speak when the Farmer looked up and Kane just couldn't lose the image of a seven foot tall Mr. Potato Head after a car crash. The Farmer's huge bulk spilled over the ornate chair and the tiny blue eyes on his bulbous, pockmarked face, framed by a ring of red hair above his ears, betrayed his Irish ancestry. He leaned over the desk and the iPad disappeared under his arms. "This better be good."

Kane cleared his throat. "If I didn't think it necessary, sir, then I wouldn't..."

"Who gives a shit what you think. It's what I think that counts." The Farmer looked for the iPad and held it up, showing the schematic building plans for Project Orbital. "Okay, talk."

"We think the Russians are now an immediate threat to the entire operation. Montrose escaped from the embassy using the pipe."

The Farmer slammed down his hand on the desk. "How the fuck did he know about Orbital?"

"Elizabeth Purley betrayed our operation. No doubt she was working with Montrose. And previously the Soviets. Whatever Montrose is looking for may still be there. Warrender was held in the cells of the Embassy. I've checked the old recordings. He didn't talk. But maybe he left a clue in that cell. And that's why I'm here. If the Russians discover it, or Montrose talks, it's game over."

"Montrose escaped, asshole. Why would he do that?"

Arkangel widened his stance and shoved a hand in his pocket. He kept a tight hold of the Nokia phone. "Purley's dead. Montrose's lifeline is gone. There's nowhere safe in London for him. This isn't going to be like Julian Assange in the Ecuadorian Embassy. Any of those bastards think of sheltering him and we'll choke their country dry overnight. But there's one embassy that would take him in. Just like Warrender. The Russians. If that happens then we can be sure he's turned. That's why I want Spanish King. There are sections of Project Orbital still operational. The automatic flood gates closed off the other pipes. They've sent in divers to clear out the flooded section, but it will take a day. And the Russians are asking questions."

"Oh yeah? The Brits can clean up their own shit."

"Their wi-fi and phone traffic are still being monitored. If he goes over to the Russians, we can still pinpoint Montrose to one room. We can be surgical. We've practised this. It works."

"If he talks, if he knows, if they work it out. Too many 'ifs'. You gotta do better than that, because what we are doing today will secure US dominance over the entire Middle East for generations. The Israelis will be crying out for help. And yeah, we might just help them, but as soon as the Iranians press the button, we're out of there. They can blow the shit out of each other and we'll sit back and watch. Egypt is ready to go. And Jordan, the Saudis and even the Iraqis. And the Israelis know every location of all the enemy forces, because we've told them. This is gonna be the mother of all battles. Maybe this is what the bible meant when they said Armageddon. But it's on our terms. Then we march in with the Saudis as a UN Peace Force and clean up. Israel will be a scorched desert. So will Iran. It's a win-win. We're never gonna get another chance like this."

Kane's throat was dry. "I understand, sir."

"What did Purley tell the Brits? What do they know?"

"Only what we tell them. They didn't know where Warrender was, only Purley did. MI5 have been directed by Downing Street to do what they're told."

"Watch out for them. They're the most devious bastards on the face of this planet. It was their weakness after World War II that led to the creation of Israel and the fucking madhouse it's become. And since then they've sheltered religious lunatics like Khomeini that fed the fires for the Iranian revolution. All that shit in the Middle East, it leads right back to them."

"We're watching them closely, since Purley..."

"Fuck that traitor." The Farmer stood up, the veins on his face pulsing and his jacket flapping around him like a marquee in a storm. "The body in the glacier? You know his name?"

"We have evidence that points to..."

"Michael MacPherson Pilgrim was his name. A goddamn hero. You might have been in high school jerking off at cheerleaders, but back then we were in a space race we could not afford to lose. Not some cock-jockey pilot walking on the moon. The satellites. We knew the Soviets were going to try to take over near space with attack satellites and when they did they could have blown us out of the sky any time they liked.

"Michael Pilgrim was selected straight from MIT. He knew what he was getting into. And we knew we had to give a little to win a lot. We set him up as a defector, got him connected with agitators and known Soviet spies. He was well-trained. He knew what to do. He made the right connections. He let them know he was working on satellite control systems. And then he walked right into a honeytrap, just like we told him. So he started to hand over information and we reeled them in. We stole software from IBM and Pilgrim sold it to Moscow. You see, if they were using our software we knew what they could do. But the Soviets got nervous. They're not stupid. So we had to go right to the wire. The Soviets told him to defect or they'd turn him over to the CIA. Pilgrim refused. He had a wife and a young family. The Soviets warned him that he stood to lose everything, but still he refused to defect. The Soviets knew he would be crucial to their program. Then they got *really* nervous. They played the endgame. So, they come bragging to us that Pilgrim is a double agent. Sure, we pretended to go crazy, but we smuggled Pilgrim to Germany, pretending that he was on the run and he handed himself over to the Soviets for protection.

"The Soviets thought they'd won, but it was all part of the plan. Now we had our man on the inside. And he did what he had to do. And they put him right where we wanted. On their satellite program. After all, he was the expert in the software. The last message we got was that the Soviets were taking him off the program. Looked like they had got what they needed from him and he knew he was dead meat. That's when we knew the Red Star was the real deal. Pilgrim knew what he had to do. He told us he was coming in. And then, nothing, until he turns up in a glacier in Norway.

"The only guy he spoke to, Roger Warrender, disappeared off the face of the earth. We looked for him for twenty years. So did the Brits. And the Soviets, but there was nothing. And that means someone was protecting him. That bitch in MI5. And when we do find him, he gets a hole in his head, just at the right time." The Farmer got up from his chair. "You know why it's called Spanish King?"

"The English?"

"Yeah. One of the best military moves in history. Called the 'singeing of King Philip of Spain's beard', over three hundred years ago. The English burned his entire Armada before it could leave port. That means 'get them before they get us'. Make no mistake, the authority now lies with you."

Kane gripped the Nokia hard as the adrenalin shot through his veins. "If Montrose goes over to the Russians, I'll personally pull the trigger."

The Farmer leaned over the desk. "Don't fuck up."

CHAPTER 22

His ribs ached as he pulled on the T-shirt, banging his elbows on the side of the cubicle.

"You okay in there?" said Kirsty, behind the partition.

"Just about." He tore open another disinfectant wipe and rubbed it against the scratches on his chest. *Last thing I need is hepatitis from all that shit*. The skin on his arms and legs was torn and specks of fresh blood appeared where the alcohol had soaked the wounds. *I'll live*. The curve of a knife and the image of Zac flashed in his head. *That's not Kane's work. No, he'd have just put a bullet through his head. Same result*. A plastic bag appeared under the door.

"Stick your wet stuff in there," said Kirsty. "Leave it."

He shoved the stinking remnants of his jeans into the bag and threw them into the corner.

"Connor?"

"Yeah?"

"Who did it? Who did that to Zac?"

He tugged on the tight-fitting cycling shorts and pulled the messenger bag over his shoulders. *The helicopter was going to a civilian airport. Not the roof of the American Embassy in Grosvenor Square.* "Kirsty, I don't know."

"Then we'll find out."

There's only one other face in this game. Arkangel. And Kane let him go.

"You ready?" she said.

He looked into the full-length mirror on the back of the door, checking the cycling shorts, distressed T-shirt, cycle helmet and new sneakers. *This could work.* He pushed on a pair of wraparound shades. "Yeah. Kirsty? Tattoos?"

"Covered."

He pulled open the door to find her holding two mountain bikes. She wore a long-sleeved baggy shirt, hi-vis vest and a white pollution mask hung around her neck.

"Hold the bikes." She pulled her iPad from the bag. "And put your mask on. They'll be in Battersea soon. But we need to stop and get a new SIM card. I've used this one long enough. And a laptop. There's only so much shit you can do on an iPad." She popped the SIM card and flicked it into a bin full of cut-price clothing. "Don't worry, I wiped it." She took her bike back from Montrose and headed for the door. "Remember, you're a cycle courier. That means you shout at anybody in your way, ignore traffic lights, ride on the pavement and generally behave like a complete twat."

The assistant stopped them at the door. "You're gonna need those helmets."

Kirsty turned. "Yeah?"

"Just came on the BBC. There's a satellite dropping out of the sky. Be lucky!"

*

"Move everything out of the way," Arkangel ordered. The technicians pushed the antique furniture to the side of the room and others dumped their steel equipment cases onto a polished wooden table.

"We have wi-fi," said one. "It's fast enough."

Arkangel checked the Nokia phone, but there was no message. He stepped over the body of the Iranian diplomat and looked out of the window to the gravel-covered drive and high-barred gate.

A guard entered the room. "Perimeter secure."

Arkangel faced the men at the table. "This is the final phase. We await instructions for the next attack. When we are done, a car will take you to a USAF base in Surrey where a jet will be waiting for the flight to New York." He pointed to the equipment. "Wipe everything down. Destroy all personal ID you carry. Your Swiss accounts have been created and will be credited this afternoon. Twenty million dollars. Passports will be handed out as you land." He nodded to the guard. "Tell the others."

*

He watched her weave through the traffic and his sneakers slipped on the pedals as he tried to keep up. The pollution mask was clamped tight to his face and felt hot as hell, but it served a purpose. Blue flashing lights appeared at the end of the road. He watched the policeman get out of a BMW and stand on the sidewalk, checking cars at the junction. Kirsty ignored them and swept through the traffic, then tore straight down the middle of the road.

The policeman looked at her for a moment then

glanced towards Montrose. He stepped hard on the pedals. *Don't look at them.* Horns sounded and the policeman turned away. Kirsty took a left and stopped outside a row of shops. He pulled up beside her and tugged down his mask. "Where are we?"

"Keep your mask up. There are cameras at the end of the street." She handed him her bike. "Wait here. I need some kit." She disappeared into the shop.

He wiped his hands on his shorts and felt the sweat chill on his neck. The shop window was full of cheap watches and electrical goods with a TV for sale in one corner, showing the BBC News channel. The rolling strapline read 'Second satellite falls to earth.'

They've done it.

Montrose stared down the street, listening to the police sirens. *This isn't going to stop here. This is way out of my league. I have to tell someone. Not Kane. No, go straight to the press. But who? If the British are working for Kane, they can slap down any newspaper they like. And the BBC will do what they are told.* A police car screamed round the corner at the end of the road and roared towards him, the wail of sirens bouncing off the buildings and rattling windows. It shot past Montrose and squealed to a halt at the other end of the road. Three armed policeman got out and covered the junction.

Montrose turned back to the TV. 'Satellites will burn up in the atmosphere say NASA. Explosion seen from International Space Station. Unconfirmed reports say US satellite is missing.'

He pulled the pollution mask aside for a moment and took a deep breath. *Jesus, would Kane shoot down his own satellite? This is bullshit. I've got to get this out. Maybe the foreign newspapers.* At the end of the street a truck full of soldiers pulled up and blocked the road. *They've got the British in their pockets.*

Kirsty came out of the shop and handed him a plastic bag. "Take this." She threw her bulging messenger bag across her shoulders. "Let's see where they are now."

Montrose pointed to the TV. "There's two satellites down. And the army are here."

Kirsty looked to the end of the street. "That isn't good. They never call out the army. We'd better move."

"*Listen* to me, Kirsty, there's two satellites down."

"Big deal."

"What? Look, this is bigger than just us."

"Really? Connor, the US lost a satellite earlier this year. Do you remember that?"

"No, look..."

"And the Chinese lost one a few years ago. The papers were only concerned about space junk littering the atmosphere. That kind of news rates lower than some vacuous celebrity with an arse the size of a planet getting her baps out on the internet. Which means we still have time." She placed a new SIM card into the iPad. "Come on, you piece of shit." She tapped the screen. "They've landed. And they still have Zac's laptop. The signal is stronger." She pointed to the map. "They're crossing the Albert Bridge. They're coming towards us."

"Okay, let me think." *If we find who killed Zac, I'm going straight to Al Jazeera. Then Russia Today. Then the French, the Germans and anyone else who will listen. That'll shake the monkeys from the tree.*

"But why the Albert Bridge?" said Kirsty.

"What? Kirsty, I don't get you."

"If they were heading north they would take Battersea or Wandsworth Bridge. Those are the main roads. But maybe they don't need the major roads to go north. And that means local. That means Chelsea or Kensington. Right here. Let's go."

She was on the bike and halfway down the road before he hit the saddle.

*

Kane had expected Cabinet Office Briefing Room 'A' to be a wood-paneled *fin-de-siècle* salon, with hanging tapestries and high windows overlooking the Thames, but he guessed he'd been watching too many black and white movies. The COBRA had no windows, just a long, wide desk that almost filled the room, with plastic chairs jammed together around its edge. The far wall was covered in video screens and he heard a low buzz that was designed to prevent recording. Several cabinet office mandarins squeezed past him, papers clasped in their hands. Kane sat at the end of the table. On the video screen he saw the rolling news strapline confirming that the Space Station had seen another explosion. His hands trembled as he felt the adrenalin rush.

One of the men approached and leaned over towards Kane. "I'm afraid, sir, that this chair is reserved for the Foreign Secretary, Mr. Gowrie."

"Fuck off." The man recoiled and Kane watched the others enter, followed by the Prime Minister and a tall man with white hair who glowered at Kane.

One of the men opened a notepad and addressed the meeting. "Thank you for coming. This is the third meeting of COBRA this year and I am the cabinet secretary, Mr. Beauchamp. I shall be…"

Kane rapped his knuckles hard on the table. "Can we miss out the best man's speech and just cut to the chase, yeah? There are fucking satellites dropping out of the sky. One of them belongs to the US and the other is Israeli. We have strong evidence that the Iranians are behind this and they are doing it right under your noses in London."

Gowrie leaned over the table and jabbed a finger at Kane. "Why is it always the Iranians with you?"

"Ah, Foreign Secretary Einstein, who else is it gonna be? It's not going to be fucking Belgium, is it? The Iranians have targeted us and the Israelis. There is no bigger enemy facing us. I mean, how shit do you have to be as a Foreign Secretary not to work it out?"

"Of course," replied Gowrie. "Your enemies. You spend so much time spreading love and peace around the globe, it's difficult to keep track."

"Yeah, whatever. But our investigations point directly to the Iranians. Absolutely no doubt."

"So you have evidence, eh?" Gowrie leaned on the table. "Care to share it with us?"

"No. This is a need-to-know basis. This is going no further."

"Really? And this evidence, of which you so eloquently speak, is it like chemical weapons plants in Iraq that turn out to be bicycle factories? That kind of evidence?"

Kane leaned forward on the table. "It's the goddamn

Iranians and it's happening right here in London because you let every fucking terrorist and religious nutjob into your country. All the Iranian presidents like Khomeini, Rafsanjani, they all built their power bases here. And the current president, whatever his name is, even went to university in your hometown. I won't even mention the succession of Third World butchers you educated in your little kingdom."

"Either you've got a selective memory," said Gowrie, "or you're as thick as shit in the neck of a bottle. I'll go for the second option. Your government asked that we bring them here, not us. Keep your enemies close, eh? We've had to put up with them so you can play your little spy games. And where is all this magnificent information coming from? Some more stellar journalism from Fox News? Or have you, as your compatriots say, just made this shit up so you can go charging around like a bunch of fucking cowboys?"

"That is confidential. All you have to know is…"

"All we have to know," said Gowrie, "is what the fuck you are up to this time. Because I think you're lying through your teeth."

"Enough!" The Prime Minister slammed a hand on the table.

An electronic alarm sounded and the video screens lit up to reveal the US presidential seal.

"Gentleman," said the President. "I have some news." They watched him open a folded piece of paper. "The Israelis have made it clear that any further attack on their satellites will be seen as an act of war. The Prime Minister and I have agreed that we will do all we can to prevent this occurring. The Israelis have fighter jets in the air and have activated their nuclear defense plan. We have assured them that we will help, but not if they go nuclear. I have to say, they are not in a mood to listen to reason. They are totally reliant upon those satellites for the operation of missiles, warplanes and the defense of their country. Therefore, they intend to initiate a pre-emptive strike if they think that those satellites are under any threat. So far we have kept the details of the attack suppressed, but we expect our enemies to brag about their success. When that happens, the US will state that it will support Israel if there is any further attack on US or Israeli assets. We hope this will bring the Israelis back from the nuclear option. Our military have allowed the Israelis access to several US satellites to cover their loss, but this will take some time as the primary satellite designed for this function was the first to be attacked. And that is not a coincidence. In addition, the Arab League is convening in Egypt and their countries have begun immediate mobilization into an attack formation directed at Israel if there is any attack on Iran. The major terrorist organizations in the region have said they will cease any military operations and join the fight against Israel." The President folded the piece of paper and stared into the camera. "We are on a knife edge, gentlemen. Mr. Kane has supplied me with indisputable evidence that the operation is being conducted directly from London, by known Iranian assets. He assures me that he can nullify these assets and the threat, but he needs your immediate and complete cooperation. What we are about to do will not be pretty. But it will be absolutely necessary if we are to stop nuclear war in the Holy Land. Let us not flinch from our responsibilities. Let us do it and let's do it now."

The room fell silent for a moment.

Gowrie leaned back in the chair, shaking his head. "With the greatest respect, Mr. President, that sounded like a shit speech from a Hollywood B movie."

"Enough, Gowrie." The Prime Minster pointed to Kane. "Do what you have to do."

CHAPTER 23

Kirsty stopped her bike under the cover of a tree and pulled out her iPad.

Montrose was out of breath by the time he caught up with her. "I know what you're thinking. Don't do it."

"Yeah, right." She held up the iPad. "They're two streets away. Follow me."

He grabbed her handle bar. "Look, I'm sure you bought a big kitchen knife in that shop, but we can't take them on."

"We're wasting time. Let go of my bike." She tugged the handlebars from his grasp.

"Kirsty, those guys are ex-military. This is what they live for. Only pick fights you can win."

She stared at the iPad, then pointed to a junction at the end of the street. "They're going to go straight past us."

Montrose looked up and saw a dark blue Audi drive past. "Okay, let's follow them. That's all. Then we work out a plan." He set off fast, but she shot past him at full speed. "Kirsty, keep your distance." He watched a black Range Rover flash past the junction. "Kirsty!"

She waited until he pulled alongside. "You see that?"

"That car?"

"Yeah, the Range Rover," she said. "Just like the one I saw outside the gates to the Russian Embassy."

"You sure?"

"Yeah. Blacked out windows and fancy rims. And the driver. Mean-looking baldy bastard with aviator shades."

"Keep your distance. These guys are marksmen." They stopped at the junction and saw the rear of the Audi, just as it turned into the gates of a high-walled courtyard. The Range Rover brake lights lit up. "Looks like the CIA are going to get there first. Let them do the dirty work." He made to put a hand on her bike, then thought better of it. *Maybe Kane is going to do it himself. He doesn't need me. He doesn't need her. This shit is over.* "Kirsty, stay back. This could be messy."

"I bloody hope so."

They watched the Range Rover slow, then accelerate and drive straight past the house. It showed no sign of stopping and disappeared from view round a bend in the road.

Shit. Is that it? No, they can't be... "Kirsty, are you sure that was CIA?"

"Same guy. I clocked him when he drove past. No doubt."

He looked back but the street was empty. *They're gonna let them do it. Kane wants this to happen. He's making it happen. No. Even the CIA aren't that crazy. They'll be back. And tooled up.* "Kirsty, the CIA know they're there, right? No need to go charging in. We just need to know who lives there."

"Let's find out. Follow me." She cycled slowly down the road, checking out the house numbers.

Montrose caught up with her. "Hey, we should stay back. The CIA could return at any moment and we don't want to be in the firing line."

"That's bollocks. Look."

Montrose saw the rear of the Range Rover come into view, parked at the end of the street, hidden by a curve in the road. Two men stood around dragging on a smoke.

"They don't give a shit," said Kirsty. "We do this my way."

"Jesus, no."

"Connor, will you fucking relax? We're not going to do the Charge of the Light Brigade on two mountain bikes." She cycled past the gates where the Audi had turned in, crossed the street and dumped the bike outside a coffee shop. "I'll check the local government voters' register and Google the address."

Montrose shoved his bike against hers and looked across the road. The front of the house had a high gate and intercom, but no nameplate. *It's a total setup. Those bastards are working for Kane. Is that why he let Arkangel go?*

"It's owned by the Iranian embassy," said Kirsty. "Doesn't give a name. Probably just a diplomat. Their embassy is right around the corner." She pulled a meat cleaver from her bag.

"Holy shit, Kirsty. C'mon, listen to me. We can't go in there."

"Hey, I'm mental, but I'm not crazy fucking bonkers mental. They have the laptop. They have the access. And they'll be online." She shoved the iPad and the meat cleaver towards him.

He looked down. *I've got what I wanted.* He tried to hide the cleaver behind the iPad. *Bit late for that.*

She took out a laptop from her messenger bag and pulled open the screen. "Let's see what they're up to."

He caught movement in the corner of his eye. "Kirsty?" Through the bars of the gate they could see two men lifting a rolled up carpet into the boot of the Audi.

"What are they doing?" said Kirsty.

"That looks heavy. I've got a funny feeling that was the guy who lived there."

"Whatever." She held the laptop in her arms. "I need to be closer." She looked out from behind the van. "No cameras. Follow me." She darted out and stood below the wall at the corner of the house, craning her neck towards the roof. "And no satellite dish or I would see it on Google maps. If they had a dish on a wall it would be on this side of the house, facing the satellite." She pointed up at the high terraced buildings. "But they won't get a signal. I'm going into their wi-fi."

"It's unprotected?"

"It is from me. I can see their IP on Zac's tracker and I can crack it from there. Listen, I'm going to clone Zac's laptop from the Cloud and then shut those bastards down. Zac and I, we have..." She stopped for a moment. "We had an arrangement. You remember I said all the evidence I had on the Westminster pedophile ring was wiped? Well, that won't happen again. Zac had my back. And I had his." She typed quickly into the keyboard. "Everything he had is on the Cloud." She jabbed a finger at the house. "And I'll get into his laptop through the coffee shop wi-fi. The best thing I can do is delete and scramble any connection method other than wi-fi before they work it out and block me." She nodded to the meat cleaver. "Stopping their wi-fi is your job, but only when I say I'm ready. Then they'll be dead in the water. Understand?"

"Kill the wi-fi? Aren't they going to notice?"

"When it goes down? Yeah. Fuck 'em."

"What if they're using another laptop? Their own access?"

"They don't need Zac's laptop to access the Red Star, but they're gonna need comms. Without wi-fi they could use a 3G phone signal, but Zac's laptop is a serious piece of kit. It's got more back doors than that whorehouse in Soho."

"You can hack it?"

"Oh, yeah. It has a cell phone signal blocker. Zac used it on trains to shut up the arseholes in suits when he wanted some peace. Blocks all cellphone signals within twenty feet. I can activate it. They'll never see me or know it's there." She stared at the house. "We're gonna shut them down."

Montrose looked along the road towards the Range Rover. "Okay, but we better keep out of sight."

She pointed to a coffee shop. "I'm going to be at that window. When I say kill the wi-fi, do it."

"How?" He looked around.

She pointed to a green communications box at the side of the café. "That's mine. Don't touch it. But see over there?" She pointed to a side street around at the corner of the house. "That's where I need you."

He saw another green communications box set against the wall bordering the house.

"You might want to use that big fuck-off meat cleaver. And the bike tools in your bag. Every phone line and internet access for the far side of the street will go through there. Open that comms box and rip out every cable you see. Ready?" Her laptop beeped. "Go!"

"Wait, what are you going to do?"

"That coffee shop has wi-fi. And a tall Americano. Let's see what these pricks can do when I have control." She closed the laptop and ran over to the coffee shop.

Montrose kept close to the wall and hurried over to the communications box. He pulled the toolkit from the messenger bag as he ran. The lock on the box was a triangular metal stub, but there was nothing in his tool kit that looked like it fitted. He took out a small mole wrench and clamped the teeth around the stub, then shoved a screwdriver into the handle of the wrench and twisted them around. The lock turned on the box and the pliers slipped off and clattered to the sidewalk.

He pulled the door open. The box was full of trays containing hundreds of tightly packed wires. He pulled a handful, but they were hardwired to the trays. Lifting a pair of wire cutters from the bag, he tried to snip every cable he could see. *This could take forever*. He traced the wires to several thick core cables leading underground. *That's it. Do the cores. No, wait for the signal.* Looking up, he saw Kirsty at the coffee shop window giving him the thumbs up. He dropped the wire cutters and gripped the meat cleaver. *Don't fuck up. Do them all.* He brought the cleaver down hard on the first core. It sliced through the insulating sleeve and bit deep into the metal wires. He chopped down hard again, straight through the core and slashed at what was left, then stepped back. Kirsty was at the window, concentrating on her laptop. He looked back along the street and saw an identical comms box twenty yards away. *Shit. I can't take the chance.* He grabbed his tools and ran down the street.

*

Arkangel hovered over the technician, holding the Nokia in his hand and checked the coordinates on the screen.

The technician sat back in his chair. "The attack plan is ready. Awaiting confirmation." His fingers hovered over the keyboard.

"Do it." He turned away and typed a message into the Nokia.

Attack underway.

He stared at the screen, waited for the 'send' confirmation, then pulled out the SIM card from the phone. He held it in his hands for a moment before snapping it between his fingers. A simple text message, he thought, that would earn him four hundred million dollars. Enough money to hide from Moscow. Though once the origin of the Red Star was leaked to the press and Jerusalem and Tehran were a nuclear wasteland, the current regime wouldn't last a week. The hawks in Washington and the outcry from the Western governments would take care of that. The riots in Red Square would be well funded. And those waiting in line to wear the crown, would do what they were told for the right price.

"Sir?" The technician spun around in his chair. "I've lost wi-fi."

"What?"

"I can't send the attack command. The wi-fi is down."

CHAPTER 24

An image of Zac's laptop flashed up on her screen. She saw the satellite control program window open, the cursor moving across the screen as the coordinates were entered. She opened the wi-fi settings and found the IP address, then flicked back to her laptop and ran an internet program to bombard it with data. Flicking back, she watched the wi-fi activity climb until it flashed red. "I need more," she murmured. She looked out of the window and saw Connor kneeling beside the communications box. "Get on with it!"

She checked the wi-fi screen and resisted the temptation to disable the wi-fi. *No*, she thought, *then they'll know I'm shadowing and they'll come looking.* The wi-fi symbol flickered then greyed out. "Gotcha!" she said.

An old lady appeared at her side with a mug of coffee. "Having fun, my dear?"

"Yeah. Kind of."

The old lady placed the coffee beside her and leaned in towards the screen. "Is that one of them 'shoot them up' computer games?"

Kirsty looked up at her and smiled. "You know, that's exactly what it is. But it's all over now."

"I'm glad to hear it. Enjoy your coffee."

She ran her fingers down the screen, trying to decipher the commands, and saw the coordinates highlighted in bold. She sat back and reached for the coffee, but her hand froze in mid-air. The command line at the bottom spelt out flashing words in red.

Нанести удар. Да/Нет?

She copied the words on the screen then flicked over to a Google translator and pasted them into the search box.

Commence attack Yes / No?

"Fucking hell."

"Language!" said the old woman from behind the counter.

Kirsty looked out of the window and saw Montrose kneeling on the sidewalk, shoving tools into his bag. He looked up and she punched the air. He nodded and began to walk towards her. She turned to the old woman and muttered an apology, then flicked back to the screen on Zac's laptop. *The Red Star*, she thought, *I can wipe it. I have control.* Her hands trembled over the keyboard. She looked down at the command line. "And then run like hell," she whispered.

Her finger hovered over the 'N' key. *Nada*, she thought, *or nyet. That's about all the Russian I know.*

She hit the 'N' key. The screen spun up a list of files then stopped at the command line. She recognized the c:\ prompt. "Bloody hell. It worked."

This is early DOS, she thought. *They must have stolen it from the Americans.* She sat back. *They must have seen me do that.* She brushed her hair from her face. *No, they're disconnected from the satellite. I'm the only one connected. They can't see me.* Her mouth dropped open. *Holy crap*, she thought, *I can kill this stone dead. Or at least long enough to get out of here.* She brought up the admin command and typed in *chgpwd. All I have to do is change the password and rename the .exe files. It would take them too long to work it out.* The new password function blinked at her, then she stared at it for a moment. *Just think of a word.*

The café door opened. Three men walked in followed by a tall man. She recognized the face from the photographs in the Soho restaurant. Arkangel. She froze.

They strode straight past her to the counter. "Do you have wi-fi?" said Arkangel.

"Yes, of course," replied the old lady. "I must say it's very popular today."

Arkangel and two technicians sat at the table and crowded around a laptop. A guard stood at the door.

"We have coffee, too," said the old lady.

Arkangel nodded to the security guard.

"Four coffees," said the guard.

"Certainly, what kind would you like, my dear?"

"I don't care."

Kirsty glanced at them. They would link to the café wi-fi in a second. And then they'd know. *Think of a password.* She thought of Zac, his face on the screen and the flash of the blade. The grief hit her and she felt her stomach tighten. *Not now*, she thought, *not yet. I will grieve. But only when they are dead*. The photos flashed up in her mind and the words written on Pilgrim's arm. *Like a tattoo*, she thought. *I'm Welsh. If I die here, they can work it out in the morgue when they look at my ass*. She typed in '*ddraig*'.

The cursor flashed and returned the prompt. She hunched over the screen and typed out the *rename* DOS command, then changed the name of every .exe file. She watched them scroll down the screen and then stop

at the cursor. *Okay, work that shit out, you wankers.*
Flicking back to Zac's laptop, she typed in the FDISK
function. The numbers started scrolling, wiping the
disk. She was reaching out to close the lid of the laptop
when she felt a hand on her shoulder. She could smell
the coffee on his breath.

Arkangel took her hand and placed it in her lap. A
guard sat beside her and took her bag. Arkangel spoke
softly into her ear. "You will tell us what you have done
and you will tell us right now."

"What do you want from me? Who are you? I'm
going to call the police." She made to get up but a hand
pressed her to the chair.

The other man leaned in and pulled a hunting knife
from his jacket. He held the serrated edge to her breast.
"You are too pretty for this blade. I will not use this side
like I used it on your friend. Zac was his name, no? I
tore open his throat." He spun the knife and held up a
long sharp bladed side. "I will use this. Your corpse will
look better."

Blinding light burst through the cafe and a pressure
wave snapped her head back. Through a blur she saw
the window shatter into a thousand glistening fragments
and glimpsed black-suited figures storm through the
door with machine pistols raised. Tumbling to the
floor, she watched the guard's head disintegrate from

the machine gun fire. Arkangel flew backwards, blood erupting from his chest.

*

Kane's shoes crunched over broken glass. Behind him he heard the rattle of automatic fire from the house as the remainder of Arkangel's team were taken out. An old woman and a customer staggered past him, holding onto each other. Kane stood over Arkangel. "I changed my mind. Can you tell?"

Arkangel began to laugh and red froth bubbled from his chest.

"Hey, I'm glad you find it funny. Cracks me up."

Arkangel shook his head slowly. "No. No attack."

"Yeah, you see, as soon as the attack began you were no longer useful to anyone. Besides, budget restrictions, you know?"

"No, there is... no second attack."

Kane stared at him. "What the fuck are you talking about?"

"It did not..."

"You texted me. You said the attack had started. If you're telling me..." He brought up a pistol and pointed it at Arkangel's face. "Tell me the second attack is underway. You're not dead yet. Think about it."

Arkangel struggled for words. "There is nothing you can do. You need me. There is no attack."

"You were holding out for more, weren't you? You slimy prick."

Arkangel grimaced. "Get me help. I will tell you."

"There is a very thin thread holding me back from kicking you to death right now. You break that thread and I will make you suffer for as long as your miserable death takes." He stepped forward and placed his boot on Arkangel's balls. "Okay, so you want to play poker. I'll show my hand. Final offer. You tell me what I need to know and I'll get you a medic. I'll hand you over to the British. They'll take care of you. Otherwise, you're mine. You've some time left. And then you'll tell me. I'll make it happen."

"Two passwords… And an activation code."

"Yeah, I know about the code. Spit it out."

Arkangel's eyelids began to close. "I had the code."

Kane pressed his boot down. "Last chance."

Campbell ran over. "Our technicians can't bring up the satellite login. It won't respond."

Arkangel smiled. "Pretty girl."

"Listen, you piece of shit, you tell me what's going on or I will rip your throat out."

The froth bubbled from Arkangel's chest. "I am dying. But I die knowing... that you... are fucked."

"Tell me!"

"Sir!" said Campbell. "This one's still alive." He dragged over a technician.

Kane pistol-whipped the man's bloody face and knelt, forcing the barrel into his mouth. "Tell me the code. Or I'll blow your fucking head off, right now." He hauled back the pistol, taking two front teeth with it.

The technician spat out blood. "I don't know. She must have changed it."

"She?" Kane stared out to the street.

CHAPTER 25

Shattered glass from the café lay strewn across the road, thousands of tiny shards sparkling in the sunlight. Montrose pushed up his pollution mask and edged forward. A taxi pulled up beside him.

The driver leaned out of the window. "Bloody hell, mate. What happened?"

Black-suited figures wielding machine pistols emerged from the café, dragging bodies behind them.

Jesus, please, not her. Then he saw her, stumbling out behind them, her arms around the shoulders of an old lady. *Holy shit.* He pulled down the mask to cover his face. *They don't know.*

"Is that the SAS?" said the taxi driver.

"Yeah," said Montrose. "SAS. Probably. Looks like they've taken out some terrorists." He kept his gaze fixed on Kirsty. Another black-suited figure ran towards her and held her by the arm, then helped both her and the old lady across the road to the wall bordering the house.

Montrose looked at the taxi. "We have to get these people to hospital." He began to run to her, but stopped. *If they see us together…*

The taxi driver stuck his head out of the window. "Wait for the professionals. They'll be quicker through the traffic."

Kirsty, just look at me. "No, we should get them out of here. Right now."

"Listen, mate, I was an army medic. I know what I'm talking about. You need an equipped ambulance, not a taxi."

Shit. He glanced behind the taxi. The road was clear. "You were a medic? Okay, help me out here."

Montrose ran over and knelt beside Kirsty, brushing shards of glass from her hair.

"Connor!" she shouted. "What happened?"

"She's deaf," said the taxi driver. "Stun grenades, probably. Her hearing should come back soon."

"Okay, but let's get them further away in case it kicks off again. We're too close." *Last chance, fella.* He could hear the taxi engine idling behind him.

The taxi driver looked at the bodies being bundled

into the back of a Range Rover and the figures standing around, machine pistols hanging loose at their hips. "Looks like they got it sewn up. Threat's over. We should wait." He pointed to the old lady. "She could go into shock. Ambulances have got the equipment. If she does, at her age you'll need oxygen and specialist care."

"Connor!" Kirsty shouted. "I can't hear you!"

He gripped her hand and pressed a finger to his lips. He flicked his eyes to the junction around fifty feet away then mouthed the words. *We go. Now. Ready?*

She nodded.

He tried to help her up, but she shook him free and grabbed onto his T-shirt.

"I'll look after this one," said Montrose. "Check the old lady. I think there's blood coming from her ears."

"Blood?" said the taxi driver. "That could be her eardrums from the stun grenades. Or it could be a serious head injury." He held the old lady around the shoulders and began checking her for injuries.

Montrose stood and Kirsty held on to his T-shirt and pulled herself up. She was about to take a cautious step forward when Montrose grabbed her and pulled her over to the taxi. He bundled her into the back, then ran to the driver's door, jumped in and slammed the stick into reverse.

"Hey!" The taxi driver stood up, but the old lady slumped to the side and he grabbed her before she fell.

The taxi shot backwards, throwing Kirsty to the floor. "For fuck's sake!" She scrambled to her feet and stuck her head through the gap in the glass partition. "Connor!" She pointed back down the street. Kane was running towards them, holding a pistol in his hands. "He's going to shoot!"

Montrose flicked his eyes between the rear view mirror and Kane. He wrestled the steering wheel and the taxi weaved from to side, striking a parked car with the fender. A side mirror flew off and sprayed glass into his open window. He heard a round thud into the headrest and looked up to see a ragged hole in the windshield.

Kane was ten feet away, his gun aimed directly at the taxi. Behind him, two men began to raise their machine pistols.

Montrose stood on the brakes and rammed the stick into first gear. "Down!" He held the steering straight and dropped between the seats. The taxi lurched forward and he heard the thud as Kane slammed into the hood. Montrose looked up.

Kane's face was flattened against the windshield. "You fu…"

Montrose hit the gas and the taxi flew backwards. Kane slid from the hood and bounced onto the road.

The gun flew from his grasp. In the rear-view mirror, a gap appeared between the parked cars. Montrose swung the rear of the taxi sideways into the gap, then twisted the wheel around and took off down the street. "Get down!" The rear windshield exploded into the cab as rounds flew past his head. He held up his arms to block the flying glass, just as the windshield exploded around him. The taxi careered around the corner and he hauled himself up. The street was clear. "Kirsty?" He hit the gas and could hear her rolling around in the back. "Kirsty!" he screamed.

A face appeared through the remnants of the glass partition. "Slow down, you bastard. I nearly broke my fucking neck."

"Are you hit?"

"What?"

He looked around to see her sweeping glass from the back seat.

"What?"

"Are you hit?" He shouted.

"No, I don't think so. And stop shouting, I'm not bloody deaf."

Houses and cars flashed past. "Kirsty, where do we go?"

"Head north."

"Which way is north?"

"No fucking idea, where are we?"

"About half a mile from the café. We have to ditch this taxi."

A car shot out from the curb and stopped in the road.

Montrose hit the brakes and his chest slammed into the steering wheel. He heard Kirsty swearing as she hit the floor. He made to grab the gear stick when a woman jumped from the Audi and pointed a pistol at his head. "Hands in the air."

Another woman got out and ran over, hauling open the driver's door. "Get out."

The first woman moved around to the corner of the taxi and kept the gun pointed at him, while the other pulled open Kirsty's door. "You too."

Kirsty held her head as the woman pulled her from the taxi and pushed her towards the Audi.

The first woman motioned with her gun. "Quickly."

Montrose stared at her.

"Do you want me to shoot her?" She pointed the gun at Kirsty.

He stepped from the taxi.

She leveled the gun at his chest. "You are Connor Montrose."

"Who?"

"It wasn't a question. Hands on heads. Get in the front." She flicked her to head to the Audi.

"In the front?" said Montrose.

The other woman helped Kirsty into the back of the Audi.

Montrose stood still.

"Get in. Now. Your friends will not be far behind."

That accent... He climbed into the Audi.

The driver got in and dropped the pistol between her legs. The Audi's engine roared and they took off down the street. The driver flicked up and down the gears as she maneuvered the car through the back streets. The pistol slid around between her legs. "I know what you're thinking," she said and reached down to grab the pistol. She held it by the barrel and thrust the pistol grip towards Montrose. "Take it."

He stared at it for a moment then took it from her hand.

She dropped three gears at the end of the road and flipped the steering left and right, sending the rear of the car into a power slide around the corner. "And if you're not going to use it, put the safety catch on."

Montrose held the warm metal in his hand. *A 9mm. Grach.* "I thought you were going to shoot me."

"If we had wanted to shoot you," said a voice from the back, "you'd already be dead. We hoped that it would not be necessary. Do not disappoint us."

"We aim to please." He looked down at the dull gun metal. "So, you guys stopped using the Makarov."

"We move with the times. Makarov is Cold War shit."

A burst of Russian came over a walkie-talkie.

"What was that?" said Montrose.

"We have a spotter. There are CIA and MI5 Range Rovers waiting for us." She slid the Audi to a halt. "Get in the back."

Montrose heard the door open behind him.

"Move."

He got out and looked along the road, but could see nothing except a busy street at the end. The second woman pushed him into the back seat and closed the door.

"Where are we?" he said.

"That's Kensington High Street," said Kirsty.

"You okay?"

"Apart from a few serious head injuries and being half-deaf, I'm just fucking peachy."

The door locks clunked shut. Dark window blinds rose up covering the rear windshield and the passenger windows. The Audi accelerated towards the end of the street.

"Whatever happens," said the driver, "don't get out of the car. And turn off your phones."

"I don't see any Range Rovers," said Montrose.

"Not yet, but you will." The Audi slipped into the traffic on Kensington High Street and indicated right.

Kirsty leaned forward. "Oh, fucking fuckitty fuck. I know where we're going."

*

Kane leaned back, his breathing ragged as he gingerly touched his ribs. "Where is he?"

Campbell concentrated on his iPad. "Montrose isn't the target. It's that bitch in the café. She's the one."

"He broke my fucking ribs."

A paramedic undid the front of Kane's shirt. "I have to bind your chest. But I need to check for fractures." He ran his finger down Kane's ribs.

Kane's head snapped back. "Jesus! You fucking idiot!"

"Listen, mate, it's going to hurt whatever I do, so sit still and don't talk. You'll make it worse."

"It's her," said Campbell. "I have the number."

"Where?" grunted Kane.

"Don't speak," said the medic. "I have to bind this properly." He pulled the shirt out of Kane's waistband.

Kane shoved the medic's hand away. "Why don't you just fuck off? I'll do it myself."

The paramedic stood up, "Yeah?" He tossed the

bandage at Kane's ribs and turned away. "Best of luck, you mouthy prick."

Kane's jaw clamped shut and he spoke through gritted teeth. "Fucking Brits, I swear..." He tried to breathe slowly through his nose. "Tell me where she is." He turned to one of the men in a black suit. "And you. Get me some fucking drugs. Lots of them." He let his head drop back against the headrest. "Okay, you find her. Leave Montrose to me. Get the team to log into the sat and start the attack."

"We can't. The Red Star is not responding."

"Then crack it."

"That's going to take at least an hour. We need her. The laptop that she used in the café is completely wiped. We can access the satellite, but we can't restart the attack. It's ready to go, but we need the password. She must have changed it. That's what Arkangel was hiding."

"Then find the bitch and drag her back here by the fucking hair."

"We're on it. We have her phone. We've checked all the other numbers in the café, but only one was a new number on the network. Connected fifteen minutes ago. It was heading north." Campbell stared out of the car window. "The last known signal was half a mile away from here. Then it dropped."

"Dropped?"

"It's gone. She's turned it off again."

"Find her. And if she doesn't want to talk, start cutting bits off her until she does. Start with her fucking hands."

CHAPTER 26

Through the windshield they saw armed police standing either side of a security barrier, flanked by high stone pillars. Behind the barrier, metal teeth stuck out from the ground.

"This car is the property of the Russian State," said the driver. "It is protected by diplomatic law. No one has a right to interfere with the passengers. Whatever happens, remember that." She looked quickly over at Montrose. "My name is Lara. Get your heads down."

He dropped onto the rear seat, catching a glance out of the driver's window. Two black Range Rovers stood either side of the pillars. Kirsty lay beside him, her head on his chest.

Lara turned towards the guardhouse and the barrier. A tall figure in a suit held up his hand and walked in front of the car. Lara blasted the horn and hit the gas. The man leapt out of the way at the last moment and slid along the side of the car. The nose of the Audi dipped as she hit the brakes and brought the car to a halt just under the barrier. She held an ID card up to the window.

The guard looked at her, then back at the black-suited figure as he scrambled to his feet.

She rapped on the window. "Open it. Open the barrier. Now!"

The black-suited man stood at her window, blocking her view of the guard. He grabbed the door handle, but it was locked.

Lara brought up the barrel of the Grach to the window and pointed it at the man's stomach. She leaned forward, looking past him towards the guard. "Open this fucking barrier or in five minutes I'll have the American Ambassador hanging by his balls from a Kremlin window!"

A loud buzzer sounded. The metal teeth slid into the ground and the barrier lifted.

She hit the gas, the edge of the barrier glancing off the top of the windshield as the Audi lurched forward. She flicked up the gears and then slowed, checking her mirrors. "Okay, they're not following. Just as well. They'd be dead within seconds." Lara looked around. "You can get up now." A Russian voice came over the walkie-talkie. Lara nodded. "They are stopping each car as it arrives at the end of the street. They are pretending it's a security incident. If they had seen you, it would not have been pretty."

Montrose lifted his head and looked through the windshield at a tree-lined road and driveways leading off to three-storey Victorian villas, hidden behind high walls. "Is this what I think it is?"

"Kensington Palace Gardens," said Kirsty. "Home of, amongst other things, the Russian Embassy." She squeezed his hand.

Montrose said nothing.

"I hear you've been here before," said Lara.

"Me or him?" replied Kirsty.

"Both of you. By the way, nice trick with the hair spray and the fire alarm."

"Thanks."

"Yes," said Lara, "and thanks to Mr. Connor Montrose for flooding the basement with raw sewage. We had to break the pipe to find out what was going on."

Montrose cleared his throat. "Yeah, sorry about that."

Lara grinned. "Well, given what we found, I think you'll be forgiven."

Montrose saw several men with automatic rifles standing in the road. "Who...?"

"Don't worry about it," said Lara. "It's the Israeli

Embassy. They're on full alert." He saw the men lower their weapons as they recognized the driver. Through the trees he could see the other gatehouse at the far end of the road, flanked by more black Range Rovers. "Why don't they just come down? It's their country."

Lara smiled through tight lips. "No, it isn't their country. This land, this whole street, belongs to the Queen. And as weak as the British Government are, they will not allow trespassing on Her Majesty's land. Diplomatic protocol. Besides, the Israelis would shoot the shit out of them if they tried and they know it." The Audi slowed to a crawl and turned right, past ornate stone pillars, into a driveway and along the side of a grand house.

Montrose noticed a Land Rover, sitting low on its fat tires and the armed guards inside.

A door opened as they approached. "Welcome to the Russian Embassy," said Lara. "The ambassador is waiting for you."

"Yeah," said Montrose, "I'm sure he is." He stepped from the car and walked around to Kirsty's side, but she was already out of the car.

"I'm fine, Connor. Let's go."

He heard helicopters and looked up, but could see nothing.

"This way," said Lara and led them up the steps. The door slammed behind them and a guard threw the bolts.

They followed Lara up a staircase towards the second floor and along a wide corridor lined with portraits. He could see an open door on the right-hand side, halfway down. The reek of sewage drifted up the corridor. *Yeah, my bad. The Brits will be going ballistic when they find out about the pipe. When they find out? They'll know. And so will Kane.*

"Christ on a bike in house slippers," said Kirsty. "What a stink."

Just as long as they don't send me the bill.

Lara stopped and pointed to an open door.

Montrose turned into the room. A tall, white-haired man stood with his back to them looking out of the high windows to Kensington Palace and Hyde Park. Montrose's shoes sank into the thick Persian rug that stretched across half the length of the room.

"Hi!" shouted Kirsty. "Sorry about the fire alarm."

The man turned around, Kirsty's voice tearing him from his thoughts. He stared open-mouthed at them for a moment and then recovered, stuck out his chin and marched around the desk, holding out his hand. "My name is Nikolayevich Ilyich Ulyanov. Ambassador for the Russian People to the Court of St. James."

Kirsty grabbed his hand. "I'm Kirsty. Do I have to curtsy? Or kiss your ring?"

The man's eyes crinkled into a smile. "Ah, the British and their humor, especially in adversity."

Montrose shook the Ambassador's hand.

"These are my daughters, Lara and Mascha," he said. "They are the only ones I trusted to complete this mission. Too many people have let me down today. Please, sit."

"Any chance of a cuppa?" said Kirsty. "I've got a raging thirst."

"Of course," said the Ambassador, "but only if you don't use it to swallow a cyanide pill."

"Eh?"

"That's Russian humor." He shrugged. "But not very good. That is why I became an ambassador."

"It's my hearing," said Kirsty. "Comes and goes. The fucking Yanks nearly blew my head off."

The Ambassador nodded to Mascha.

"Actually," said Kirsty, noticing a decanter at the side of the desk. "That'll do." She hefted up the heavy glass decanter of clear liquid and poured herself a glass.

The Ambassador held up a hand. "Wait, it is not water, it is..."

"Vodka," said Kirsty and toasted him with the glass. "I'd just like to say I love your country." She took a gulp. "Wow! You keep that on your desk and you're my kind of fella. Oh and thanks for capturing us. Cheers!" She downed the glass in one.

He looked at her empty glass. "You know, I think you may have a career in the diplomatic service."

"Well, if Wales ever opens an embassy in Moscow, I'm your man."

Montrose cleared his throat. "What do you want from us?"

The ambassador sat behind his desk. He exhaled slowly, then reached over to the desk and refilled Kirsty's glass and poured a drink for himself and Montrose. He sat back in his chair, downed the vodka and thumped the empty glass onto the desk. "Before I answer that, Mr. Montrose, I have to know. Can I trust you?"

Kirsty leaned over the table. "Frankly, mate, it's not him you have to worry about."

*

"We've found Montrose. And her." Campbell pointed to the map on the iPad.

Kane tried to lean over, but the pain in his ribs made him sit back and gasp. "Where?"

"Kensington Palace Gardens. The Embassy. They must have been smuggled in by the Russians."

Kane twisted his head to look at Campbell. "You better be sure about this."

"The parts of Project Orbital that are still functioning have recognized his voice. And that of the Ambassador." Campbell held up the iPad for Kane to see. The red dot on the map moved around the screen and stopped. He flicked the map to a 3D grid. "Second floor. According to our plans, that's the Ambassador's office."

Kane's face turned bright red and his breathing quickened. "That piece of shit traitor. Okay. Let's do it."

"Sir?"

"Operation Spanish King."

"If we initiate the attack, the consequences could be very severe. The Farmer was very clear, sir. But it's your choice. He also made that very clear."

"Spare me the blame game, you fucking weasel. Grow a set of balls. If Montrose and the girl are in that prick's office, then the whole of goddamn Russia is going to know all about it any second now. We get this right and they'll think the whole satellite attack shit is still being run by the Iranians. And they'll have no evidence otherwise. So, we do this now or a whole world of shit will come down on me. And you."

"But sir…"

"Shut up. The plan is ready. They'll think it's the Chechens, Muslims, Ukrainians or whoever else the

Russians have managed to piss off. It's a long list. Jesus, even the Dutch want to kill them. They'll know who to look for when they trace the weapons back. You told me the team is trained and ready, yeah?"

Campbell stared at his iPad. "Standing by, sir. I had hoped it would not be necessary and that…"

"Yeah, well it is, so just fucking do it. I want to see them burn."

CHAPTER 27

The Ambassador drained his glass. He slumped in his chair, eyes closed, then sat up and leaned forward on the desk, carefully placing the glass beside the decanter. "What I'm about to say to you is not the voice of Moscow. It is the voice of a Russian who lives in the real world. What is happening is not the action of a modern Russian nation. It is Cold War lunacy. We have a lot to learn in this new democratic age and there will be painful lessons before we become a free and just society. But this will put us back generations. When Arkangel discovered the access to the Red Star, something we had lost many years ago, Moscow thought we had regained control. And regained the power that it brings." He dropped his eyes for a moment. "That prospect terrifies me. But that is nothing to the nightmare that is unfolding. There are people in Moscow who would let the world burn to regain control of near space. And they will."

Kirsty refilled her glass.

The Ambassador tapped the tip of his finger on the desk. "There is an opportunity, right now, to save the Middle East from nuclear war." He pointed to Montrose and then around the room. "Moscow may come to their senses, but it will be too late. There are those in the Kremlin who are drunk on power. They care nothing about death and destruction on a global scale. All of that is an acceptable price for power. But they are not the ordinary Russian, who just wants peace and a stable country to bring up his family in." He stood up, staring at the far wall. He shoved his chair back and marched to the window. "Moscow will soon discover your whereabouts. My daughters will say nothing, but you know how these things work." He turned around. "You must understand, I make no apology for the aspirations and actions of the Russian government. We need no lessons from the USA in self-interest and hypocrisy. You are not the guardians of democracy, only of your fragile control of the world economy and self-interest, for which you will commit any crime. Right now, we have criminals fighting for the chance to initiate destruction. But it is not too late. We will find out who did this. And what we do with that information..." He shrugged. "That is for another, perhaps bloody day." He cleared his throat. "Moscow has told me that another attack plan is ready and waiting in the Red Star. And despite the lunatics baying for blood in the Kremlin, I cannot believe our President would initiate an attack. But the Americans? Only God knows what you would do."

Montrose began to rise from his chair. "Hey, hold on, fella..."

The blood gathered in the Ambassador's face. "Do not dare to lecture me on the innocence of the United States. They would irradiate the entire Middle East if it suited their plans. Your presidents, your Congress, they come and go, but the hawks, they still circle Langley. They still lust for absolute, imperial control. They would create a blood-soaked desert and call it democracy." The Ambassador closed his eyes for a moment. "Moscow will find you. They will know that you have talked to me. What happens now, well, I will live or die with the consequences." He walked slowly to his desk and pressed the flat of his palms on the polished wood. "If you have the power to stop this madness then I implore you, in the name of humanity, do it now."

Kirsty took a gulp from her glass and tapped her ears. "You know, I didn't get a lot of that, but you're kinda sexy for an old bloke, so what have you got in mind?"

Montrose leaned over. "He wants us to destroy the satellite."

"Sorted." She downed the vodka. "Give me the internet and ten minutes on a PC."

The Ambassador dropped down into his chair and pointed to a door at the side of the room. "There is a computer in there. It is not connected to the network. It has unidentified internet access. I'm sure you understand."

"Whatever," said Kirsty and jumped to her feet. "Let's do it."

Lara opened the door and Montrose followed Kirsty through to a small room with only a desk and computer in it. Lara stood in the doorway. "I will prepare an exit for you. When this is done, you'll have to move."

Kirsty sat down and began to type. "Fast jet to St. Petersburg, baby. That'll do for me."

Montrose watched Lara close the door, then spoke directly into Kirsty's ear. "Can we do it?"

Her head jerked back. "Fuck off, Connor, I got my hearing back ages ago. I just wanted to wind him up. Right, leave me alone and I'll sort this out."

"What are you going to do? Wipe the software?"

"No, that's amateur shit. I'll do much better than that. All I need is Google translate and the coordinates of the Red Star. And I've got those. So, what do you think will happen if I told the Red Star to target its own coordinates?"

Montrose stared at her blankly for a moment. "It'll attack itself?"

"You win a coconut. Now, bugger off and leave me in peace. I've got to untangle all the changes I made in the café. I'll try not to take out any friendly US satellites. Though if I can find the one that the BBC uses, I'm going to blow the shit out of that."

"The BBC? Why?"

"I'm Welsh. Shut up and go away. Your sexy talk is distracting." She hunched over the PC.

Montrose looked out of the small window and gazed over the Kensington Palace Gardens and beyond, through the trees to Hyde Park. *She can do it. Maybe. What happens next? They just let us go? Maybe we'll end up in Moscow. Because when we step out of here, Kane will be waiting. They'll work it out. Maybe the guards on the gate saw something. Whatever, they'll be waiting.* He looked down to a concrete yard and a high wall and through the razor wire, to a track which led from the main road into the gardens. A pickup truck piled high with branches and logs trundled along the lane towards the park, a golden crown emblazoned on the door. He turned back to Kirsty, but she was staring at the screen while her fingers moved quickly across the keyboard. The blaring of horns made him turn back and he saw a white panel van behind the wall, blocking the pickup truck. The truck driver shouted out of his window and hit the horn.

A man stepped out of the panel van.

Montrose felt a stab of adrenalin as shock kicked up his spine and into his brain. *Why is he wearing a mask?*

The man brought up a pistol and fired two rounds through the pickup's window. The driver slumped in his seat.

Montrose's legs shook and his breath stuck in his throat. Four men jumped out of the van, each carrying an RPG. They crouched behind the hood of the pickup. Another masked man emerged from the van, carrying a square-shaped frame and trailing a cord. He disappeared behind the wall. *Shaped charge. Det cord. They're going to blow the wall.* "Get down!" He spun around and grabbed Kirsty by the shoulders, throwing her to the floor. The chair slid sideways and clattered into the wall.

"Connor, what the fuck?"

He shoved her below the desk and held her tight as the blast hit the window. The glass shattered and spewed fragments across the room as plaster fell from the ceiling.

Kirsty shoved him aside and lunged for the desk. "I'm nearly there! Just let me finish this." She tipped shards of glass from the keyboard and pulled her chair close.

Montrose scrambled to his knees and crawled to the window. A cloud of dust lifted from the scene and he saw the gaping hole in the wall, dust and rubble scattered across the yard and bricks embedded in adjacent cars. Two men rushed through the gap, knelt on one knee and pointed their RPGs towards the windows. "Down!" He grabbed Kirsty's chair and pushed her to the far corner of the room, then pulled her to the floor as the door to the ambassador's office blew out and landed on top of them. He held her tight as a fireball burst over them. He could smell the paint scorching on the door. They lay still as smoke and plaster dust settled on the floor. Then the screaming began.

"Stay there." Montrose kicked the door aside and ran to the window. The panel van was gone.

Kirsty scrambled over to the desk. The keyboard lay twisted and smoldering and the PC was shattered and broken. "I was so close!" She grabbed her bag from the floor and slung it over her shoulder. "Connor, we're fucking out of here. Go."

Montrose kicked aside the broken doorframe to the Ambassador's office. The room was thick with smoke and dust, the curtains and furniture ablaze. At his feet lay the twisted and bloody body of Mascha, her arms missing and her head twisted around, her features blackened and torn. Lara ran in from the corridor and dropped to her knees beside her father, trying to smother the flames from his burning clothes. She cried out and sat back, tearing her gaze away from his body. She looked up and saw Montrose, then got to her feet and slowly turned her head. "You," she said, pointing at Kirsty. "You are the one. This is because of you. You must stop this…" She looked around at her sister and began to hyperventilate, screaming. "No! It stops now." She skirted the remains of her father and stood in front of Kirsty. "You have to do this."

"But I couldn't do it," said Kirsty. "I didn't have time."

"Then we will find a way. If they find out you survived, they will come back. They will kill us all. If they do this, they will never stop. Come with me."

"Where are we going?" said Montrose.

"Safe house," said Lara. "Not far. How long do you need?

"Five minutes," said Kirsty. "And the internet."

"That's all?"

"Yeah."

"I will keep you alive for that long. After that, it's

up to you. We go. Not through the gates, they will be blocked. Follow me."

Montrose ran after them into the corridor, past guards carrying fire extinguishers, and down the staircase. Lara threw the bolts on the door and stepped into the car park, looking left and right. Montrose stood behind her. The Audi was still there, its windshield shattered and bricks strewn through its interior.

Lara pointed to the Land Rover. "We'll take that. It's armored. Get in the back," she said to Kirsty. "And get undercover. There's a blanket on the back seat. Remember, you are the target."

Kirsty said nothing and pulled open the door, then dived into the rear, dragging the blanket over her head.

Montrose got in front.

Two men approached with machine pistols at the ready. Lara shouted at them in Russian. She listened closely then fired up the engine. "They've gone. We'll go through the park," said Lara and fired up the engine. "All other exits will be blocked."

The two men ran to the gap in the wall and took up position. The Land Rover knocked the Audi out of the way, bumping up over the ragged stumps of the wall. The Land Rover crashed down, narrowly missing the gardener's body, then spun right, heading down the lane, hemmed in by trees on one side and the high brick wall on the other.

Montrose could see the exit where the road emerged into Kensington Gardens. The lane narrowed and trees closed in behind them. The Land Rover picked up speed as they neared the gardens.

A black Mercedes appeared from the corner and slewed to a halt, blocking the exit.

Lara blasted her horn. The driver jumped out and crouched behind the hood of the Mercedes, waving an ID card.

"Who the hell is he? A Brit?" said Montrose.

"Not in a blacked-out Mercedes," said Lara. She kicked open the door of the Land Rover and held up a pistol. "Get out of my way. I will shoot!"

The rear door of the Mercedes opened and a man with a machine pistol rolled out and brought it up towards the Land Rover.

Lara dropped him with a single shot to the heart, then turned and fired at the first man, who ducked behind the Mercedes. She fired several rounds into the hood, where they pierced the metal skin, disintegrating against the armor plating.

A burst of fire came from under the car. A round caught Lara in the ankle and she fell back against the Land Rover. She returned fire, blood pumping from her leg as she slid back from the fender.

Montrose launched himself over the seat and reached

out, dragging her back. She kept her pistol raised and steady.

The first man rolled out from behind the Mercedes and began to bring up his gun when Lara shot him square in the head. The breech on her gun slid back empty. He tumbled to the ground and lay still as the propellant smoke drifted across the lane.

A voice came from the open door of the Mercedes. "восемнадцать." Kane stepped out from the rear door of the Mercedes. "Timing is everything." He pointed the gun at Lara. "Drop it."

She let the empty pistol fall from her hands.

Kane kicked it across the lane. "восемнадцать. Eighteen. The number of rounds in a Grach pistol. Or nineteen, if you've got one up the spout." He nodded his head towards the first man lying beside the Mercedes. "Which he forgot." He pointed the gun at Montrose. "Get out of the car. Hands on your head." He flicked the gun towards Lara. "Right fucking now."

Kirsty's head emerged from under the blanket. She edged her shoulders between the front seats, then took out her iPhone, hit the camera function and slid it over the top of the seat. On the screen, she could see the guy in front of the Mercedes, a gun in his hand.

Montrose stepped from the Land Rover, supporting Lara by the arms.

Kane fired two shots into Lara's chest. She slumped to the ground.

"No!"

"Now it's just me and you, asshole. If I didn't get you in the embassy, all I had to do was flush you out. The gatehouses are barred. Why do you think they blew a hole in the wall?" Kane held his ribs as he edged forward. "You damn near killed me. But I'm not dead yet."

Neither am I. Montrose glanced down at Lara's pistol. *Empty.* The bodies of the men lay beyond Kane. There was no way to get to their guns without going through him.

Kane's features twitched as he walked.

You're hurting. Come closer. Montrose dropped his hands to his side and edged closer to the side of the Land Rover.

Kane stopped. "Hands on your head. Now!"

"Fuck you. I haven't got a gun."

Kane smiled and held his pistol steady. "I'm gonna cut to the chase 'cos I'm kinda busy today and I'm getting really pissed chasing you across town. We know what happened in the café. We know what she's done. You're just a pretty boy. Women, eh? Who gives a shit. Where is she?"

Kirsty tugged the blanket over her head and pushed

herself between the seats, keeping below the high dashboard of the SUV. She braced her feet against the rear seat then grabbed the auto stick and tried to pull it back. It wouldn't move. She looked down and realized that it wouldn't engage unless the footbrake was pressed. She slithered between the seats and pushed her hand flat on the brake, then reached back and gently pulled the auto stick into drive. The Land Rover gave a slight shudder, but didn't move. Keeping her whole weight on the brake, she pushed her hand across her chest and reached for the accelerator.

Montrose took a step forward. He could see the thick strapping under Kane's shirt.

"Stay where you are."

Montrose nodded towards Kane's chest. "That's gotta hurt."

Kane grinned. "I can't feel a thing." He tapped his ribs. Montrose caught the flickering movement of his eyelid.

The noise of rotors filled the air and trees and bushes flattened in the lane. "The cavalry are coming." Kane pushed his feet apart and widened his stance. "But not for you."

They'll find her. He felt his shoulders sag as the realization kicked home. *There's no choice. It ends here.* He let out a long, slow breath then stretched up on his toes.

"I would kill you in a blink of an eye. You're worthless to me. Now, you tell me where she is and you tell me right now or I'm going to empty this clip into your gut. One by one. Until you tell me. It takes a long time to die from stomach wounds, if you know what you're doing and believe me, I do. And then you'll be screaming for a medic. And you know, I'll get you one, because I want you back in the States and I want to hit the switch and see you fucking fry in a chair like the traitor that you are." Kane adjusted his grip on the pistol. "You betrayed your country. You went over to the Russians. People will be lining up to piss on your grave. But I'll be the first. Now, I will ask you, one last time. Where is that bitch?"

Montrose felt his legs shaking. *He's going to shoot me whatever I do.*

"I'm waiting."

Montrose looked up to the sky.

"Tell me and tell me right fucking now."

"You know," said Montrose, "I met a man today. A brave man. And he said something to me just before he died." The steady whump-whump of the chopper came closer. Leaves and dust blew around them as the chopper hovered over the gardens. Montrose raised his voice. "He said, if I had to choose between betraying my country and betraying my friends, I should hope I have the guts to betray my country."

Kane leveled the pistol towards Montrose's stomach. "Then you're a dead man. But let's see how brave you feel when your guts are ripped open."

The engine of the Land Rover roared and it lurched forward. Kane tried to move, but the edge of the hood caught him in the chest and threw him to the side.

Montrose ran over and booted Kane in the face. Blood spurted from his mouth and he crumpled to the ground. Montrose searched around in the undergrowth for the gun.

Kirsty climbed into the driver's seat. "Forget it! Go!"

The rotor wash blew him against the bodywork of the Land Rover. He tugged open the door and jumped in.

Kirsty hit the all-wheel drive button and jerked the stick into reverse. The Land Rover shot back a few yards until she stood on the brakes. She pointed to the Mercedes wedged across the exit. "Hold on. We're going over." She stamped on the gas and drove straight for the Mercedes, then at the last moment she swung the steering right and left and hit the Mercedes. The Land Rover's engine screamed and the armored fender tore up the hood of the Mercedes, the front wheels scrambling for grip, until the rear tires caught onto the crumpled metal and launched them over the hood.

Montrose held on to the dashboard as Kirsty kept her foot hard to the floor and the Land Rover dropped down the other side of the Mercedes, pitching him forward. His head smacked the windshield and he was thrown back as Kirsty spun the steering to the right and headed for the gardens.

"That's for the taxi," she said. "Bloody hurts, doesn't it?" She turned out of the lane, then stood on the brakes. A black helicopter hovered six feet from the grass. The pilot remained motionless behind aviator shades. At the cargo door, two men with automatic rifles leaned out. Montrose saw the missile tubes beneath the chopper. *We're covered. They'll cut us down.*

The chopper advanced slowly towards them.

"So, you wanna play chicken?" said Kirsty.

"No…"

She revved the engine. "A few more seconds and then he can't use the missiles. He'll be too close. You see them?"

"Yeah, listen..."

"A few more feet, come on, big boy!"

The chopper slowed.

Kirsty gripped the steering wheel. "Who's got more to lose here? Me or him?" She floored the accelerator and the wheels spun, then found their grip. The Land Rover shot forward.

The look on the pilot's face said it all. He pulled the stick hard, but the roof of the Land Rover caught the landing gear as it shot under the chopper and flipped the nose of the helicopter forward. The pilot reacted quickly, hauling the helicopter back.

Montrose saw the spinning tail rotor flash past his window as it crashed to the ground and bounced. A piece of rotor blade flew past his nose and embedded like a knife in the glass.

Kirsty didn't look behind, but drove straight for the trees and the park beyond.

Montrose twisted his neck and saw the helicopter pirouetting wildly, its tail rotor shattered, before it pitched to the side and smashed into the trees. "Get your head down!"

Shards of broken rotor blades and branches flashed past them and frosted the back windows.

Kirsty held on to the steering wheel and bounced over a road, scattering pedestrians in all directions.

Montrose brushed the broken glass from his pants. "Where are we going?"

An explosion kicked the Land Rover forward.

"North."

"Where?"

"I've only got one idea left. Paddington."

*

Kane rolled onto his back, screaming through the pain. He fumbled around in the pocket of his pants and brought out a pressurized syringe. He jabbed it into his stomach and held it firm. His head dropped back as the morphine kicked in and coursed through his veins. He grabbed a syringe from his other pocket and forced the amphetamines into his blood.

Campbell knelt beside him. "Sir, are you hurt?"

Kane's pupils dilated and he looked up at Campbell. "Am I hurt?" His whole body began to tremble as the amphetamines took hold. "Campbell, when I'm finished with Montrose, I'm going to start on you." He jerked his thumb towards the park. "Green Land Rover. Get them."

CHAPTER 28

A Frisbee bounced off the windshield and the Land Rover ploughed straight through a flower bed. Kirsty headed for a gap in the trees. "I guess a stealthy exit is out of the question." She leant on the horn and stuck her head out of the window. "Get out of the way!" The Land Rover slewed sideways across the grass and she pointed the hood towards the high railings and main road bordering the park. "We need to find a gate."

His head cracked off the roof as the Land Rover bounced over a rockery. "Yeah, a normal road would be good."

She craned her neck to look up at the sky. "We've got about four minutes before a copper in a chopper takes off and is all over us."

Montrose held on to the grab handle on the dashboard

as the Land Rover slewed past a group of picnic tables. "Just four? You know these things?"

"I know these things. It's not the first time I've had to run from the Old Bill."

Yeah, but it's not the cops I'm worried about. They're just the spotters. "There!" Montrose pointed to high ornate gates leading to the road.

"No, that's blocked by a bollard. It's a Land Rover, not a tank. Next one." She turned right and weaved around a group of tourists running in all directions. "I got it. Check that road."

Montrose tried to keep his head still as they bounced over the grass and through a row of bushes. In front was a tarmac road leading to a narrow gate. A Parks Department truck was slowly negotiating the gap and blocking the exit. The driver busied himself closing the gates.

Kirsty pulled the Land Rover onto the road and hit the gas.

Montrose pushed himself back in the seat. The Land Rover accelerated straight towards the truck. "Jesus, Kirsty, don't!"

She stood on the brakes and slid to a halt in front of the truck, then hit the gas and slammed the hood of the Land Rover into the truck's fender.

The driver ran to Montrose's door.

"Point a gun at him," said Kirsty. "I don't have time

for a chat." She revved the engine and the Land Rover pushed the truck back through the gates.

"I don't have a gun."

"Then punch his fucking lights out, but don't just sit there like a wet fart."

The driver made a grab for the door and Montrose hit the lock.

"Stay out of this!" shouted Montrose. Or I'll… shoot you."

Kirsty gave him a look as the Land Rover pushed the van through the gates and across the sidewalk. "That's possibly the most threatening statement I've ever heard."

"Can we just get out of here?"

She jabbed the accelerator and the truck shot into the road. A black taxi locked all four wheels and slammed head-on into the truck. She threw the Land Rover to the left and joined the traffic.

"We're heading back to the Embassy," said Montrose. "Go south."

"Not a chance. We need the back streets. Now." The line of cars came to a halt and she looked around, ready to mount the curb.

"Kirsty, we need to get some speed up." He peered out of the windshield towards the sky. "This isn't going to work."

She twisted the steering right as far as she could. "You're right there, *boyo*. In a few minutes every copper, chopper and spook is going to seal this place tighter than a nun's chuff. Containment zones, remember? And frankly, Connor, we either get off the streets or we're dead meat." She kept her eyes fixed on the oncoming traffic.

He saw a red double decker bus coming towards them. Montrose braced himself. "Kirsty!"

The Land Rover shot into a gap in the oncoming traffic. The bus squealed to a halt and caught the edge of the Land Rover, knocking them sideways. She held on tight to the wheel and headed for a side street. "Don't worry, we're going to the hospital."

"What?"

"Just keep an eye out for the coppers. We've got about three minutes left."

The Land Rover accelerated down the street, lined with parked cars and bordered by high apartment buildings. Montrose could hear sirens. He stuck his head out of the window, trying to gauge which direction they were coming from, when Kirsty turned off, down one street and then another.

"Two minutes." she said.

"What hospital are you talking about?"

"Not far, just keep your eyes peeled."

"What are we going to...?" Blue flashing lights appeared at the end of the road.

The Land Rover took a hard left and then right onto a broad avenue. Kirsty held a line in the middle of the road, weaving in and out of the traffic. "Enough with the back streets. We don't have time." She pointed through the windshield. "There!"

Montrose saw the grand, stuccoed façade of a railway station. "Paddington Station?"

"No, next door."

He saw the sign for St Mary's Hospital as Kirsty turned left, blasting the horn at a crowd of people heading for an Underground entrance.

"Down there. See that building on the corner? Red doors, three storeys high."

He looked towards the railway sheds and saw a red brick building with wide doorways. "Got it."

"The loading bays, are they boarded up?" She was watching both the taxis parked outside the station and the rear view mirror. "If they spot us now, we've had it."

As they got closer he could see that all the doors were covered in metal sheets, fixed to pillars at each side. "Yeah. We're not going to get through them."

"Good news. That means it's still deserted."

"We're going in there?"

"Yeah, but not through those doors. Hospital first. Up there." She jabbed a finger up towards a line of windows. "That's where they invented penicillin." She slowed behind an ambulance and followed it into a car park.

"Yeah, great, but…"

"What? They're the ones to thank for getting rid of the clap."

"The clap?"

"V.D." She tapped the steering wheel, as the ambulance pulled to the side. "You're telling me you've never had a dose of the clap? Jeez, Connor, you need to get out more. Are you still a virgin?"

For once Montrose was dumbfounded.

She pulled the Land Rover into a parking slot. "We're here. Follow me." She threw open the door and ran to the rear of the Land Rover. By the time Montrose had unfastened his seatbelt she was hauling a cyclist's hi-vis vest from her bag. "Put this on. And bring those tools."

He lifted the tool roll from a compartment in the trunk and grabbed the tire lever.

Kirsty pulled a few sheets of paper from the truck's logbook and held them out in front of her. "If anyone asks, I'm the boss and we're from the Town Council, here to check emissions, right?"

"Yeah, but…"

She ignored him and headed down an alley between two buildings. "Chin up. Act like a bored worker. Let's go."

Montrose followed her past temporary huts, lined with pipework, to a corner where a rusting iron ladder was pinned to a wall. Kirsty threw the papers aside and scaled the ladder. He tucked the tool roll into his waistband and grabbed the rungs, hauling himself up. The sound of sirens came closer and he could see the gleaming new railway sheds behind Paddington Station as he scanned the sky for a helicopter. "Kirsty, we go up there and they're going to…"

She didn't look back. "Then we'd better be bloody quick. Chop chop!" She clambered on to the top of the wall and held out a hand to pull him up.

"Kirsty, that's a mainline railway station. They're gonna target it and then they'll find the Land Rover."

She turned and ran across the roof. "Good. That'll keep them busy."

They find the Land Rover and they will tear this place apart. He saw her scramble over a wall onto an adjoining roof.

Montrose could see blue lights flashing, converging on the station.

"Connor! Move it!"

He ran over and pulled himself over the wall. She was standing beside a small brick hut set into the roof with a graffiti-covered wooden door. "Kirsty, they're gonna close that station in seconds."

"They certainly will. But we're not taking the train. Well, not the one you mean."

"Where are we going? We need to either get the hell out or stay low."

She pointed at the roof below her. "This is the old Royal Mail Sorting Office for Paddington Station. Closed down and sold off. That's the place I pointed out to you. We used to hold illegal raves there, but they boarded the place up. We need to be in there. I know what I'm looking for." She pointed to the tools. "Okay, Mr. Muscles. Do your thing."

He looked down at the two thick steel padlocks. "That's impossible."

"Not the padlocks. The hinges. That's the weak point."

He dropped the tool roll, took out the tire lever, punched it into the brick beside the hinges and watched as the brick powdered. After several blows the screws to the hinges were exposed and he dropped to his knees and started on the lower hinge. "Kirsty, they're going to search every inch of this area to find us. Whatever we do."

"Yeah, but they'll do the railway station and the Underground first. There are five Underground Lines that go through Paddington and a shitload of railway platforms. That's where they'll look first and by that time we'll be well clear of here. If you manage to get through that door, that is."

He jammed the tire lever into the gap beside the hinges and wrenched it back. The damp wood disintegrated and the brick crumbled at his feet. He hauled the edge of the door towards him and let his weight drop back, opening up a gap. "Ladies first."

"Ta!" Kirsty slid through the gap, then leaned against the other side to let Montrose through.

He grabbed the tool roll and squeezed into the gap. The sound of sirens died away and Kirsty reached into her bag and brought up a torch, playing the beam across narrow steps leading into the darkness.

"What are we looking for?"

She ran down the steps with Montrose close behind and stopped in a corridor.

"Kirsty..."

"Quiet, I'm thinking. Last time I was here it was very dark." He watched her close her eyes and trace a map with her fingers. "Through the door, turn left, first, second...Got it! Follow me." She ran to the corner of the corridor and pressed herself into a low archway.

She disappeared from view and Montrose turned into another corridor, lined with half-open doors, where fissures of light appeared around the edge of boarded windows.

"We need to find the door. An old door. There is an elevator alongside it, but it's ancient and I'm not going anywhere near that."

Halfway along, she stopped and pointed the torch, silhouetting the metal gates of an elevator, its handles fixed with a heavy chain "This is it." She moved the torch to the right. "And behind that is the door."

Montrose looked at a sheet of metal stretching from the roof to the floor, bolted to the wall. "Kirsty, we're not going to get through that."

"I know. This is… disappointing. That's a structural wall. They'll go straight into the stone. Okay, we'll do it the hard way. Follow me."

What the hell? She disappeared from view through an office door adjacent to the blocked exit. Montrose stepped through.

Kirsty stood at the wall playing the torch beam over the dusty, flaked plaster. She knocked on the wall.

Montrose heard the hollow thud.

"That wall in the corridor might be stone, but this certainly isn't. Hundred and fifty year old plaster and some crappy wood. Okay, Connor," she nodded to the wall. "Time to do your macho thing again."

"Where the hell does this go?"

"Down. Way down. And yeah, I've done this before. That's why they seal the doors and windows with steel. To keep out urban explorers like me. We'll make our own door. Give me a wrench." She pulled it from the tool roll, then stabbed into the plaster which broke away in large flakes, falling to the floor. Thin dust drifted through the torch beam and wooden lattice work appeared where the plaster had fallen. "Right, Connor, see that tire lever? Get stuck in. I'll be back in a moment." She placed the torch on a dust-covered desk and directed it at the wall.

"Where are you going?"

"Do it!"

Montrose brought up the lever and slammed it into the plaster. *Twice in one day with this shit. I'm going to have to learn how to use a door.* The plaster fell away and he shoved the edge of the lever through the lattice, twisting it to the side. The dry wood splintered and cracked, then broke away and fell to the floor. Sweat began to form on his brow. *This is going to take forever.*

"Out of the way!"

He turned and saw Kirsty running towards him holding an old fire extinguisher above her head.

She slammed it into the hole and it burst through the lattice, wedging itself into the wall. Kirsty tugged it back and it fell at her feet. She grabbed the torch and shone it through the hole.

Montrose glimpsed a stairwell.

"That's it," she said. "Keep going."

He picked up the extinguisher and smashed the plaster, then attacked the lattice with the lever. The ancient wood shattered and he worked his way down methodically until a two foot hole appeared through the plaster dust.

"That'll do," said Kirsty. She ducked her head, then stuck one leg into the hole and squeezed through. "Hand me the torch." She shone the beam through the hole and he followed her onto a metal spiral staircase. "Go!" She pointed her torch at her feet and headed down the staircase.

He kept his eye on the steps as they descended. The beam of the torch played over the edge and he saw the staircase descending into darkness. "Where are we going?"

"Concentrate," she said. "One slip here and you'll end up at the bottom, head first and you'll take me with you."

The air became warmer as they descended until they came to a door. Kirsty stopped for a moment and took a few breaths, then gently pulled the door open. "It's clear."

Montrose followed her into a dimly lit train platform. It was deserted. "What is this? The Underground?"

"Yeah. In a way. But not the one you're thinking about."

CHAPTER 29

He looked over a dusty platform to a narrow gauge railway line. Along the other side, glass-fronted offices lay empty and strewn with discarded boxes and broken furniture.

"This is what's left of the Mail Rail," said Kirsty. "The Post Office built an underground system to deliver tons of mailbags across London. It ran for ninety years. All the major train stations are linked up north of the river. And more importantly, it goes directly east."

He looked up at the roof where a few strip lamps cast a dark yellow glow over the platform. "How do you know all this?"

Kirsty laughed. "I told you. I'm an urban explorer. London has many secrets. All you have to do is kick down a few doors and you're in."

The rail tracks were only a few inches below the platform and he looked along to where they disappeared into a low, dark tunnel.

"Over here," she said. "This is the inspection train, at the end of the line. Engineers use it to check the tunnel."

Montrose turned and saw Kirsty at the edge of the platform, pulling a tarpaulin aside to reveal a small, roofless engine, about four feet high, with faded, peeling red paint and a louvered, oil-stained engine cover. "This works?" In his mind, he remembered a kid's train at a fairground.

"Oh, yeah. They have to keep the line open for inspections. It's the law." Kirsty opened a thick wooden door which came up to their knees and was emblazoned with the faded ornate symbols 'E II R'.

The image clicked in his mind from red Post Office boxes. "This belongs to the Queen too? She's got her own train set?"

Kirsty ignored him and sat on the driver's seat, looking at the levers. "Let's go."

Montrose squeezed in beside her and stuffed the tool roll between his legs, shining the torch on the track. He saw the dull brass of the deadman's handle with a cracked wooden knob. *This is Victorian.* The glint of fresh oil gave him some confidence. *This steampunk shit might work.*

Kirsty prodded a red button and the electric motor hummed into life. She jabbed around at several smaller buttons and a yellow safety lamp began revolving behind their heads. "Crap, wrong one." She hit the button to switch it off and tried the others until the headlamp flickered into life and gave off a dim glow. She grabbed the deadman's handle and the train jolted into life. The motor whined as they began to pick up speed, moving towards the mouth of the tunnel.

Montrose kept his eyes fixed on the platform, but there was no sign of life, only padlocked shutters and dark doorways to offices crammed with broken office chairs, cracked oil lamps and stacks of yellowing paper. They entered the tunnel and darkness closed in around them. The train's headlamp brightened as their speed increased, giving about ten feet of visibility. He covered his mouth against the clouds of dust that kicked up around them.

"The line hasn't been used for ten years," said Kirsty, "but they have to do regular inspections." The track opened up and she pulled the handle all the way back.

He held on tight as they rattled along, the roof a mere foot above their heads. "How fast does this thing go?"

She shouted above the noise. "Thirty miles per hour, at least."

"You been down here before?"

"Yeah, a few times. On foot. It's the first time I've stolen a train."

Her hair swept back in the slipstream and Montrose caught her grinning. "How long does it take?"

"No idea. Enjoy the ride."

"What about the other stations?" He felt her ease off the power for a moment and begin to turn towards him, but she stopped and hauled the handle back hard. The train jolted forward. The tool roll spilled from his lap and onto the tracks. Montrose held on tight as the line banked to the left. A light appeared in the distance. "Kirsty? What about the other stations? Are they all deserted?" He pointed down the tunnel. "What about that one?"

"Could be. No idea."

"What if there are people there? The line is still connected to Post Office depots, right?"

"We'll see." She didn't take her hand from the deadman's handle. "We'll blag it."

"What?"

"We'll pretend." She let the handle slip forward and the train slowed as they approached the end of the tunnel. "Relax," said Kirsty. "You're just a guy inspecting the tunnel, right?" She pointed to his hi-vis vest.

The train rolled out of the tunnel and Montrose looked out over a short, narrow platform, only a few feet wide and lit by dull strip lights. The headlamp showed rusty fencing enclosing another track and bare metal ribs vaulting the tunnel. He shone the torch onto the dusty platform, but there was no sign of life and no footprints, only tiny mouse tracks.

"This must be the Western Parcels Office," said Kirsty. "I'm trying to remember the map. It closed down years ago. The entrance and exit were sealed with concrete. I think it's a hotel or an office now." She pulled back the lever and the train shot forward into another tunnel.

"What's next?"

"Not sure."

The side of the tunnel was inches from his head. It opened for a moment and they rattled through another cramped station with a short platform, a foot wide, hemmed in by a wall of concrete. "What was that?"

She shouted over the noise. "Can't remember. Closed off."

Blue light sparked beneath them from the power rail. The line straightened up and the train gathered speed while he covered his eyes with one hand against the blinding dust. The train slowed when another light appeared at the end of the tunnel, this time brighter.

Kirsty brought the train to a halt before the tunnel's exit. In the distance they could hear the banging and crashing of metal trolleys. "Shit."

"What?"

"This is the District Office. It's still in use." She edged the train forward. "Blag it. Ready?" She jabbed the button for the yellow safety light. "Look bored." She pulled back the lever and let the train trundle into the station. Strip lights buzzed into life above their heads. "Trip switch," said Kirsty.

A wide platform opened up in front of them, lined with glass-fronted offices which were dark and empty. The crashing of metal cages became louder as they rolled past scattered railway equipment and broken cages. Montrose looked right and saw a wide exit leading to a warehouse full of metal trolleys. He heard voices in the distance.

Kirsty shot him a smile and pulled back the lever as they got the end of the platform.

Dust caked on the sweat above his lip and forehead. He tried to spit, but his mouth was dry. *It's only going to take one phone call and they'll have a reception committee waiting at the next station.* "Okay, what now?"

"Next station's closed. Then Western Central. I remember that one. It's not far."

Montrose held on with one hand and squinted along the track. He ducked as a line of broken stalactites appeared in front, hanging from the low roof. The tunnel suddenly opened up to a long, dark station, the headlamp flickering against bricked up exits and rusting signs.

Kirsty pulled the handle back hard.

The train jumped about the tracks and blue flashes illuminated the sides of the tunnel as the line swept hard left. The line straightened up and he spotted a light in the distance. "Where are we now?"

"North of Oxford Street. Next stop is Mount Pleasant."

"Abandoned?" In the faint light he saw her shake her head.

"No." She eased back on the handle. "This one is going to be more tricky."

Montrose fixed his gaze on the tunnel and the light grew brighter.

"We get through this one, we're home and dry. Every other station is abandoned and cemented up. There's no access."

And no escape. I've had enough of this underground shit.

She jabbed at the buttons until the lights shut off and let the train slow to a halt just inside the tunnel.

The noise of power tools echoed around them. "Crap," said Kirsty. "They've started already."

"What's going on?"

"They're turning it into a tourist attraction. I heard about it, but I didn't know they were working on it."

Montrose stepped from the train and crept towards the tunnel exit. Construction workers under bright lights crowded the platform. He turned back to Kirsty. "This isn't going to work."

She tightened her grip on the handle. "Fuck it. What about if we just go for it?"

He pointed down the line where a series of points in the track moved left and right. "No. Doesn't matter, they've taken the track up. We have to find a way out."

Kirsty stepped from the train and moved along the wall. "Over there. The elevator." Near the end of the platform the elevator doors opened and two constructions workers emerged, carrying toolboxes. "Do it."

Montrose moved forward, just as the doors closed. "Wait until it comes back and then we go straight for it." He watched the lights above the elevator doors. There were only two stops. It flashed 'G' for ground level and then blinked off. "It's coming. Ready?"

"Yeah." She pressed herself against the tunnel wall. "Go."

They edged forward out of the tunnel and walked quickly towards the elevator door. Montrose pulled the high vis vest tighter around him and held the tire lever low.

"This'll work," she said. "We'll be outside the containment sector. We can head to Holborn and down into the East End. We'll keep to the back streets. I know how to do it."

The elevator thumped to a halt and the door slid open. Kirsty stepped forward but was met with a black gloved hand. Two men in uniform stood facing them, machine pistols raised.

Montrose froze.

A man in a light blue suit stepped forward between the two men, his face a mask of concern. "Please, don't run. My name is Lockhart. Mr. Pilgrim sends his regards. Now, if you wouldn't mind, come with me. Quickly."

*

"Just give me the shot," Kane squeezed his eyes shut and took small, shallow breaths. The medic gingerly inserted the needle. "Hurry up. And double the dose, it hurts like fuck."

He sat on the edge of the desk and lifted a hand to Campbell, but the pain made him pull it back. "Where are they?"

"They were last seen heading towards Paddington Station. The whole area has been turned upside down. The Land Rover was abandoned nearby. Every train and underground line has been stopped."

"And?"

"There are hundreds of carriages, sir. No sign so far."

"What about her phone?"

"No signal. It's either switched off or on the Tube."

"The Tube?"

"The Underground, sir. The subway. They're searching every line and station connected to Paddington and all the CCTV. If they're on the Underground then they have to come up sometime. And we have all the cameras monitored."

"Be there when they do. I want a man at every station. And every airport. I want London sealed tight."

*

The Jaguar sat low on its fat tires as Montrose followed Kirsty and Lockhart into the rear seat. The two soldiers sat in the front, their machine pistols on their laps. The driver pulled the stick into drive and the Jag edged into the traffic.

Kirsty pulled out her phone. "I'll check for messages from Mr. Pilgrim."

"Use the blues and twos," said Lockhart. "Every police car in London seems to be using them today, so we may as well follow fashion."

The Jag's blue lights lit up and the siren whined. The driver swung into a gap in the traffic. The engine growled and the car shot forward.

"How did you know?" said Kirsty.

Lockhart shrugged. "I did a bit of Urb-ex in my youth, long before it was fashionable and long before it had a cool name. I never managed to crack the Mail Rail, though. When we saw that your car was parked near the old Post Office building, I made a guess. And directed all other efforts elsewhere."

"I'm impressed," said Kirsty. She gently elbowed him in the side. "We must compare notes sometime. How is Mr. Pilgrim?"

Lockhart cleared his throat. "As well as can be expected. We've arranged for him to be transferred to a clinic on the Continent as soon as his condition is stable enough to allow travel. The United Kingdom is a little too hot for him right now."

"Can I talk to him?"

"Best not," said Lockhart. "It's essential that all communication is kept to an absolute minimum.

Everything is being tracked. And I mean everything. Besides, your phone won't work in here." He tapped the roof. "Armor plating. Plays havoc with the signal."

"Fair enough," said Kirsty and switched off the phone.

Montrose eased down in the leather seats. "Tell me your story, Mr. Lockhart."

Lockhart smiled. "What I can tell you would not be terribly illuminating, I'm afraid, though I'm sure you understand. There is, how can I say, a growing distrust between certain areas of British Intelligence and the actions of the US security services. The revelation of Edward Snowden showed the British, and, might I add, the Canadians, New Zealanders and Australians, that their own security organizations were at risk due to the actions of certain Cousins on the other side of the pond and that a lot of information that was supposed to be shared, was not. This is of great concern, especially to our Foreign Secretary. He has close ties with a number of people in the Security Services from his army days. Let's just say we are members of a rather more independent division and Mr. Pilgrim has been a friend for many years."

"Where is he?" said Kirsty.

"Whitechapel. Some of our old friends from the East End are looking after him."

Kirsty grinned. "East End boys? I think I'd rather mess with your lot than those geezers."

"Geezers?" said Montrose.

"Gangsters," replied Kirsty.

Lockhart coughed. "Or rather, independent businessmen who have a very high regard for their country." His smile vanished and he looked distraught for a moment, before he leaned over and spoke in a low voice. "If I may, and of course this is just my opinion, bearing in mind I am not totally *au fait* with both the situation and the facts of the matter, I…"

Jeez, spit it out. "Go for it," said Montrose.

"I think it better if… whatever information you hold, if any, should be destroyed."

Montrose nodded. "That's the first sensible thing I've heard all day."

"Thank you," said Lockhart. "Miss Purley was a very dear friend of mine. I shall miss her enormously." He cleared his throat and stuck his chin in the air. "Of course, if I can help in any way?"

Kirsty gently patted his thigh and Lockhart blushed. "I've got it covered. Trust me."

*

Campbell pushed open the glass door. "We have a signal. Her phone."

Kane jumped up and winced in pain. "Where?"

"Some place called Mount Pleasant. Near the main Post Office. It was only for a few seconds. But it was there."

"When?"

"Two minutes ago."

"Find them!"

"The signal's gone. We're tracking the whole area."

"Close all the roads. All the containment sectors. Shut this fucking town down!"

Campbell's iPad beeped and he looked out to the office where his team pointed to a technician. "I think I know why." He gestured to the men and two of them lifted an MI5 technician from his chair and marched him over to the office. "In here," said Campbell and shoved the technician in front of the desk. "Talk."

The technician shuffled his feet. "Well, the signal disappeared near Paddington and then briefly reappeared near Mount Pleasant."

"We know that. What else?"

"Both of them are old Post Office distribution centers. And the only thing that connects them is the secret railway."

Kane edged around the desk. "The fucking what? You have a secret railway?"

"It's a disused underground railway for the Post Office. It goes right across London. Hasn't been used in years. But it's still there. It still works, most of it."

"So why the signal at Mount Pleasant?"

"Maybe they were nearer the surface. You know, when you sometimes get a signal on your phone in an underground station?"

"No, I don't fucking know," said Kane, advancing towards him. "Where does it go? After Mount Pleasant?"

"Liverpool Street, I think. And then Whitechapel. The East End."

Kane jabbed a finger in the technician's face. "Get the fuck out of here." He turned to Campbell. "Get me a helicopter."

CHAPTER 30

The stained ochre brick walls closed in and the Jaguar rolled from side to side on the uneven cobbles. Through the windshield Montrose looked along a narrow, dingy alley lined with shuttered windows.

"We'll get out my side of the car," said Lockhart. "There are no cameras here. The proprietors are, shall we say, not too keen on surveillance." The Jaguar pulled up beside rusting iron gates. Lockhart got out of the Jaguar and held the door for Kirsty.

Montrose shuffled across the seat behind Kirsty and stepped into a small courtyard, stacked with metal beer kegs and wire cages packed with flattened cardboard.

Lockhart leaned in towards the driver. "I've organized transport for our guests. Secure the exit, then report back."

The driver nodded and the Jaguar rumbled down the lane.

Montrose whispered to Kirsty, "What is this place?"

"Deepest, darkest Whitechapel," she replied.

He heard a bolt being thrown and looked down a path carved out between the beer kegs to see a fire exit door open and a huge, shaven-headed man in a long, dark coat fill the doorway. "Welcome to Whitechapel," he grinned. "Home of Jack the Ripper and the best curry in the world."

Lockhart nodded to the man. "This is our host, Mr. Kent."

Kirsty walked towards the door. "He's not here, is he?"

"Who?" said Kent.

"Old Jack."

"Nah. He was, though." Kent pointed to a corner of the yard. "That's where they found one of his victims. She was a sorry mess." He stepped aside and held out a hand. "Your friend is upstairs."

"Jack?" said Montrose.

"The Ripper," replied Kirsty.

"Lovely to see you again, Mr. Kent," said Lockhart.

"And you, Mr. Lockhart, if only these were happier times."

"Such is the way of the world."

Kent slammed the fire door behind them. "Straight ahead. Lead the way, young lady."

Montrose followed Kirsty through a heavy black curtain and down a narrow corridor, paint peeling off the walls and floorboards squeaking under his feet. They emerged into a long, wooden bar. He stared at the fading grandeur, sumptuously decorated mirrors, tiled walls and etched glass, lined with mirrors and bottles. But for all the Victorian opulence, the bar was pitted and stained and the air reeked of beer and sweat. In a corner, a steel pole was bolted into an unvarnished wooden dais, grimy metal stretching to the roof. *This isn't the Playboy mansion.*

"End of the bar," said Kent.

Kirsty turned into a low doorway, then up a steep staircase.

Montrose bowed his head and followed her through. He lost sight of Kirsty for a moment then heard her running.

"Kirsty?" It was Pilgrim.

Montrose looked up to the top of the stairs. At the end of the hall was a bedroom, where he could see Kirsty hugging Pilgrim on the bed. Half the room was filled with camera equipment and open bags of lingerie. He did a double-take when he spotted a woman by the bedside, squeezed into a latex nurse's uniform. At the other side of the bed stood an Asian doctor in long white robes and a *taqiyah* skull cap.

Pilgrim slowly raised a hand as Montrose entered. "I hear you have had quite a day." He nodded towards Lockhart, standing in the doorway. "Thank you for delivering them safely, Mr. Lockhart and give my regards to both your team and the Foreign Secretary."

Kent appeared beside Lockhart, his head grazing the top of the doorframe. "The transport is here. When you're ready."

"Thank you, Mr. Kent," said Lockhart. "I wonder if it would be wise to wait until things are a little quieter out there?"

Pilgrim tried to sit up on the bed. "I heard the helicopters. They're a bit too close for comfort. What's the latest?"

"They're over the central Post Office," said Kent. "That's the final destination of the Mail Rail. They must have worked it out. The place has been sealed off. And I don't think they are going away anytime soon."

"I might be able to help with that," said Kirsty and pulled a phone from her bag.

"I would strongly advise that all mobile phones are switched off," said Lockhart.

"This has never been used," she replied. "The number is untraceable."

"I've got some clothes for you next door, young lady," said Kent.

Kirsty jumped off the bed. "Cheers, mate. Any knock-off designer gear?" She looked down at the bags. "You have a nice line in lingerie."

Kent laughed and stepped aside for Kirsty.

"How are you?" said Montrose.

"Hurts like hell," said Pilgrim. "But I'll live."

"He needs specialist care," said the doctor. "There's always a risk of secondary infection. We need proper facilities and he's not to be moved, if at all possible."

Lockhart raised an eyebrow. "Unless they stop re-enacting *Apocalypse Now* outside, I think that's going to be unavoidable."

"I understand," replied the doctor. "I must go. Please call me if I can be of any help." The doctor closed his bag then laid a hand on Pilgrim's head. "*Ma'a as-salaama*, my friend."

Pilgrim closed his eyes for a moment. "*Ila-liqaa.*"

The tiles on the roof rattled as a helicopter swooped overhead.

"That's too bloody close for comfort," said Lockhart.

"Kirsty's phone," said Montrose. He rushed from the room and shoved open the first door he saw.

Kirsty spun around, holding a T-shirt to cover her naked body. "Well, at least close the bloody door."

"Your phone!" He grabbed it from the bed and thumbed the power button. The windows rattled as the helicopter hovered over the building and then moved away.

Kirsty looked down at the phone. "But I've never made a call with it. It's totally untraceable."

"Did you have it switched on next to mine? Or in the Russian Embassy? Or one you had used previously?"

"Maybe, I don't know..."

"Get some clothes on. We've got to move."

Kirsty turned away from him and pulled on the T-shirt.

From the corner of his eye, Montrose saw the bright red Welsh dragon tattooed on her ass.

She pulled on her panties. "Hey, no peeping. You've seen enough for today. And get me a clean phone. If we're going away for the weekend, I need to phone a friend."

Montrose opened the door. Lockhart and Kent shuffled along the corridor with Pilgrim on a stretcher.

"There's an ambulance waiting," said Lockhart. "Let's go."

"Where?"

"London City Airport. Six miles from here. We have to take off before the net closes."

"We've lost it. We had a good signal, but it dropped before we could complete triangulation." The technician adjusted her glasses and leaned into the screen, drawing her finger across a map.

"Where?" Kane leaned into the screen.

"Somewhere in Whitechapel. It was only for a few seconds, so it didn't triangulate with all the transmission posts."

"Find it, you asshole."

The technician's fingers froze on the keyboard. "What did you say?" She turned the chair around to face him.

"Hey, less of the drama, sweetcheeks. Just do your job."

She nodded slowly. "Sweetcheeks, eh?" She looked directly at him. "Do you want any more broken ribs, you fat, Yankee arsehole?"

Kane leaned over towards her and stuck a finger in her face. "Hey, I don't need your shit. Find that fucking phone."

"Yeah? Or what? What you gonna do?"

"What the hell? Just do your..."

Campbell leaned into the keyboard. "I'll do it."

The technician spun around in her chair and brought up her elbow hard, powering into the bridge of Campbell's nose. His head snapped backward and blood splattered across his shirt.

Two black-suited guards reached for their guns.

The technician logged off and stood up, facing the guards. "What are you gonna do? Shoot me? Yeah? Well, why don't you just do it, so I won't have to put up with your *shite* anymore." Other technicians rose from their desks.

"What is this?" said Kane. "A fucking revolution?"

Several of the technicians leaned down to their keyboards and logged off.

The technician grinned as she looked around. "What if it is?" she said and leaned in towards him. "*Sweetcheeks*." She held out a finger, pointed at his ribs.

"Get the hell away from me! You fucking assholes, you fucking second-rate Limey jerk-offs!" He turned to the guards. "Get everyone to Whitechapel. Seal all the roads. Go!"

CHAPTER 31

The ambulance cut the sirens. Montrose looked out the rear window and saw the signs to the private jet terminal. "Is this secure?"

Lockhart pulled a pistol from his jacket. "Yes. My two men in the Jaguar are waiting for us. Any more would attract too much attention." High steel security gates closed behind the ambulance. Lockhart stood ready at the doors. "The airport have been alerted that we have a passenger being transferred for urgent medical treatment, so we have priority. The jet will be waiting. No pack drill, no tickets, we just go." The ambulance pulled up at the terminal building. Lockhart held his gun low and threw open the doors.

The Jaguar came around to the side and two soldiers jumped out, machine pistols raised, scanning the tarmac.

A Learjet stood twenty feet away. A flight attendant emerged from the door, beckoning them over. Another rushed down the steps of the jet to help Lockhart as he pulled the stretcher from the back of the ambulance.

Montrose looked up. He could smell the River Thames close by and hear the faint noise of helicopters, but they were blocked from sight by the skyscrapers in the financial district of Canary Wharf. He looked down the runway. The old Victorian sea dock stretched directly in front of him, about a hundred feet wide, with dark water on either side.

Two businessmen carrying suitcases emerged from the terminal. "Hey!" said the first, pointing to the ambulance. "How long's this going to take? We've been delayed long enough. How come that guy's taking off and we're stuck here?" He pointed to a Learjet emblazoned with the livery of an oil company, edging past them, heading for the runway.

A young woman in a flight uniform appeared from the terminal doors. "Gentlemen, please, I asked you to stay in the terminal. This is a medical emergency and has priority. We'll ensure you take off as quickly as possible."

The two soldiers glanced around and then returned to scanning the runway. One ran over and stood guard at the door as Lockhart and Kirsty lifted Pilgrim into the jet. The other headed for the runway.

Another member of the terminal staff appeared at the doors with a telephone in her hand. "Major Salter?"

The soldier turned around. "Yes?"

"I have a call for you. They say it's extremely urgent."

Salter looked quizzically at her and then took the phone. "Major Salter here." He listened for a moment and then barked into the receiver. "I am a British soldier and I do not take orders from Washington." He cut the call and handed her the phone.

"Who was that?" shouted Lockhart.

"I didn't wait to find out. Some bloody Yank shouting his mouth off."

Kirsty screamed. "Connor!"

Montrose turned and saw the businessmen drop their open suitcases and pull out compact machine pistols.

They opened fire and Salter crumpled to the tarmac. He rolled onto his back and tried to get to his knees, firing his weapon in short bursts, taking down one man, but flew backwards as several rounds caught him in the face. He lay motionless on the ground.

Montrose hit the deck and scrambled towards the jet.

The second soldier ran over, weapon raised, but was cut down as a burst of automatic fire tore through his legs. Bullets pinged around the tarmac and caught him in the neck. A spray of arterial blood spewed out. Lockhart came running from the jet, pistol raised and slotted two rounds into the second man's chest. The man twisted backwards and slammed into the ground. Lockhart ran over and placed two more rounds into the man's head, then turned to the jet and pointed to Kirsty. "Go!"

The sound of helicopters became louder, echoing off the buildings. Montrose could hear the flight attendant shouting from the open door of the Learjet.

Kirsty knelt behind the steps of the jet, looking at the sky, and brought out her phone.

Montrose grabbed Salter's gun and raced over to her. "Kirsty, get on the fucking plane."

She didn't look up, but stared at the screen as the phone booted up. "Not yet."

The sound of helicopters filled the air. The flight attendant began to pull up the steps to the jet. Montrose stamped on the bottom step to hold them down. He gripped Kirsty's arm. "They're not going to wait, we need to get the hell out of here!"

She thumbed a number on the phone. "It's too late, Connor, they'll be on us in seconds. I have to do this." She lifted her phone to her ear and shouted, "Do it!", then scrambled to her feet and ran up the steps of the jet.

Montrose stepped back and lifted his machine pistol to the sky. *They'll come in low. And firing. I need some cover.*

"Connor!" Kirsty stood in the doorway as the flight attendant tried to close the door.

He turned to the pilot at the window and pointed down the runway. The engines wound up and the flight attendant shoved Kirsty inside and hauled the door shut.

The downblast of the helicopter blew Montrose to the ground as it swept over the terminal building at head height. Another followed behind and they took up position either side of the runway. The water in the dock churned and blew clouds of spray into the air.

Lockhart kept low and pulled Montrose to the side as the jet straightened up and faced the runway. "Get behind the Jag," shouted Lockhart over the noise. "It's armored."

He ran with Lockhart and knelt behind the hood, then brought up the sights of the machine pistol.

"Go for the pilot," said Lockhart.

The cargo doors on the helicopters opened on both sides and automatic rifles pointed straight at them. The Learjet squealed to a halt at the start of the runway.

He saw Kirsty at the window, frantically pushing down her palm to tell him to keep his head low. *Yeah, kinda worked that out. Doesn't matter. We're fucked.* He looked over to her again and she was pointing across the dock. He glanced over the water, to the far dock, where a group of kids in long black trench coats stood, each wearing identical Guy Fawkes masks, with flashing red lights at their feet. *What the hell?* He watched the red lights rise and fly straight towards the helicopter before he realized. *Drones.*

The first drone kept low on the water, barely skimming the surface and then rose up to the nearest helicopter. Another followed close behind, but as soon as they touched the downward blast of the rotor wash, they tumbled over sideways and crashed into the water. The kids wrestled with their remote controls, but it was useless. Two more drones took off, arcing high into the sky above the dock, edging towards the airspace over the helicopter. *Holy shit, they're going to be pulled down.* The lights dropped fast as the drones were sucked into the rotor blades.

"Get down!" He grabbed Lockhart and pulled him beneath the fender of the Jag as the rotor blades shattered, sending shards of metal in all directions. He looked up as the helicopter keeled over on its side then plummeted into the dock. Water flooded in through the open cargo doors and burst up from the hot engines. It sank like a stone.

The second helicopter swung low across the runway and turned sideways, automatic fire pouring from the cargo door.

"Protect the jet!" shouted Lockhart. "I'm going to

draw their fire." He rushed out from the side of the Jag, firing his machine pistol from the hip, but was cut down in a spray of bullets.

Montrose looked up and saw Kane in the cockpit. A rake of heavy fire tore across the armored Jag. Montrose dropped to the tarmac just as more red flashing lights appeared in the sky.

The pilot saw them too and swung the helicopter towards the kids, raking the area with gunfire. The kids scattered and ducked behind the corner of a warehouse, except for one, who stood still and pushed up his mask, concentrating on the drone in the air. He dropped to his knees behind a metal bollard as bullets spattered the tarmac around him.

Kane pointed to the kid and the pilot swung the helicopter hard to the right, searching for the drone. The helicopter dipped and twisted in the air and a black-suited figure toppled from the door and bounced on the ground, then lay still. The helicopter swung away towards the kid, who looked up, his eyes fixed on a point in the air above the helicopter, then dropped the controls. The drone fell out of the sky.

One rotor blade shattered and the helicopter lurched to the side and hung in the air for a moment as the pilot wrestled with the controls; it plunged down, smashing into the edge of the dock before toppling sideways into the water, churning the surface to foam and disappearing from view.

The Learjet's engines screamed as it shot forward down the runway. Montrose hit the tarmac as the jet wash blasted over him and looked up as the jet rose steeply into the sky. He watched it bank hard between the skyscrapers then rise up into the clouds.

He stood up, machine pistol still in his hand, then ran over to the edge of the runway and looked down into the water. He could hear screaming sirens.

Kane's body floated to the surface, a gun still grasped in his dead hand. Montrose stared open-mouthed at the carnage around him, then heard shouts from the kids on the opposite bank. They were pointing at the water. *I don't understand.*

His legs began to shake and the gun dropped from his hands. He looked behind as the sirens became louder and a police car slid to a halt outside the terminal gates. He turned back and caught the eye of the kid without the Guy Fawkes mask. *Oh, yeah. I've got it.* He took two steps back and dived into the water.

CHAPTER 32

He closed his eyes and let the aroma of bitter coffee and wet stone drift over him. The murky water lapped gently against the worn steps leading into the canal. In the near distance he could hear gondoliers crying out, vying for the tourist trade. Montrose looked along the water, where the buildings seemed to slump together, holding each other up against the tide and the assault of the sea. The canal was so narrow he could have jumped across it. At his feet the rising tide had edged higher, threatening to flood the tiny café terrace and the small hotel on the far side of the canal.

He sipped his coffee and watched two tourists drag their luggage towards the hotel. They checked the map in their hands and he could hear their relief that they had found the address. Montrose grinned. Being hard to find was a good thing. Pilgrim had given him the address of a safe house which had turned out to be a two room attic at the top of a six-hundred-year-old building that had sunk ten feet into the Venetian lagoon since it was built.

He stretched his legs out below the table, listening to the incessant dialogue between the Italian mamma behind the zinc counter and the waiters scurrying around with orders. For the first time, he began to relax. He had spent his first day working out escape routes over the maze of roofs, discovering hidden attics through unlocked skylights and nearly killing himself on moss-covered slates. The next few days had been spent navigating the blind alleys and hidden courtyards that laced the buildings, threading out to every corner of Venice. And then he did it all again: in the dark, under flickering lights, memorizing the doors, the graffiti, the nameplates and windows, the smell of restaurants and dinner cooking in the apartments, until he was sure he could do it blindfolded.

He sat up and leaned forward in his chair, but there was no-one watching, no new faces on the corner. The canal was too narrow for anything other than a gondola and he had photographed every boat that had come down, checked their numbers and logged them in his notebook. The sour scent of the sea caught in the back of his throat. The only escape from it was deep between the buildings, down alleys so cramped his shoulders brushed the sides. He closed his eyes again and mentally retraced a route he had taken the night before, the sights and smells ingrained in his memory. *Yeah, I could do that with my eyes shut*. He remembered the hidden entrance to a courtyard, just behind a perfumers, where they had sold the same brand of perfume since the Middle Ages. A right turn, through another courtyard and there was the low exit towards a vaulted, crumbling archway, leading to the tannery with its tang of ammonia, past a cheap restaurant redolent with the lingering aroma of rosemary, fried tomatoes and garlic, then sideways along an unlit alley, reeking of piss, garbage pails and yesterday's fish, before emerging into a wide palazzo.

A waiter stood at his shoulder and held out a newspaper. "Signor?"

I wrote the damn news, I don't need that crap. He shook his head.

"No, Signor, it is for you." He placed the newspaper on the table.

Montrose looked down at the headline of *The Herald & Tribune. Hell, this I've got to see.* The front page was emblazoned with the story of an old Soviet satellite exploding in space and taking out several other military satellites before it burned up in the atmosphere. Conspiracy theorists were having a field day, but by the end of the week it was old news and prime-time TV had moved on from how some decrepit space junk had nearly brought the Middle East to war. The born-again environmentalists in the White House were having the most fun, having a go at the Chinese and Russians. *Like they give a shit*. He pushed the newspaper aside. *She is safe.*

His phone buzzed and he pulled it from his pocket. The text message showed a list of double digits, in groups of five. He sat up in the chair. *If Pilgrim thinks this is funny...* He glanced around, but no one looked his way. He slowly reached for the newspaper and opened it at the crossword. It had already been completed. *What the hell? Pilgrim could just phone me. Unless my phone is compromised.* He flicked his eyes left and right, then hunched over the table and began to decode the first numbers, using the newspaper as his notepad.

I have become a butterfly.

He stared at the message. *Kirsty?*

A light breeze ruffled the pages of the newspaper. He looked up, but there was no one around. The tourists had gone. He spotted a curtain move, high up in the hotel across the canal. A figure stood at a long window, behind lace curtains, her back to the canal. A flash of short, red hair and a towel slipping down to the waist to reveal pale, almost faultless skin on her arms and back. *No, it's not her. You're crazy. She'll be long gone.*

He turned back to the crossword, trying not to look up at the window.

Tomorrow I fly away forever. What you saw before? Lipstick, powder and paint.

He lifted his head.

The towel dropped from her waist to her feet, to reveal a bright red tattoo. She pulled aside the curtain and pressed her ass to the window.

A snort of laughter escaped as he scribbled the final words.

Except for one. Now, come up and kiss the dragon.

NAMES OF THE DEAD

Connor Montrose is running for his life. All that he held dear has been ripped away. Every Western intelligence agency and all the police forces of Europe are looking for him, with orders to shoot on sight.

The only man who can prove his innocence, is the man that most wants him dead. Only one woman, a Mossad sleeper in Paris, will stand by his side. With her help, he must now turn and fight.

Read the brilliant debut from Mark Leggatt, introducing the first action packed thriller with Connor Montrose.